SHERLOCK HOLMES

AND

THE KRAY TWINS

There's a debt to be paid

SHERLOCK HOLMES AND

THE KRAY TWINS

There's a debt to be paid

David C Phillips

Table of Contents

Acknowledgments

My thanks to

The Queen of Gangland-Kerry Barnes for her belief.

My son Christian for the things he taught me.

The late George Dwyer for being my friend.

Dedication

For

Kyle and Demi

Don't ever give up trying.

Preface

This is the story of the great grandsons of Sherlock Holmes and Dr.Watson and their association with the Kray twins and the Firm in the years 1963/4. I have written it exactly as it was told to me by John Watson in his own words. If his poor opinion of the original Sherlock or of the Firm offends anyone, I apologise on his behalf.

Introduction

When Sherlock Holmes pays the Kray twins to settle a blackmail matter, they ask him and Watson to do a couple of jobs for them to return the favour. This leads to the pair spending time in the East End and associating with the Firm. Unfortunately, the twins fail to resolve the blackmail affair and won't pay back the money they'd been given.

Holmes is now determined to be repaid, and with interest. The story takes place in the latter part of 1963 and early 1964, when Holmes and Watson are involved in the social and business affairs of the Firm.

They meet Sonny Liston at a club opening.

Watson meets and has a relationship with Kathy, who he last knew as a prostitute in Soho four years previously.

They fall foul of Adolf, Benito and Tojo, the Morris brothers, which results in murder.

Holmes re-enacts The Musgrave Ritual in a search for buried treasure.

After two visits to Nigeria and their part in the disastrous Enugu project, Holmes is finally prepared to accept the debt has been paid.

CHAPTER 1

Avery Goodman

Was it really all those years ago that me and Sherlock Holmes were involved with the Kray twins? It was 1963; when you could buy a house for four thousand pounds, or a new car for eight hundred quid, and the average weekly wage was about twenty-five pounds. I was 25 years old then; back living in Penge and renting a nice flat in one of those big Victorian houses in Thicket Road, opposite the park.

It all started on a Tuesday morning. I was having breakfast when the doorbell rang. I opened the door to find a skinny little geezer in a grimy fawn raincoat, with a corduroy cap on his head, and on his top lip, he had one of those thin pencil mustaches.

In those days there were two types of people who wore those mustaches, and they were mostly men. The first type were the ones who wanted to look dashing and romantic, like Errol Flynn or Clark Gable. The second type were the officious ones who wanted to have an air of authority, and that's the category that this geezer was in. He had a briefcase tucked under one arm and a pad in his other hand, and his nose kept twitching like a rat who'd smelled food.

I said, "Yeah."

He gave me a slimy sort of smile. "Good morning, I'm looking for Avery Goodman."

I shook my head. "No, sorry mate, he don't live here."

With that he put his briefcase down on the floor, looked at his pad, looked at me again, frowning. "Are you sure?"

Now, he's implying that I'm either lying or else I'm stupid and don't know who lives in my own flat. So I said, "No mate, I'm not Shaw and I'm not Avery Goodman. So fuck off." And slammed the door in his face.

I hadn't got back to the kitchen before the bell rang again, and this time it didn't stop. I flung the door open and he's standing there, grinning. Except now, there's no mustache, there's no cap on his head, he's about six inches taller and not so skinny anymore. It was Sherlock Holmes.

"Hello, John, I see your manners haven't improved." His nose twitched again. "That coffee smells good. May I come in?"

And he's already sliding past me into the hallway. As I followed him down to the kitchen he was looking all around, making an inventory of everything, the way he always did.

Now, when I say it was Sherlock Holmes, it obviously wasn't the one in the books cos he's been dead for donkey's years. No, this is his great-grandson or his brother Mycroft's great-grandson; there's always been some doubt in my family about that.

Not many people know the real story of what happened when Sherlock Holmes retired. He wound up living in Sussex somewhere,

2

with the old mort out of Baker Street, who he'd been having liaisons with for years and thought no one knew about it.

I happen to have all the original drafts and manuscripts that my great grandfather, Dr. John Watson, wrote, and I know what Sherlock Holmes was really like

What happened in Sussex, was Sherlock had got a young girl pregnant; I think she came from Brighton. So the one from Baker Street, Mrs. Hudson, chucked him out of the house.

He then made his way up to Norwood, where his old mate, Dr. Watson, was living with his wife and family, and begged them to put him up. Well, old Dr.John had always been a bit soft and easy-going, so he let him move in with them. Within a very short time, Sherlock had rowed the little mystery from Brighton into the house as well.

Not very long after that Mycroft turned up with a hard-luck story, and my great grandfather let him move in too. Luckily, it was a big house, but not big enough, as it turned out.

Holmes soon got up to his old tricks, firing bullets into the bedroom wall, getting drugged up, playing a violin at all hours of the night, and carving his initials in the furniture with a pocketknife.

All that was bad enough, but the worst thing was at mealtimes when he'd give his lectures on the different types of fag ash. These could go on for hours sometimes, but if anyone got bored, or showed disinterest, he'd get the hump and threaten 'em.

Needless to say, Dr. John and my great nan had enough of it in the end. They didn't do what anyone else would have done and flung the three of 'em out on their necks. Instead, they bought another house down the road in Penge, packed up all the furniture and everything, and moved out, leaving the house to Sherlock and his brother.

How do you think them two repaid the doctor for what he'd done for 'em? Somehow, they managed to secure the rights to the books that my great grandfather had written and copped all the dough for it. Old Dr.John wasn't bitter about it though, he said, "Sherlock Holmes cannot help being what he is, any more than a jackal can help being what it is."

I thought that was very nice of him to be like that.

Our family stayed in the house at Penge; my dad was born there and so was I. Sherlock and the Brighton trollop stayed in the house at Norwood with Mycroft. I don't know if they ever married, but she had a son, another Sherlock. He grew up, married, and had a family, and so it went on. The old Sherlock and Mycroft were both dead and gone by the nineteen-thirties. After that, the families gradually came together and tried to forget their differences; they did, but I never did. We came to think of them as family, so me and the latest Sherlock grew up almost like cousins.

I heard a lot of stories about the old days from my nan. She knew Mycroft and the old Sherlock, and she didn't have a good word to say about either of 'em. She never really took to the young Sherlock either;

although she was always nice to him when he came round. But she said to me, "never ever trust him, John," and I never did. He used to come down to Penge sometimes in the summer holidays, and he'd invite me up to Norwood, but I never went cos I still considered that house as ours.

As we got older, we drifted apart. He went from private school to public school to university, and I got a job in a warehouse in Croydon. Later on, I heard he'd left university and joined a Guards regiment. I got called up for national service and got to go into the RAF cos I thought it would be easy. Then I wound up in the RAF Regiment, which is like the army, and it wasn't easy at all.

Once my national service was over, it was hard for me to settle into civvy life. After a couple of jobs which I didn't like, I found I could get by wheeling and dealing, and ducking and diving. Through a pal of mine who's dad had a betting shop I was getting dog racing tips; and through another friend, an assistant trainer at Newmarket, horse racing tips.

So all in all I was getting a reasonable living. As well as all that, I'd invested some money with a pal of mine who was into long firm fraud, and now and then I'd get a dividend off of him. Life really wasn't too bad.

The next time I met Holmes, he had left the army and set himself up as a private investigator, or a consulting detective as he liked to call himself. He never asked what I was doing, and that made me think he already knew. Sometimes I'd help him in his work, driving, or plotting up, waiting for someone to come in or go out. A few times I'd force an entry into a place, where either he couldn't do it or didn't want to get caught doing it.

He must have been getting hold of some good money, cos he always paid me well for doing next to nothing. And now he'd turned up on my doorstep.

CHAPTER 2

Teddy Kray

I'd followed him into the kitchen and found him shaking his head and smiling to himself.

"I didn't think I'd still be able to fool you, John, after all these years."

That is him saying you've always been a dope and I'm clever. And he's still smirking. I have to admit he was good at disguising himself, so I said, "Holmesy, getting dressed up may be the one thing you are good at, and I admire you for it. There, does that make you happy?"

He nodded, "I must admit I was disappointed John that you're not a very good man"

Now, this is him with riddles.

"I don't know what you're talking about."

For some reason this perked him up a bit, he came closer, still smiling. "I said I'm looking for, Avery Goodman. A- very- good-man."

He found that very funny, and started sort of gurgling to himself, while I poured two cups of coffee from the percolator on the stove.

"Yeah, hilarious,"

I'd poured his coffee the way he liked it, black with no sugar, put cream in mine, and we sat at the table.

7

He hadn't changed at all since I last saw him. But then he never did. He looked pretty much the same as he did when he was a kid, and not too far off the geezer in the old black and white Sherlock Holmes films in the 1940s.

Slim, about six feet tall, brown hair combed back and sideways, high cheekbones and a thin nose, straight and slightly hooked. His eyes were a grey-blue, and a bit starey sometimes like he's trying to hypnotise you without you noticing.

I said, "so to what do I owe the pleasure of this visit?"

He stopped smiling now and looked serious. "Business John, business."

From an inside pocket of his grimy coat, he took an envelope, put it on the table, and pushed it over to me. There were photographs inside, and I only had to look at the first one to guess what the others were. There were four men, maybe five, cos I didn't look that close, and they were a bit tangled up. And they were all naked as the day they were born. I pushed them back, a bit disgusted.

"Don't tell me you're selling pornography."

Well, he got all red and puffed up and indignant. "No I'm bloody not."

"Please tell me then you're not blackmailing someone."

He got even redder, more indignant, and slammed his fist on the table. "Fuck you, John. No, I'm not blackmailing anyone, someone else is."

He then went on to tell me the story, how his friend Adrian had been lured from a gaming club in Kensington to a party at a nearby flat. There, he'd been drugged, abused, and was now being blackmailed. I'd met Adrian before and recognised him in the photos, and he seemed to be the only one with a smile on his face.

"That was obviously the result of being drugged, the poor fellow's absolutely distraught," Holmes explained.

Now, I know a little bit about drugs, not everything, but I'm sure there's no substance I've ever heard of that could make me smile in a situation like that.

He told me then, that the blackmailer was a man named Teddy Kray, and it was his family that was running the gaming club, Esmeralda's Barn.

"I've been doing some research," says Holmes, and he starts pacing about the room and holding his head like he's got a headache or something. "The Kray Twins, d'you know anything about them?"

I said, "I know they come from the East End and they're very dangerous".

He stopped walking about then and sat down at the table. "Why do you say that, John? Why do you say they're dangerous?"

I had to think then, cos I didn't know why I'd said it. All I knew about the Kray twins was what I'd read in the News of the World. They were sporting personalities who did a lot of charity work. Then I remembered:

The West End 1959. Before Chinatown became Chinatown.

When Bernie Silver and Big Frank Mifsud ran nearly all the strip clubs and clip joints in Soho.

Back then, if you'd crossed the road from the Flamingo in Wardour Street and walked along the left side of Gerrard Street you'd pass three or four of those clip joints; until you came to the last one, in a basement opposite Peter Mario's restaurant, called The Top Hat. That's where Carole worked. She was someone I was seeing at the time, but it didn't end well, so I won't talk about it.

Sometimes I'd go downstairs with her before they opened for business and chat with the girls, or maybe Sheila, who ran the place. There would be touts down there too; these were the ones who steered the punters off the street into the clubs.

I always found it pretty dismal down there. Three of the walls were painted or papered in a dull yellow, and the fourth was a deep red. On the floor was a red carpet to match the wall and that was brand new. But unfortunately, a new carpet, cheap perfume, and cigarette smoke couldn't take away the damp, basement smell.

There was a bar to the left of the stairs, some tables and chairs, and on the far wall was a jukebox, which churned out the hits of the day. And even now, if I should hear Elvis singing, "One night with you," I can see in my mind, little black-haired, dark-eyed Maria slow dancing with her boyfriend, Johnny Scouse.

I'd got friendly with one of the touts from there; his name was Ted, Manchester Ted. That's what he was known as all round Soho. I couldn't describe him now, except for saying he was about twenty-four years of age, wore a trilby hat, and had a Manchester accent. Other than that, he was the most average man I've ever seen. He was average height, about 5'9", average build. Medium brown hair, average complexion. He was Mr. Average. The only thing that set him apart, was his personality; they might call it charisma today, I don't know. He could charm hardened prostitutes into giving him money. He could talk angry punters into not beating him to death after he'd steered 'em into a clip joint and they'd been fleeced. And he never really took things seriously. One night one of the street girls lurched out of the White Bear and nearly bumped into us. Straight away Ted got hold of her hand, got down on one knee and started singing:

"Ah sweet mystery of life at last I've found thee

Ah I know at last the secret of it all

All the longing striving seeking...."

He stopped about there, cos the girl said, "Fuck off Ted," pulled her hand away, and stomped off towards Leicester Square. I don't think she enjoyed the attention of the small crowd that had stopped to watch.

Anyway, Ted stood up, got a round of applause, brushed his trousers with his hand, and said, "She didn't mean that you know."

That's the sort of things he'd do. Another night, and this is how I came to hear about the Kray twins, we were in Doris's Cafe, which was

11

just around the corner in Lisle Street. It was just an ordinary sort of working-class cafe, but sooner or later everyone went there; gangsters, cab drivers, pimps, prostitutes, thieves, runaways; the elite, and the dregs of Soho drank tea in Doris's.

This particular night it was busy. We were having a cup of tea when two of the girls came and sat at our table; we didn't invite them, they just sat there. I knew 'em to talk to, and so did Ted. They were brass who used to hang around in Wardour Street, Kathy and Marilyn, if that was her real name. Marilyn was what you might think of as a typical streetwalker, plenty of make-up and plenty of attitude. She was a bit older than Kathy, probably about twenty-two, and very protective of her, perhaps cos they both came from up north.

Kathy was nice, always friendly. She was tall, had fair hair cut short, and dimples, and her eyes always seemed to be half shut like she was on the verge of falling asleep. She wasn't all that pretty till she smiled; then she was beautiful, more than beautiful. She had an honest smile like she really meant it. Not like some of 'em, "hello how ya going whaddayawant". Not that sort of smile. She could actually make you feel better.

We said hello and carried on with our conversation and they carried on with theirs. I'd often wondered about these two. What had made 'em leave their homes and their families up north, and come to London, and wind up on the game. Perhaps they didn't have families. What did they think they'd grow up to be when they were kids, a secretary, film star, in the mill like some of the older girls? I bet they didn't think they'd be on the streets of Soho, doing what they do.

I was staring at a crucifix Kathy wore on a chain round her neck, and I looked up and saw that she'd been watching me. She was smiling to herself and nodding her head like she knew something. Then she looked at Marilyn and they were smiling at each other.

Ted nudged me. "Oy, I'm talking to you"

We carried on our conversation, but I was thinking, 'What the fuck was she grinning about.'

The girls were talking and both smoking. I noticed that Kathy had left her cigarettes on the table, with the packet open; Ted noticed it too. He reached over, picked up her fags, took one out, and offered the packet to me, which I refused. Both of the girls had watched him do it, and as he was lighting the fag, Kathy, in a loud indignant voice said. "Oy Ted, what's your game?"

Quick as a flash Ted winked at her and said, "Plating and charvering darling. What's yours?"

Well, Marilyn was trying not to laugh and was spitting tea all over the table. Even Kathy had to smile She pushed the fags back to Ted and said, "Go on, you might as well have 'em."

The conversations resumed in the cafe, someone said, "Nice one Ted".

That's what it was like in Doris's in those days.

The story went about in the area and Ted got a bit of stick. The girls in the club used to tease him, "Ted are you really good at your game?" And they'd all start giggling.

One of the doormen, "Oy Ted what's your game?"

Ted wasn't his usual self, and then a couple of days later, we were walking on Shaftesbury Avenue, and he told me why. "I don't know if I should have said that to her."

I guessed what he was talking about, though I didn't see any harm in it, but he looked really miserable. I said, "Why not? She didn't mind. What's the problem?"

He looked worried, gnawing on his top lip. "She's one of Adie Morris's girls."

" So is he someone you've got to worry about?"

"No," he said, shaking his head "It's not him. It's his mates, the twins."

That was the first time I'd heard of 'em, and I pictured two identical twelve-year-old kids playing with a train set on the floor. I don't know why I thought that, but I did.

"So, who are the twins, what's so special about them?

And that's when Ted said, "The Kray twins. They come from over in the East End and they're very fuckin dangerous."

I must have been daydreaming because now I've got Holmes staring at me with his hypnotic eyes. "You say they're very dangerous John. What does that mean?"

I knew, in his world, dangerous means someone who returns a tennis serve too hard. Or someone who don't shout fore on the golf course. So I said, "Well, dangerous is someone who could physically hurt you if you give 'em the hump. And very dangerous, is someone who could, and would hurt you, and no question about it."

He thought about this for a while, then he got to pacing about again, posing. "You know John, danger is a narcotic to me. Do you know what Euripides said…?"

I stopped him there. "No, I don't, and I don't want to." That was rude I know, but he has these imaginary friends that he keeps quoting. I said to him, "I don't need to take advice from a geezer who's been dead for a hundred years, and never even knew what a flush toilet was."

He never had an answer to that, and it shut him up. We talked then about the problem at hand, and it turned out, his mate, Adrian, had given Sherlock a certain amount of money, he wouldn't say how much, to pay off Teddy Kray. Holmes decided he was going to go undercover, whatever that means. And I was to talk to people I knew, to find out about the Kray family. To go undercover, Sherlock said, he needed me to teach him some slang. In his words, he wanted to learn: "The way you people converse with each other."

Don't you love it when someone says, 'you people?'

So I said, "We people talk the same fuckin way you people talk to each other, except we generally mean what we say."

He got a bit apologetic then and said that's not what he meant, and could I just teach him some slang. I had to think about that because I don't use it much myself and I don't really know anyone who does. I advised him to forget it, cos he wasn't going to fool anyone, not anyone who mattered, anyway. This upset his vanity and he said, "Gawd blimey guvna, watcher mean?"

Now that is exactly what I was talking about. He could do the accent alright, but not the dialect, the words we use; no more than I could fool his toffee-nosed mates, if I tried to talk posh.

"Oh hello Claude hisn't it perfectly hawful."

They'd twig it in two seconds. So I told him the basics. The least said the better. Just say, "Gowan, is that right. Nah? like you can't believe it. And never say, 'The old bill or the bill", call 'em coppers, cozzers, gavvers, policemen, even call 'em the filth if you want to, although I never used that myself. There's no "the' in it, it's Old Bill and that's all. Is that old Bill just drove by like it's your mate or something. Not 'Is that the Old Bill?'

I thought he finally understood it, till he said, "Oh, so old Bill isn't just one particular policeman?"

I gave up then and we talked about motor cars for a while. When he was ready to go, I walked with him to the main front door. He went down the steps and through the gate. I was closing the door when I thought I heard him call out, "Tally Ho".

During the next few days, I tried to find out what I could about the Krays. The first person spoke to was an old pal of mine, Big Harry. He was a bit younger than me, but he knew a lot of important people.

We met in the bar of the Robin Hood. It's gone now, but it used to be on the corner of Croydon Road and Elmers End Road.

Harry was already at the bar when I arrived. "Hello John, whatcher having?"

I had a light ale and we sat down at a table by the window.

"So what are you doing with yourself?" That was always his first question.

I told him, "I'm doing a bit of work for Holmsey."

I knew Harry wasn't his biggest fan, he said, "Don't bring that fuckin idiot down here will you".

I stopped him there before he reeled off all of Holmes's faults to me. I said:" Yeah I know, but that ain't why I'm here. Harry, what do you know about the Kray twins?"

He looked at me a bit serious then. "You don't want to get involved with them."

"No," I said "why not? D'you know 'em?"

He gave a short laugh. "No, I don't, and I don't want to."

17

He agreed to put me in touch with someone who knew them well. I knew the name he mentioned; I'd heard all about him, but never met him, Johnny Gresham. from Croydon. Using the phone behind the bar, Harry made the call, and after speaking for a while, passed the receiver to me. From the way he spoke, I don't think Johnny Gresham. was a very jolly man. He was polite enough, most of 'em are, but he more or less said, "If you want to know about the twins go to Bethnal Green and ask 'em yourself, cos no-one else is gonna tell you."

"If you like," Harry said afterwards, "we can go and see Harry Haward, he knows 'em".

Another phone call and we drove down to Harry Haward's spieler at Loampit Vale, just outside of Lewisham.

Godfather wasn't a term used in those days, but that's what Harry Haward was in a way. He was known as Flash Harry, and he was proper old school. And if people went to him with problems, he would solve 'em if he could, or if it was in his interest to. In his time, he was a good thief, a publican, club owner, and a gambler. And he wound up championing the rights of the old pensioners in Deptford.

Big George Cooper was on the door. He was an ex-heavyweight boxer, and I knew him from years ago. Harry came over and greeted us, smiling. "Hello Harry. Hello John, how are ya son?" And he's got his arm round my shoulder like I was his best friend. He knew what I'd come down there for, and he said, "I ain't gonna talk about 'em, but I'll tell you all you need to know about them two. Keep away from 'em and stay on this side of the water."

Then he called George over. "Here George, he wants to know about the twins."

George came over. He was big, about six feet two and big with it. And with a voice to match, never loud but deep. He looked at me shaking, his head, "Ooh they're a bit naughty. You wanna stay away from them." Then he said, "They're a miserable pair of bastards."

I said, "Why d'you say that?"

He smiled and looked around, like someone else had spoke. "What? I didn't say anything."

And that's what it was like. Nobody had anything to tell me about the Kray twins. After all the asking around, the most information I got was from a fellow in Bermondsey who'd grown up with the twins in Bethnal Green. He described them as: "Too unpredictable to do business with."

And that was all he wanted to say on the subject.

The next time I heard from Holmsey, he was in a police station at Bethnal Green. That was in the afternoon, a few days after I'd last seen him. Sitting in my front room, I'd just got a beer out of the fridge and put on a Sarah Vaughn record, when the phone rang. It was Bethnal

19

Green nick, and would I take a call from a Hershel Coombs. I had to think for a bit before I said yes, and then Holmes came on the line.

"Hello John, I can't say much at the moment. Get me a solicitor and get me out of here as quickly as you can."

I said "Hold up, what are you nicked for?"

He didn't answer for a while, then, "I'll tell you later. Just do it and don't worry about the money." And he hung up.

In those days, nearly every police station in London, or every one that I knew of, had corrupt coppers. If you had enough money you could buy yourself out of almost anything. Funny thing was, they were a bit hotter on drink driving than they were on robbery, especially if they'd had to chase you. Anyway, I phoned a solicitor we knew, and he phoned a copper he knew, who may have been in Penge nick or Catford, I don't know. But, within two hours Holmes, or Hershel Coombs, was out on the street with no charges. I had to take three hundred pounds down to the solicitor, and that was that.

Holmes rang to thank me, but never came round, and wouldn't tell me what he'd been nicked for. A couple of days later I got a cheque in the post for four hundred pounds, which was nice. But if I'd known the trouble that phone call to the solicitor would cause me, I never would have made it.

CHAPTER 3

Arrested

It was late when I got up the next morning. The sun was shining through my kitchen window, warming the whole room as I made breakfast.

After I'd washed up, had a shave, had a bath, got dressed and smiled at myself in the hall mirror, I walked out to the top of the steps which led down to the front garden. From there I had a good view up and down the road.

There was a Ford Zephyr parked on the other side a few doors up, with three geezers in it, two in the front and one in the back. Old Bill. I guessed they were looking for a fellow who lived along there, Ronnie something. The story was, that he'd escaped from a cell in the police station and embarrassed every copper in Penge.

As I patted Holmes' cheque in my pocket, walked down the steps, and turned towards the High Street. a car door slammed behind me. I turned to see one of the coppers crossing to my side of the road. Then the Zephyr slid slowly past and stopped about fifty yards further on. Another copper got out and crossed the road to wait for me. He stood on the path smiling as I approached him.

" Hello, John"

I said, "Yeah, what do you want?"

With that, he's flashed a warrant card at me. "John Watson, I'm arresting you on suspicion of obtaining credit by deception. You do not have to say anything, but anything you do say ...."

I'd stopped listening to him by now, and muttered: "Yeah, nothing to say."

The other one had come up behind me and pushed my arms up so he could pat me down; satisfied, he said," Put your right hand out."

Then he's handcuffed me to his left hand and pushed me over to the car. The driver had got out and opened the back door. So in no time at all, I was sitting in the back between two of 'em, and driving down Penge High Street. Past the Adelaide on the right, then the Crooked Billet, down to the traffic lights by Penge nick. The lights turned green, and we turned left, but instead of pulling into the police station yard, we went straight on.

I asked the driver: "Where we going?"

"You'll find out "

He said this in a thick Scotch accent, and not a happy one. We drove toward Sydenham, then round Bell Green and down into Catford.

The one I was cuffed up to said, "What do you know about long firms, John?"

This was the first time I'd really looked at him. He was a lump, mid-thirties with a big jaw and eyes that sort of sloped down. He reminded me of a sad bloodhound. I didn't answer and he leaned in front of me and said to his mate on the other side, "He knows but he won't tell us." That amused the pair of 'em.

We went down through Catford into Lewisham; and looking out of the car window, it suddenly hit me, what a horrible feeling it is to be nicked when you're not expecting it. Your mind starts racing and your mouth goes dry, mine does anyway. And you're thinking, 'What do they know? Who could have told 'em anything? Did I leave anything indoors that might help 'em?' But the worst thing about it is, you've lost the power to communicate. You're cut off from the world.

Ninety-nine times out of a hundred, or more than that, you're put into a motor car or a van. And that's it. Your mother could be standing on the pavement next to you, and there's no way you can talk to her, or anyone else. You're separated from the world. You can talk to the coppers who've nicked you if you want to, but you don't.

That man walking his dog on Rushey Green, you're not part of that world anymore. Those people standing at the bus stop. You might see someone you know, but you can't communicate with them. A car pulls up alongside at traffic lights and someone looks over. They don't know that you've just been nicked, and even if they did, you're not part of their world right now.

This wasn't something I was worried about, cos I was confident I'd be out on the street in a short time, but it's still a horrible feeling.

The car took us through Deptford down to the Rotherhithe Tunnel. Then we were through and out the other side, in the East End. It was only then, that I thought, 'Bethnal Green police station;' that slimy, skinny bastard Holmes, had put me in it to save himself. My old nan was right when she said not to trust him. We drove about in some back streets and finally pulled up outside a pub called The Old Horns.

I was thinking, this ain't right; although I'd heard of people meeting coppers in a pub to have a deal. I knew for sure it wasn't right, when I was pushed and dragged through the door, and saw the crowd at the bar. They weren't Old Bill.

The fellow I was cuffed up to looked at his mates, and in a loud voice so they all could hear, "Avalook. Does he look like someone who's just found out we ain't policemen?"

That made 'em laugh, and another comedian amongst 'em said, "Ello ello ello , who have we got here then?" And that made the fuckin idiots laugh some more.

I was taken over to a table away from the bar and cuffed up to the table leg. I said," What's all this about?"

"You'll find out in a minute." he said, "Someone wants to talk to you."

As he went back to the bar I looked around. It was not a pub I would have chose to drink in, but it was like thousands of other backstreet pubs that were about in those days. The chair I was sitting on was upholstered in either red leather or plastic, whatever it was, it squeaked if you moved. The table and chairs were stained to look like oak, probably pine underneath. That's what I was thinking when I suddenly heard the sound of traffic from outside.

Looking round, I saw the door open and two young men in identical grey suits came into the bar. One of them went to talk to the group at the bar, and the other one came and sat at the table opposite me. He was a miserable-looking bastard, about 30, thick black hair, thick eyebrows, and an unpleasant scowl, staring at me with dark brown, almost black eyes. I tried to lighten his mood and gave a nod. "Y'alright?"

He didn't answer, just kept staring, which was a bit creepy. My mind was on Sherlock Holmes now, the skinny no-good sloppy bastard. This was all his fault.

Then the other one came over and sat at the table, and I could see they were twins. Not identical twins though. This one was better looking, not so miserable, and it was either his eyebrows or his eyes, that gave him a look of being puzzled. I felt that I knew him from somewhere, I'd met him before. So these were the Kray twins.

He spoke first. "Hello John, I'm Reg and this is my brother Ron".

I tried to smile, "Hello"

No reaction from Ron. My mind was racing with the things I'd been told. 'They're very dangerous. Ooh they're naughty. Stay on this side of the water. They're unpredictable.'

Reg was talking. "John, you've heard of good cop bad cop, ain'tcha?"

I nodded.

"Well, we're bad cop, worse cop. And we're gonna ask you some questions, and we're gonna want some answers. So don't fuck us about, will you?"

I shook my head, licking my lips, cos my mouth had gone dry. "No course not, what do you want to know?"

Ron leaned forward and his voice was quiet and a bit high pitched. "Who's this Hershel Coombs and why's he asking questions about us?"

I said, "Hershel Coombs?"

Ron's scowl deepened and his eyebrows got close together. He whispered very menacing, "Yes, Hershel fuckin Coombs, who got nicked for importuning men for an immoral purpose. Who phoned you up from Bethnal Green police station. That Hershel Coombs."

As soon as I said it, I knew it was the wrong answer. "Oh him, no there's no such person."

Ron's scowl got deeper, and he took a flick knife from his pocket and laid it on the table. My mouth was really dry, but I said, as quick as I could, "What I meant by that is, it's not his real name. His real name's Sherlock Holmes."

There was a dull click; Ron had pressed the button and the blade had come out. He touched it on my right ear and said, "see your ears. You can go home with 'em on your head, or in your pocket. Now stop fuckin about and tell us his real name."

I don't get frightened too easy but he was scary. I turned to Reg. "That is his real name, feel in my pocket."

I leaned forward and Reg took Holmes' cheque out of my pocket. He looked at it, turned it over, held it up to the light, then passed it to Ron. After putting on a pair of glasses and scrutinising the cheque, Ron put it in his top pocket. He whispered to Reg and they both got up and went to the bar. I heard one of 'em say, "Dick, go and undo him, and see if he wants a drink."

Dick came and took the cuffs off of me and off the table leg. He gave me a warning not to think of going anywhere, and I ordered a light ale. It was about five minutes, before the twins came back with their drinks, and a bottle for me. They took their seats, and I have to say the mood seemed a bit lighter. Reg said, "So who is this Sherlock Holmes?"

I'd decided honesty is the best policy, so I said, "He's the great-grandson of the one in the books. He does a bit of private detective work sometimes."

Ron said, "So what's he want to know about us for?"

I said, "I don't think it's you so much as your brother. He wants to have a deal with him."

Then both of 'em together, "Who, Charlie?"

"No Teddy."

They looked at each other and Ron whispered in Reg's ear, while he's nodding his head like he knew what he was going to say. Reg was looking at me again, serious. "We ain't got a brother Teddy. So what's it all about?"

I told them then, the story of poor Adrian and how he'd gone from Esmeralda's Barn to the party, and got drugged, pumped up, and then blackmailed, by a person calling himself Teddy Kray. But in between, I kept saying, "This is only what I've been told by Holmes."

How he'd been authorised to pay Teddy off. Really, I knew nothing much about it. All I'd done was put up some money to get Hershel Coombs out of Bethnal Green nick. Holmes was the one they needed to talk to.

"So where can we get hold of him?"

That was the question I'd been dreading. I think they knew by now that I would have told 'em anything they wanted to know; and I guessed they believed me when I said, "I don't know"

I explained that the only way I could get in touch with him was through his office phone number, which was some sort of answering service. I gave them the number, and Reg wrote it down. Then he was staring at me and smiling a bit. "I know you now," he said, "You're a mate of Tommy McGovern ain'tcha."

Without saying anything, I nodded, trying to think. That's when I remembered where I knew him from. It might have been a couple of years ago, an ex-professional boxer's do at the Thomas a Becket in the Old Kent Road. I'd arranged to meet a couple of pals of mine there, Bev Chapman and Sweeny Wilson. They'd come down from Norwich with Ginger Sadd, who was a highly rated middleweight in the 1940s;

had a hundred and eighty-seven fights and beat Freddie Mills before the war.

We were drinking at the bar, and I noticed a fellow near the door keep looking at me. I didn't want to look straight at him cos in those days "Who you fuckin looking at?" was often the last thing you heard before you got a right-hander. In the end, I did get a clear look at him and recognised him, it was Tommy McGovern, a good ex-lightweight fighter from the forties and early fifties. He'd retired from boxing, and took up managing, and he'd managed my pal, George. I went over to him. "Hello Tom," we shook hands and he used both his hands, it was a thing he always did. "Hello er er"

He'd forgot my name, so I said, "John"

He was smiling and agreeing with me, "That's right, course it is. How are you, John? How's George, is he alright?"

We talked for a while, the usual waffle. His wife was alright, his kids were alright, he was alright. Then he introduced me to the young fellow he was with. "I'm sorry, this is Reg. Reg, this is John, mate of George Cooper's"

That's when I shook hands with Reg Kray without knowing it. He said, "say hello to George when you see him. Say Reg said Hello."

Ron was smiling now, which made him look even more sinister. "You should have said you were a mate of Tommy's. Would have saved all this unpleasantness."

I should have said!!

If I'd have known it would have made a difference I would have said, but I didn't know. But I know now. So, every time in the future when I'm swagged off the street by bogus police, taken to a strange pub miles away, handcuffed to a table, and confronted by two gangsters, I'm gonna say, "I'm a pal of Tommy McGovern".

I wasn't even a mate of Tommy's; I liked him well enough, I'd met his wife and kids, and he was always nice and polite, but he didn't even remember my name. The few times I'd been up his flat was with George Cooper when Tommy was his manager, but I wasn't going to tell them that. Now we were like dear old pals having a drink together and chatting about old times. I'd finished my light ale, and without getting up, Ron signaled one of the goons at the bar to get me another one.

"What was that funny little motor he used to have?" Reg said

"Nash metropolitan." I knew this cos they were pretty unique at the time, and I think I only saw two of 'em all my life.

"That's right, funny little thing wasn't it,"

Ron was smiling now at the memory, and that made me feel a bit better. My other beer came over, and we talked then about Sherlock and his work; Reg was interested when I said that I sometimes forced entries for him. Then Ron took over, taking my cheque out of his top pocket, he wrote a number on it. "Give this to your mate and tell him to come and see us. I'll sort out that blackmail nonsense for him. I don't like blackmail myself, it's the sort of thing women do." Then out of the blue, he said, " How's old Charlie Dickson doing? I ain't seen him for ages."

Alarm bells went off in my head. This is what coppers do sometimes to trick you. I tried to look like I was thinking, shaking my head slowly. "No, don't think I know him".

Ron looked surprised, or he tried to. "What, I thought everyone knew Charlie on your side of the river"

"Nah" I said, "What does he do?"

Reg piped up, "He's a rag and bone man. Got a scrap yard"

"No," I said," never heard of him."

Ron said, " Don't matter it's not that important, just thought you might have known him."

Then he looked at me a bit concerned, forgetting he wanted to cut my ears off half an hour ago. "I bet you want to be getting home don'tcha."

Without wanting to appear too anxious to get away from 'em, I nodded. "Yeah, I do."

We talked a bit more and they swore me to secrecy. "Don't breathe a word about what we've spoke about to anyone. You can tell your mate but no one else, because everything comes back to us."

I was nodding as they said this, and I knew now, why nobody wanted to talk about them. We left the pub and they saw me out to the car where Tommy, the one I'd been cuffed up to, and the Scotch geezer were sitting in the front. I got in the back and off we went.

On the way back we passed through Lewisham, and I looked out at the snooker hall where I first met Charlie Dickson. That would have been in the late 1950s when the cream of that part of South London visited it at some time or another. It was situated over Burtons the tailors, and a walk up those stairs took you into a den of iniquity. Certain times, you might see the aristocracy of South London there, Hawards, Hennessys, French's, Johnny Carter from Peckham and Kyle Greener from Bromley, people like that. Patsy Houlihan, who Jimmy White said was the best snooker player he'd ever seen; and was described as the greatest hustler of all time played in there a lot. Charlie Dickson used to pop in now and then.

When I first saw Charlie, I had no idea who he was, but people knew him, and he seemed to be well respected. In those days he used to get pills. He'd have pills to keep you awake, pills to knock you out, and they were only slightly more popular than the pills to loosen your bowels, or what was usually the case, someone else's bowels. The rumour was that he owned a pharmaceutical warehouse.

I came to be in Charlie's debt one night through a game of snooker. I'd played a fellow from New Cross, called Lennie something, for a fiver and the table money, and beat him. Then he wanted to play double or nothing, and even though I hadn't seen any money, I stood for it. It was a busy night, and there were no empty tables, so Charlie and a fellow named John were waiting to get on our table. He said he'd mark up for us and have the table when we finished. Well, I beat this Lennie again, and then he didn't want to pay me. He said he'd owe it to me till the next time we played. When I pointed out that he had the dough on him to pay me now, he started cutting up a bit rough, until Charlie said

"Oy, why don't you pay him? It's only a tenner."

I only knew this Len from the snooker hall. I knew him to be a bit mouthy and he liked to hang around with the heavy people, but this night he only had two mates with him. "And why don't you mind your own fucking business?" He said this to Charlie and looked at his mates for backup if he needed it.

Charlie nodded. "Alright" He took out a roll of notes from his pocket and gave me £15. "That's his tenner for the game and a fiver for the table."

Turning to Lennie, he said, "Now you owe me fifteen quid. Next time I see you in here, if you don't pay me, I'll throw you down those fucking stairs. Now fuck off".

Len had been staring at him while he said that, and now he looked round for his mates, but they must have known something that he didn't, and they'd drifted off. I don't know if Lennie ever paid Charlie the £15 or if he got chucked down the stairs, but he was always very polite to me after that night.

I hadn't seen Charlie Dickson since those days at the snooker hall and hadn't thought of him till Ron Kray brought his name up.

The two gangsters were talking to each other in the front, and I didn't bother listening to 'em. We were coming up to Sydenham when the one called Tom turned round and said, "So what did the twins want to see you for?"

I looked him in the eye and give a little smile. "Why don't you ask 'em?"

He didn't like that at all and put on his tough voice, "Cos I'm fuckin asking you".

Shaking my head, I said, "You wouldn't want to know mate. It's embarrassing."

Then the Scotch geezer who was driving said, "Well tell us anyway."

"Alright," I said, "They wanted to know, when you picked me up, which one of the three of you I thought was the dopiest; and I said, him," pointing to Tom.

Well, the Scotch fellow couldn't stop laughing at that. He had trouble controlling the car. And I knew he was going to tell all the others when he got back. Tom wasn't amused though; he realised his tough voice hadn't worked, and he muttered, "Yeah, you think you're very fuckin funny."

I leaned forward so they both could hear. "No Tom, you don't get it. I think you're very fucking funny."

I knew then that me and him were never going to be friends. But I had no way of knowing what a rat he'd turn out to be.

The first thing I did when I got in was to ring Holmes; it was a Mayfair number, but the girl who answered would never give me an address or tell me her name. I used to call her Maud. "Hello Maud, would you tell Mr. Holmes that Mr. Watson has received the charge sheet from Bethnal Green, and it's very interesting."

In less than ten minutes my phone rang with Holmes on the line. "What's all this about a charge sheet?"

I didn't answer straight away but rustled a piece of paper like I was reading. "It says you were importuning men for an immoral purpose. What's all that about?"

"That's not what happened at all." He was shouting now, and I imagined him getting red in the face. "I was offering a young man some money for information when two old bills came out of nowhere and arrested me, but there wasn't any charge. So how come you've got a charge sheet, what's going on?"

I didn't tell him that I never had a charge sheet, but I did tell him I'd been swagged off the street by bogus old bill, and about meeting the twins, and Ron's offer to sort out Adrian's problem. I could hear his excitement through the telephone line. At last Sherlock Holmes was going to meet the Kray twins.

CHAPTER 4

178 Vallance Road

The next day was sunny. I was up early, washed dressed, breakfasted, and waiting for Holmes when the doorbell rang. I opened the door to find a postman, or someone dressed as a postman, holding a parcel. He said, "Sorry to trouble you sir but I can't get an answer from the flat above."

Thinking it was Holmes, I half-turned to go back to the kitchen, and said, "You're making a fool of yourself now mate. It's only funny once. Are you coming in?"

He was still standing in the doorway holding out the parcel saying, "This parcel sir."

Now I was getting fed up. I said, "If you ain't coming in you might as well fuck off."

And when I looked, he was walking backward, with his mouth open, holding out the parcel; till he bumped into Holmes, who'd just walked through the main door. The postman apologised and was muttering, "I've had enough of this." as he went down the steps.

We went down to the kitchen, and I made coffee while Holmes rang the number that Ron had given me. Whoever he spoke to, said we could come as soon as we were ready, and gave the address as 178 Vallance Road, Bethnal Green.

Using my car, it only took Holmes one quick look at the A to Z to give me precise directions. It was a different route to the one the three goons had taken me. This time we went over the top of Sydenham, Lordship Lane, Barry Road, Peckham, Old Kent Road, and finally over Tower Bridge and into the city. In less than an hour, we were outside 178 Vallance Road.

Standing by the door was a scruffy pale-faced geezer with a suitcase. I said, "I wonder what he's up to"

Holmes was nearer to him than me. He wound his window down and really scrutinised the man. "Who, John Ripley, the malacologist? Perhaps he has business with the Kray family."

I was a bit shocked by this. "Do you know him?" As soon as he gave his slimy superior smile, I wished I hadn't said anything.

"No, I don't know him, John. But from his suitcase I can see his name is J. Ripley, James or John, probably John. From the paleness of his skin, I can see that he has not been in this country during the summer months, more likely in one of the Nordic countries. And the snail trails on his sleeve tell me that he's a left-handed malacologist, a studier of snails. From the size of the trails, I would guess that they were made by Helix Aspersa Maxima, a large edible snail; though I've no idea why he should be at this address."

He wound the window up and we got out of the car. I said to the man, "Hello John."

He looked blank, "What?"

37

I said, "James, are you James or John Ripley?"

A look of understanding came on his face. "Oh, the suitcase. No, I found this on a trolley at Liverpool Street station. D'you wanna buy it?" His nose was blowing bubbles of snot as he spoke, and he wiped it on his sleeve, adding to the glistening trails. I guessed then; he wasn't really a malacologist. And I was sure of it when he went on, "I've just got out of Chelmsford Prison. Someone told me if I come down and see the twins, they'll give me a few quid till I get on me feet."

Holmes had hold of my arm, pulling me away. "Come away John, you'll catch something."

I knocked on the door and it was opened straightaway by Ron. " Come in. Come and say hello to our mum."

We were taken down the hall to the kitchen and introduced to Mr. and Mrs. Kray. They looked to me, what I would expect an East End couple of their age to look like. He was about fifty, receding hair, and reminded me of a picture I'd once seen, of John Dillinger, the American bank robber. Mrs. Kray had a nice honest face that might have been attractive once. Her blond hair was waved and showed darker roots, but she looked nice. In her kitchen, in her pinafore, she looked how a mother should look.

Holmes did what I might have expected him to do with Mrs. Kray. "You're their mother, surely not?" in his fake shocked voice. "I thought you were the sister."

Mr. Kray shook his head and carried on reading his newspaper. He obviously knew a bullshitter when he saw one. After saying no to a cup of tea, we went into the front room and sat down, with the twins sitting opposite. The room was decorated in a style that was probably 1950s East End chic; wallpaper and curtains, with trees all over 'em. The furniture though was mostly modern, and we had two comfortable armchairs. I introduced Sherlock Holmes to the twins.   Ron said, smiling, "So, shall I call you Shirley?"

Holmes smiled grimly, "I'd much rather you didn't".

Ron laughed and nudged Reg "Nah, I was only joking. So, what's all this about blackmail?"

Holmes took the photos from the envelope and passed them to him. They took turns in looking at the pictures, and each one of 'em nodded as if this is what they expected to see; as if they recognised someone. Reg passed the photos back to Holmes, saying, "What's the deal you wanted?"

"Well, Adrian is prepared to give this Teddy person £200 as a one-off payment and that's the end of it."

Ron took one of the pictures from Holmes, looked at it then gave it back. "Give us £250 and we'll sort it. He'll never hear from him again. What do you think?"

Holmes took an envelope from his pocket and gave it to Ron. "Two hundred and fifty, it's all there."

Reg looked at his brother, and he didn't look too happy, but he didn't say anything. Now Ron carried on. "Right, we've done something for you. How about you do something for us. That'd be fair, wouldn't it?"

Holmes smiled. "And what would that be?"

"Well, a friend of ours has had a robbery..."

"Or says he has." Reg interrupted him, looking first at Ron, then Holmes, with that puzzled look on his face.

"Or says he has." Ron went on, "We wondered if you might have a look into it, cos it's a bit of a mystery."

I knew that word would get Holmes' interest, and it did. He got up holding his jaw like he'd suddenly got a toothache. But I'd seen it all before, this is him posing. "A mystery, in what way is it a mystery?"

We soon found that out when the twins took us to some offices over a hardware shop in the Bethnal Green Road. Mr. Edmunds, the tenant, and owner of the Great Metropolitan Loans Company had been briefed and was expecting us. He was a big man, about fifty, with a red face and a ginger mustache to match his hair. And he insisted on addressing everyone formally as Mr.. Ron, and Reg were each Mr. Kray, and they called him Mr. Edmunds.

After being introduced as Mr. Coombs, Holmes stood inspecting Mr. Edmunds. From his brown brogue shoes to his brown tweed suit, to his

40

country check shirt, till finally, his eyes settled on the tie. "I see you had a full English breakfast this morning Mr. Edmunds?"

Edmunds looked at me, then at the twins, then back to Holmes, " Yeah, so what. What's that got to do with anything?"

Holmes was staring right at him with his scary hypnotic eyes. "I expect you're wondering how I could have known what you had for breakfast."

"Not really," says Mr. Edmunds, "I should think everyone in Bethnal Green knows what I have for breakfast. I've been having the same thing in Pellicci's for the past twenty years."

Holmes was frowning now, "Yes, but I'm not from Bethnal Green."

"Well I can see that."

This is when Holmes should have given up, but he wouldn't. Folding his arms, he said, "So you're not curious as to how I know?"

Mr. Edmunds looked pissed off. He went and sat at his desk. "No, I'm not. What I am curious about, is how I'm missing six hundred pounds and you want to talk about my fucking breakfast. That's what I'm curious about."

"Well I'll tell you anyway, it was the grease spots on your tie. Now tell us about the robbery."

So Mr. Edmunds told us about the robbery. The thief or thieves had picked the two locks on the street door, then picked the lock on the safe, and taken the six hundred pounds. The evidence was there to see; two pieces of wire each of 'em bent over half an inch at one end and two inches at the other end. These had been left sticking out of the keyhole of the safe. As Holmes was inspecting them Reg asked, "Could you pick a safe lock with them?"

Holmes smiled, and shook his head, "No, and neither could anyone else,"

He held them up a bit theatrical, for us all to see. "These are a red herring or red herrings. Can I see the safe key Mr. Edmunds?"

Edmunds reached in his desk drawer, took out some keys on a ring, and passed them to Holmes. The safe, which stood wide open close to Mr. Edmund's desk, was an old Milner 212. Before he inserted the key in it Holmes took a small magnifying glass from his pocket and inspected all the keys one by one. He must have seen what he was looking for 'cos he gave a little smile. After locking and unlocking the safe a couple of times Holmes returned the keys to Mr. Edmunds.

"Mr. Edmunds, does anyone else have access to the keys?"

Looking up at Holmes, he shook his large ginger head. "No, only me. I open up in the morning and lock up at night."

"What about staff, I heard a typewriter clicking in the room next door?"

"No, that's Rosemary, she never has any reason to touch them; why, what are you getting at with the keys?"

Holmes didn't answer him, but said, "Do you mind if I have a word with Rosemary?"

"No, I don't mind," said Mr. Edmunds, " but I can tell you now, she has cereal for breakfast."

"Very droll," says Holmes and nodded to me to follow him.

We were about to join Rosemary when Ron stopped us at the door, " We're going now. Let us know how you get on with this." They said their goodbyes to Mr. Edmunds and left.

Rosemary's office was not what you'd call inviting; the theme was brown. On the floor was brown and green patterned lino, cracked in places and frayed at the edges. A large brown desk took up the centre of the room, and one wall was lined with filing cabinets. On the opposite wall was brown wood panelling, waist-high, and above that, a sliding hatch window, looking out onto the top of the stairs. A window on the far wall looked out onto the Bethnal Green Road.

Rosemary stopped clacking away on her typewriter, put her cigarette down, and turned in her chair to say, "Hello."

She was a very pretty young lady, probably in her mid-twenties shoulder-length light brown hair, no make-up, and wore a wedding ring on her left hand. Somehow her voice seemed out of place to me, it was refined, and didn't seem to belong in Bethnal Green. Holmes noticed it too, his eyebrows twitched. "Hello Rosemary, I suppose Mr. Edmunds told you why we're here, about the robbery."

She stared up at him with a concerned look. "Yes, it's awful isn't it. It's frightening to think that he might have been watching our movements. It's one of those things you think will never happen to you."

Holmes asked her a few meaningless questions, but all the time he was studying her, making a mental note of everything about her. As we left the room, I noticed him casually drop his notebook just inside the door. Mr. Edmunds was still where we'd left him, in his chair. "Do you occupy any other rooms here Mr.Edmunds?" Holmes asked him.

Heaving himself out of the chair Edmunds said," Yes, we've got a small kitchen and a toilet on this floor and a bathroom and two more rooms upstairs."

Holmes smiled. "A bathroom?"

"It was living accommodation before I took it over. Most of these places still are."

"Interesting," says Holmes, "Do you think you could show us upstairs."

Mr. Edmunds snorted, he hadn't wanted to get out of his chair in the first place, now he had to walk up some stairs. "I don't know what you expect to find up there. They came in through the front door."

We were at the bottom of the second flight of stairs when Holmes patted his pockets.

" Oh dear, I think I've left my notebook in Rosemary's office. If you can just show the rooms to Mr. Watson 'I'll be up in a minute."

Mr. Edmunds grunted, "Huh, come on."

At the top of the stairs was a landing leading to three open doors. On the left was a bathroom with a toilet and basin, that had the usual damp musty smell that unused bathrooms have. The other two rooms were bare, both papered in that old 1940s roses and leaves wallpaper.

I was wondering, 'What am I doing in this stinking rotten building, with this miserable ginger bastard? What am I getting out of it? I'm here cos of a whim of Holmes's, cos he heard the word mystery.'

He interrupted my thoughts when he came to the top of the stairs with his notebook in his hand. Standing there, he seemed to be staring at the far room. ''Interesting,'' he said. Then he started peering at the skirting boards on either side of the landing. "Right Mr. Edmunds, we'll be off now. I think I've seen enough."

Mr. Edmunds' red face got redder. "Seen enough? You've dragged me up here and you ain't even looked in the rooms."

Holmes gave him his sneery smile. "I don't need to look into the rooms, thank you, I can smell them. I've seen all I need to see in this squalid building, and so we'll bid you cheery ho."

We went down the stairs, listening to Mr.Edmunds getting abusive as he waddled down behind us. I knew this would amuse Holmes; he liked that sort of thing.

Outside, we got directions to the Bethnal Green public library and drove down there. It was a depressing building, and from the outside, it had the look of an old workhouse. I was sitting on a bench outside for about half an hour before Holmes came out grinning. "I think we've solved the mystery John, well, I have. But we're a team aren't we, so let's say we've solved it."

But we hadn't solved anything cos I still don't know who did it, if anyone did it at all; or if they did, how they did it. He obviously knew or thought he did. We found a phone box and he invited me in while he phoned the Great Metropolitan loans company. Rosemary answered, "Hello Rosemary, this is Mr. Coombs again, I wonder if you'd be good enough to give a message to Mr. Edmunds. Would you tell him that we've found out who did the robbery and we'll come to your office tomorrow at exactly twelve o'clock. Thank you, Rosemary, we'll see you then, bye."

We were in the car driving back to mine and I asked him, "Are you going to tell me who did it or what?"

He gave the self-satisfied smirk that I fucking hate so much, "Of course I am John, it was Terry Marshall, their next-door neighbor."

"So who's Terry Marshall, and what makes you think he did it?"

He touched my arm and gave me his creepy stare, "John will you indulge me?"

I didn't know what indulge meant then, and I'm not sure now, but it sounded like one of those pervy public school things they used to get up to. Like the time he said once, he might want me to be his Boswell. What's a Boswell? That definitely sounds pervy to me.

Anyway, I just pulled my arm away and didn't say anything, and neither did he. I think he must have been embarrassed.

The next morning, Holmes was round early. He'd already phoned the twins and made arrangements to meet them at Pellicci's Cafe, just a short walk from The Great Metropolitan Loan Co. Ron was already there when we arrived at eleven forty.

"Is Reg going to be here?" Holmes asked him as we sat down.

Ron shook his head, "No."

But he didn't say why, and he didn't say anything else for a while, just kept looking at the door and inspecting whoever came in. Without our asking for them or being given a choice, three teas were placed on the table. Occasionally Ron would look away from the door to me and Holmes, and he'd frown a bit like he was trying to remember something.

After about the weirdest ten minutes of my life, sitting in silence, Holmes said, "Shall we go."

Ron sprang up from his chair. "Yeah, why not, come on."

As we got near to Mr. Edmunds's office Holmes said to me, "John, I want you to cross the road and observe the first-floor window to the left of the offices. At exactly twelve o'clock I expect you to see a young man at the window watching Ron and me. If that happens, I want you to nod once, walk off, cross the road further down and join us."

I crossed the road, glad to get away from Ron, cos I found his silence a bit creepy. Two minutes to twelve I was standing opposite, and sure enough bang on twelve the curtain went back, and a fellow had his face pressed against the window looking down at Holmes and Ron. I gave Holmes the nod, walked down, crossed back over, and joined them.

Mr. Edmunds was in his favourite position, sitting at his desk. He was wearing the same clothes that he had on yesterday. "So, you say you know who stole my money."

Right at that moment, Rosemary came into the room with some papers in her hand. "Sorry to interrupt, these are the applications from yesterday."

She placed the papers on the desk and was about to leave when Holmes held up his hand. ''Please don't go Rosemary, this might interest you too." Turning back to the desk he said, "Can I see your safe key again Mr.Edmunds."

The fat man sighed, leaning back in his chair he opened the drawer, took out the keys, and threw them on the desk, like a big sloppy sulky kid. "Phew, what now?"

Holmes smiled, but his cold stare said he didn't mean it. He selected one of the keys and held it up so we could all see it. I knew that the theatrics were about to begin. "Is this your safe key?"

Mr. Edmunds nodded. "Yes, it is."

"And is the safe locked?"

"Yes, the safe is locked," He was looking questioningly at Ron. Ron was looking questioningly at Holmes, and I was looking at Rosemary, who looked a bit troubled.

Holmes slammed the keys down on the desk, "Watch this." He patted the keys with his left hand, went to the safe, and bent over it with his back to us. Then, like a chef pulling the lid off a flaming rice pudding or something, " Et voila." Stepping back, with his trademark smirk, he pointed to the open safe.

Mr. Edmunds grabbed at the keys on his desk, then, seeing the safe key still on the ring. "How did you do that?"

"Quite easily really. In much the same way that Terry Marshall did it to steal your money."

Ron had been staring at Holmes, definitely impressed. "And who's Terry Marshall, where can we get hold of him?"

Holmes was looking at Rosemary. "You won't have to go far Ron, just next door."

I don't think the others noticed, but I'm sure Rosemary whispered the F word when he said that.

"No," Mr. Edmunds said, "that can't be. There's only a Terry Mitchell lives next door. You know him, don't you Rosemary. He's always trying to chat her up, but I've told him she's married."

All eyes were on Rosemary now, who'd gone into her office and returned with a lighted cigarette. She looked distraught.

Holmes carried on, "I'm afraid Mr. Mitchell isn't Mr. Mitchell at all. He is Terry Marshall. He is on the voter's list as Terry Marshall. And he was Terry Marshall when he was sentenced at Bow St Magistrates Court to one years' probation for going equipped to steal."

Mr. Edmunds had got out of his chair and locked the safe, testing the handle to make sure. 'So how did he get in and open my safe."

"Well, he didn't need to pick the door locks downstairs because he came in through the loft hatch upstairs. And he didn't need to pick the lock of your safe because Rosemary had given him an impression of the key, from which he made one of his own."

Poor Rosemary burst into tears, and she looked a pitiful sight. For all her sobbing and trying to catch her breath, she wouldn't stop puffing on her cigarette, and smoke was coming out of her mouth and her nose, almost hiding her face.

Holmes took a handkerchief from Ron's top pocket. "D'you mind Ron." Without waiting for an answer, he went to Rosemary and wiped some of the tears from her cheeks. "I'm sorry Rosemary, I suppose he told you he loved you." She nodded and made more horrible gurgling noises. Holmes pressed the handkerchief on her face and left her to hold it. He turned to me then, " I suppose you're wondering how I knew what Rosemary had done."

He said it to me, but he was really addressing all of us. I was tempted to say 'no', but I was a bit curious, so I nodded. He picked up the keys again from the desk and held them up.

"When I examined these keys yesterday, I found minute grains of a white substance on one key only. The key to the safe. From that, I gathered that an impression had been made of that key using cuttlefish bone. I asked myself, 'Why only that key, and why not the keys to the front door locks?' My conclusion was that the thief had an alternative means of entry. You must have noticed, John, when you looked upstairs, a loft hatch in the ceiling."

I shook my head, "No, I didn't."

"I didn't either," said Mr.Edmunds.

"That's because you looked but you didn't see," said patronising Holmes, "But I did, and I also saw the marks of a ladder on the skirting boards. The ladder that Mr. Marshall used to gain access to his loft space and to descend into your property. I assume that these buildings have no partitioning walls above eaves level."

Edmunds was looking a bit distraught now, probably thinking he's got to hire and train a new secretary. "But how did you know that Rosemary was involved?"

"Well, while you were upstairs with Mr.Watson yesterday, I opened your desk drawer intending to take an impression of the safe key, which I did. Inside the drawer, I found minute grains of cuttlefish bone, which indicated to me that someone had already taken an impression, in or over the drawer. Someone who had access. And on the floor, I found this." He'd taken a matchbox from his pocket, opened it, and

51

tapped it out on the desk. "Cigarette ash, but not just any cigarette ash, this is the ash from an Embassy cigarette. Isn't it Rosemary?"

Poor Rosemary started gurgling again, holding Ron's sodden handkerchief to her face.

He went on, "All my suspicions were confirmed when at precisely twelve o'clock Terry Marshall appeared at his window to see who it was that had discovered him. And that information could only have been imparted to him by this sad lady."

Everyone was looking at Rosemary now, and if she hadn't impressed us enough with her sobbing and gurgling, she now started howling and more tears ran down her cheeks. Ron had been sitting on the edge of the desk, he got up now, and he was scowling. "Right, so how do we get our money?"

I'd thought it was Mr. Edmunds's money, and I think he did too, but he didn't say anything. Holmes spoke calmly, the way you might talk to an excitable child. "Give me half an hour Ron and I'll get the money. Why don't you go and have a cup of tea in Pellicci's and I'll bring it to you, or should I give it to Mr, Edmunds?"

"Give it to me, and I'll sort it out, and try not to be too long."

We watched him strutting up to Pelliccis as Holmes rang Terry Marshall' doorbell. After all that had gone on, we didn't expect an answer, so Holmes took a piece of celluloid from his pocket, slid it into and down the door jamb, pushed, and the door was open.

Terry Marshall was sprawled on his sofa, wearing a sort of knee-length dressing gown over his trousers. And he wasn't pleased to see us. He jumped up and started flexing his shoulders like he meant business. "How the fuck did you get in here?"

Holmes looked him up and down smiling, "We just want the money, Terry. Rosemary has told us everything. So, if you'd like to give us the money you stole, that will be the end of the matter. What do you say?"

He was a big lump, about as tall as Holmes but bigger built, and very good looking. His hair was dark, almost black, but the most striking thing about him was his eyes, they were a deep blue, and seemed to shine out of his face. Coming a bit closer and moving his shoulders like he was going to do something, he shouted." Now. Do yourself a favour and just fuck off. Now."

Holmes wasn't intimidated by him at all. "I expect you're wondering how I knew it was you, Terry. It was the ladder marks on the skirting board."

He didn't get the answer he was expecting. "No," said Terry, "What I'm wondering, is will you bounce when I throw the fucking pair of you down them stairs. I'd better tell you," he went on, "I work for the Kray twins, so you'd better fuck off now, and forget about any money."

Holmes said, "I don't believe you. Why don't you just give us the money?"

There was a phone on a coffee table next to his sofa. He sat down and dialled a number, looking up at Holmes, "You don't believe me."

We could hear the ringing tone, then someone picked up. Terry spoke into the phone, "Hello, is that Ron, Ron Kray?" there was a pause, then, "It's Terry, Ron, I've got two mugs round my flat demanding money off of me. I've told 'em I work for you, but they don't believe me, alright."

He handed the phone to Holmes. "Ron Kray wants to talk to you."

I was nearer, so I took it off him. "Hello."

A deep voice, nothing like Ron's answered me. "This is Ron Kray. If you ain't out of that flat in two minutes I'm gonna come down there myself, and I'm gonna fucking hurt the pair of you."

I looked at Holmes and he nodded ever so slightly, so I played along, "Oh, sorry Ron, we didn't know he was a mate of yours. We must have made a mistake."

"Yeah, you fucking did. And don't call me Ron, it's Mr. Kray to you, dickhead."

I put the phone down then. I was trying to look sheepish and stop myself from laughing at the same time. "Sorry Terry, I think we must have made a mistake, no hard feelings I hope."

The bully was coming out in him now, you could see it in his face. "Just fuck off you pair of fucking mugs. And think yourself lucky he didn't come down here."

Holmes couldn't help himself; he touched his forelock as he pushed past me to get out of the room. "Thanks, guvnor".

I was relishing the thought of telling Ron what had gone on, and I didn't have to wait long to do it. We were just about to close the door when he came strutting back from Pelliccis; he'd got tired of waiting. Listening to the story of what had happened in the flat Ron's eyebrows were getting closer. "Let's go and talk to him," he said.

Terry was surprised to see me and Holmes again. He jumped up from his sofa. "I thought I told you to fuck off, you......"He stopped then, and his mouth fell open when Ron walked in the room. "Oh, no."

"No," said Ron, "It's oh yes. Now, where's my fucking money?"

"It's all here Ron, It's in the kitchen"

He was shaking and nearly ran out of the room, with his silly dressing gown flapping round his knees. In about two seconds he was back with a brown paper carrier bag. Putting it on the sofa, he took out six bundles of notes, each one secured by a heavy elastic band, and put them on the table.

"It's all here Ron, six hundred. I didn't know it was your money, no-one told me."

Ron picked up the bag and emptied it onto the table. Three more bundles fell out. Ron gave one to me, and one to Holmes and stuck one in his pocket. "Expenses," then he took another two. "Commission," The rest he put back in the bag. He was smiling now, and passed the bag to me, "Do you want to wait outside for me, I'll be along in a minute."

I glanced at Terry Marshall, and he looked thoroughly distraught, and with good reason. We hadn't got out the door before Ron had suddenly punched him somewhere below the belt, knocking him onto the sofa; then he was kneeling on top of him talking, but rhythmically punctuating each word with a punch to Terry's face. "You –will—not—fucking tell—people....... ."

And Terry was keeping up the rhythm with his groans, "Oof.....ugh....ooh...

I stopped watching when I saw the blood splattering up in the air, but Ron didn't seem to mind. We could still hear him as we went downstairs.

When he came down, he seemed happier, now that he'd got blood all over his white shirt, and on his suit. "Let's hope that's taught him a lesson. Where are you parked?"

This was the first of many lessons we saw taught by the twins over the next few months. The lucky students got away with a beating, the ones who weren't so lucky would get cut, or shot in the leg; it depended on who was the teacher of the day, and what mood they were in.

We'd parked just over the road from Pelliccis, so it didn't take long to get back to Vallance Road. Mrs. Kray Answered the door, shocked at the sight of Ron.

"Oh Ron, what have you done now?"

"Fellow got a nosebleed mum; I gave him my hanky, but it couldn't stop it."

She accepted this; probably she'd heard it before, or similar, and it was better than hearing the truth. "Go upstairs and get changed; give that suit to your dad, he'll get those bloodstains out.

We waited in the front room, and he came down in a clean white shirt and a different suit, not a sign of blood anywhere. Reg was with him, and I guessed that he'd been told about all that had gone on. He winked at Holmes, "You've had a busy day then. Good result though, you happy with that?"

I think he meant the money, but I knew the money was nothing to Holmes compared to the satisfaction he got from solving something like this. Not waiting for an answer Reg went on, "we've got another little job if you're interested."

I nodded to Holmes, and he nodded to Reg, so he told us what they wanted, and that was for us to watch someone in a few days' time. They wanted to know where he went, and who he met. The man's name was Leslie Bishop, and he lived in South London. They were also anxious that no one should know Holmes' true identity or his profession. At a later date we might be meeting some of the staff, and the least they knew the better.

After those arrangements were made, we chatted for a while. The twins told us they owned a couple of nightclubs, did a great deal of unpaid charity work, and supplied security men for various clubs and businesses in east and west London. All this naturally led to them meeting showbiz personalities, and other important people. If we were interested, they could probably put some very lucrative work our way.

About an hour after we arrived, we were getting ready to leave, when Reg answered a knock on the door and admitted their brother, Charlie. He was taller than the other two, and where they were dark, he was fair, but it was easy to see the family resemblance. We were introduced, but Ron didn't use Sherlock's name, he called him Hershel.

Holmes was looking Charlie up and down in a way that I thought was a bit rude. He said, "I see you've just come from an upholsterers shop in Wapping."

Charlie looked a bit puzzled. "Why would you think that?"

"I observe," said Holmes, "strands of horsehair clinging to your trousers, and...." He bent down and ran his finger along the edge of Charlie's shoe.

"And on your shoe the yellow clay of Wapping."

Charlie smiled, brushing his trousers with his hand. "No, that's not horsehair, it's dog's hair. I stopped to stroke one outside. And I'm sorry but that on your finger is not clay."

Holmes winced. "Uurgh."

I was trying hard not to laugh, but Holmesy, without batting an eyelid, picked up some hair from the floor and said "Yes, I think you're right. Deutscher Schaefer Hund, if I'm not mistaken."

Charlie shook his head again. "No, I'm afraid you're wrong there, it was an Alsatian; I saw it walking off afterwards."

That's when Ron interrupted, "No he's right Charlie. That's what the Germans call Alsatians. He knows what he's talking about."

"Thank you," said Holmes, at the same time, taking a handkerchief from Charlie's top pocket, "D'you mind?" Not waiting for an answer, he wiped his finger on it, and then handed it back to Charlie. I tugged Holmes' sleeve and we made our exit, but not before he'd poked his head around the door to say goodbye to Mr. and Mrs. Kray.

When we'd arrived, I never had a chance to look at Vallance Road, cos of the malacologist, and Holmes' eagerness to meet the twins. Now I had a chance, and it wasn't impressive. Identical drab terraced houses, with only the difference in some of the doors and curtains giving them any sort of individuality. On the pavement, two doors up from the Krays, there was a huge Alsatian sitting and looking at us.

Holmes nodded at the dog. "There's your culprit. There's the answer to the mystery of the yellow clay of Wapping." He smiled as he said this and the fucking dog smiled back at him.

We were in the car driving back when I said, "Did I imagine it, or did that dog smile at you?"

Then came his self-satisfied smirk again. "Yes I think it did."

I said, "Holmes, dogs can't smile. Their brains ain't adapted for smiling."

"Alright John, perhaps it didn't, but I will tell you this; and not many people know it, but I share with Adolf Hitler, a strange power over women and dogs."

Now I knew it was time to talk about something else so I said, "what do you make of them twins then?"

He didn't answer straight away but closed his eyes and started moving his lips about like he was chewing something. "Well," he said, "they're certainly an enigma."

Like I'm supposed to know what an enigma is. All I know is it's something to do with going to the toilet. So I said, "Yeah, I thought that as well."

He went on, "The thing that I find strange, is why two very successful young men should choose to live with their parents, in what is essentially a slum."

"What, d'you mean?" I said, "Cos it's got an outside toilet?"

He didn't answer, just nodded, and turned to look out of the side window. That same thing had occurred to me. Why would anyone choose to live at 178 Vallance Road?

CHAPTER 5

Surveillance

Three days after our meeting with the twins Holmes rang me to say the Leslie Bishop thing was on for tomorrow. The next morning, he was round mine early; in a London taxi that he'd bought at auction, and had a new engine fitted.

He assured me it would blend in anywhere and outrun anything it might need to and at 10.15, we left for Mr. Bishop's house at Tulse Hill.

Reg had told us that he never left home before 10.30, so we didn't have to wait long before he was picked up by someone in a two-tone Singer Gazelle. They hadn't gone far before they stopped in a side road off of Tulse Hill. We swung round past them and Holmes got out to follow them on foot. He came back to say that they'd just ordered breakfast in a cafe on the main road. It was nearly an hour before they came round the corner and got in their car. Back into Tulse Hill, we tailed them, heading north to Effra Road, through Brixton, past the Oval into Kennington Road, then on to Westminster Bridge.

A couple of times we thought we'd lost them in traffic but managed to pick 'em up again. It was driving round Parliament Square that we did lose 'em properly. I was gutted and ready to go back home, but

Holmes wouldn't give up. He had us driving round these streets, doubling back on ourselves, till finally, in a little road called Storeys Gate, there was the Singer Gazelle with the driver still in it, parked outside of a pub, the Westminster Arms. We pulled into a side road and Holmes got out; he walked down and turned the corner.

After a while, I got fed up with watching people walk by, so I switched on the radio, hoping for some music. I got "Workers Playtime" from a company up north that made aluminum clogs or something like that. Half a minute and I turned it off and went back to assessing the passers-by. It wasn't too long before Sherlock came back, grinning. "I'm pretty sure we're finished for the day. Go and stand on the corner, he should be out soon."

He was right; in a couple of minutes, Bishop came out of the pub, clutching his briefcase. I ran back and jumped in the cab. Holmes had already started it and we pulled up to the corner of the road and waited. Sure enough, the Singer came sailing by, and we tailed it back over the bridge into south London. "He'll be going home now." Holmes seemed quite pleased with himself.

I said," How do you know?"

"Because he's got what he came out for, what this day has been about, trust me."

He was so confident that he let their car get away in the traffic while he told me what had gone on in the pub. Bishop had met with a smooth-looking Jewish man and they'd gone to a table to talk business.

Don't ask me how he knew the man was Jewish. Anyway, they'd studied some papers together, and the name Enugu was mentioned twice. Bishop had stuffed the papers into his briefcase, and they shook hands. "The question is," says Holmes in his dramatic voice, "Who or what is Enugu?"

He was right about one thing; Bishop had gone home. The Singer Gazelle was just driving off as we passed his house. Holmes dropped me at mine and didn't want to stay because he had film to develop. It turns out, he'd managed to take photos of Bishop in the cafe and in the pub. I was beginning to get a bit more respect for him than I had before.

Later that night he rang me to say he'd spoken to Reg, who was pleased with what Holmes had told him and it was arranged that we'd go back to Vallance Road tomorrow with a full report, photos, and all.

Holmes arrived almost without incident the next day; apart from the fact he was dressed like a beatnik, and now driving a mini cooper. When I say like a beatnik; he had on a navy corduroy jacket over a roll neck jumper, blue jeans, and brown Hush Puppies. And he didn't seem embarrassed by it at all. We sat in the kitchen drinking coffee, and I said to him,

"Are you really thinking of going over there like that?"

His eyebrows went up. "And why shouldn't I?"

I didn't care to have an argument about it, so I just said, " Don't matter," and left it at that.

He showed me the report on Leslie Bishop that he'd made out, and I couldn't believe it. Besides photos, there was a list of every road they'd travelled and times, what they'd had for breakfast at Tulse Hill, and what they'd drunk at the Westminster Arms. There was no doubt about it, I had underestimated him.

I rang Ron at Vallance Road and told him we were on our way. Holmes wanted to take his Mini Cooper, but I talked him out of it. I had a theory about those cars. Nobody ever bought one because they were comfortable to drive. They were a "look at me I'm different" car, like a Rolls Royce, except they're: "I've got more money than you lot." Who in their right mind would want to drive one of them about? Different if you've got a chauffeur, or if you was the only car on the road.

Anyway, we went in my car, a Rover 100, which was 10 times more comfortable than a Mini, and probably just as comfortable as a Roller. To stop him sulking I let Holmes drive, and I've got to be honest, he was a good driver; probably the only thing he was good at. That and disguising himself.

We took the same route as before, Tower Bridge, Mansell Street, turn right into Whitechapel High Street and we were outside number 178 in just over 35 minutes. As I knocked on the door, I noticed that

Alsatian dog sitting in the same spot where we'd last seen him. I nudged Holmes. "Avalook, there's your mate."

Holmes turned to look, and the fucking dog winked at him. Just then, the door opened, and Mrs. Kray invited us in. "Come in love, The boys will be down in a minute. Would you like a cup of tea?"

Holmes couldn't stop himself. "No thank you, Mrs. Kray, that's awfully kind of you but we've only just had breakfast. You've had your hair done haven't you".

She smiled and patted her hair. "Yes, I have, d'you like it?"

"Well, if I didn't know Grace Kelly was in Monaco, I would have sworn she'd just opened the door to us." He said this with a smarmy leer on his face; but it pleased her.

"Yeah, I'm sure you would," she said, smiling. She was laughing as she showed us into the front room.

As soon as she was gone, I said to Holmes, "Did that dog wink at you or what?"

He didn't answer at first, just raised his eyebrows and shrugged. "I don't know, did it?"

The boys came into the room then, and I guessed the surprise on their faces was because of what Holmes was wearing. Reg said, "Hello chaps, how'd it go? "

Holmes took an envelope from his briefcase and passed it to Ron. "Not too bad actually."

The contents were tipped out onto a small table, and while Reg went through the photographs, Ron was reading the first of two typewritten pages. When he'd finished, he passed the papers to Reg, and he looked at the photos. They both seemed satisfied, and Ron said, "Very nice, very professional. Now if that had been one of our firm he would have said, 'He went into a pub met a geezer got some papers off him, and went.' That's even if they managed to tail him to the pub"

They both laughed at that. And that lightened the mood enough for me to say, "Here Ron, who's is that Alsatian sits outside a couple of doors up?"

He went to the window and drew back the net curtain. "Oh, that's Nero, poor old thing. He got hit by a van and it's fucked his face up, keeps twitching and blinking his eye. I used to have his grandfather years ago."

Looking at Holmes I said, "Oh so he don't actually smile at anyone."

Ron said "No dogs ain't got the mental ability to smile. They either lick you or bite you. That's as far as it goes with 'em."

Holmes was nodding his head "Ron, that's exactly what I've been trying to tell him."

Then he went on to talk about them living in Jack the Ripper territory, and how he was surprised that his great grandfather hadn't investigated the murders. I didn't want to say, "Cos he might have done 'em himself." That was a belief that had been passed down in our family over the years.

Reg said, "Yeah, there was one of 'em done just around the corner from here, mind that was years ago wasn't it."

Holmes was nodding again, and Ron said, "Things ain't changed that much in the East End you know. There's always some nutter with a knife, cutting and carving people up."

They both found this amusing, Ron more so than Reg, he sat for a long while, looking down at the floor and chuckling to himself.

We were getting ready to go when Reg said they had another little job for us if we were interested. Apparently, a fellow called Big Albert Donaghue had been threatening to shoot them, not to their face, but to other people.

The twins had no idea who he was, or why he should wish to harm them. In their business, they did get gangsters trying to take over their clubs, or demand protection money, perhaps he was one of those. If we could find out where he lived, where he drank, and who with, perhaps a meeting could be arranged to settle the differences.

We were given the name of one pub that he used. This all seemed simple enough, so Holmes agreed we'd do it, and we were about to go when Reg said, "I ain't being rude, but you might want to think about wearing a suit around here."

Holmes's jaw dropped. "Oh"

Reg went on, "Dressed like that people might think you're old bill or a fuckin landscape gardener or something. They wouldn't take you seriously." From his pocket, he took an envelope, and from another pocket, he brought out some five-pound notes. "That's for yesterday, and there's a few quid extra, buy yourself a suit."

On the drive back I gave Holmes the name of my tailor, Sam Arkus in Berwick Street, nearly everyone in Soho went there, I don't know if the twins did. He said he'd give it a try. Then he started babbling about Jack the Ripper again.

I don't think he knew it, but I'd read up about the Whitechapel murders and I happened to know that Jack the Ripper hadn't done 'em. It annoyed me the way people were so ready to believe that Jack the Ripper was the killer. No one ever questioned it. No-one ever stopped to think; could it have been somebody else that done 'em. I put this to Holmes, and he got a bit pompous, which is what I expected.

"Oh," he said, "So who did kill those women?"

I knew he wouldn't like the answer. "Queen Victoria's grandson and her doctor."

He didn't take his eyes off the road but pulled a face like he'd just had a migraine attack. "And you believe that?"

I said, "I know that. There's no way Queen Victoria would let her grandson be nicked for murder, so they had to fit someone up for it. So they picked on a geezer who happened to have the name, Jack the

68

Ripper. If he'd been Jack the baker, or Jack the chimney sweep, or Jack the train driver, you'd never have heard of him."

I looked at Holmes for a response, but he was staring at the road, although he kept screwing up his eyes like he was in pain. I carried on," It's funny ain't it; he was never tried in court, never found guilty, and yet everyone is quite happy to say Jack the Ripper done it. No wonder he went into hiding, I would have done too, so would you."

He turned his head quickly to look at me, "Well John if that's what you believe I can't really argue about that."

Now that's what I've always found, not just with him, but with people like him. You confront 'em with facts and they've got no answer. We were coming up Barry Road, and nearly home when I mentioned Adrian's money.

"What about it?" said Holmes.

"Well, what's going to happen to it? Even Reg knew he'd given you more than two hundred and fifty quid. What are we gonna do with the rest?"

He was drumming his fingers on the steering wheel. "I had thought about giving it back to him".

"Yeah," I said. "that sounds fair. I'll phone him when I get home, and we'll do it tomorrow." I looked at Holmes when I said this, and his eyes were rolling about a bit in his head like he was trying to get his thoughts together. Then he said, "a hundred and fifty."

That was a nice few quid in those days, so I said, "What, each?"

"No," he said, "a hundred and fifty for your share. Do you want it or not?"

I was happy with that, plus there was a hundred and fifty for us to split in the envelope Reg had given him, so it was a nice day's work. I switched the radio back on and we drove up towards Crystal Palace, listening to the Beatles singing, "Listen, do you want to know a secret.....I've known a secret for a week or two. Nobody knows, just we two..."

Holmes switched it off. "I don't know John," he said, "why people would say the twins are dangerous. They seem like two normal healthy young men to me."

It took just over a week for him to find out one of them at least, wasn't as normal as he'd thought.

CHAPTER 6

Esmeralda's Barn

It was another five days before Holmes rang to say he was on his way round. The sun was up, and as it was a warm day, I was sitting on the front steps drinking coffee when he arrived. This time he was driving a dark blue 2.4 Jaguar with the new A registration: the car of choice for the smash and grab firms and bank robbers in those days.

I had to look twice as he climbed out of the car and walked towards me, wearing a suit that could only have come from Sam Arkus. And not only that, he'd adopted the swagger and mannerisms of the Kray twins. He looked pleased with himself. "Well, I didn't want to look like a fuckin landscape gardener, did I?"

Now, not only did he walk like them he sounded like 'em too. If I didn't know better, I would have sworn it was Reg talking. We went back into the flat and I made more coffee.

When I asked him how he'd got Sam Arkus to make him a suit in such a short time, he leaned forward in his chair and looked at me the way Reg had done, and he spoke in Reg's voice. "It was quite easy actually. I persuaded him."

The radio on the worktop was playing. "And here's another song from the Beatles Please Please Me album, this one's entitled Misery."

We only heard a few bars of the introduction before Holmes was on his feet. "Why didn't they call the whole bloody album Misery? D'you mind?" And he sauntered across to the radio and switched it off. Now, he didn't just look and walk like one of the chaps, but like one of the chaps who was doing very well for himself. From the way he kept adjusting the knot in his tie and hunching his shoulders I got the impression that he liked his new look. We finished our coffee, and while I washed up Holmes went to look at himself in the hall mirror. Then we jumped in his Jag and headed for Bow.

On the way over, he told me he'd been having cockney gangster lessons. He wouldn't say who taught him, only that he was a far more capable teacher than I was. No one could deny that cos now he could have fooled anyone.

It always occurred to me that once you crossed the river you were in an older part of London. This was London when Catford and Penge and Lewisham were country villages; but compared to our side of the water it was grey and dreary. And I knew why, it was because there wasn't any trees. Well, there was a few, but they were pathetic straggly things compared to what we had in South London.

Holmes had made a list of the pubs in Bow and it was in the third one, The Wentworth Arms, that we got some information, "Try the Black Swan."

This was another street corner pub in the Bow Road, and we got a few looks when we went in. I ordered a light ale for Holmes and a gin and tonic for myself. Holmes nodded the barman over, in his cockney gangster voice, "Big Albert been in lately?"

"D'you mean Albert Donaghue?"

It was a lesson in intimidation to watch Holmes. He didn't answer at first, just touched the knot in his tie, and all the time staring at the barman with his creepy eyes, then he said, "Yeah Albert Donaghue."

It don't seem possible how those three words could be frightening, but they frightened that barman alright. He was gulping and looking round like he wanted someone to help him.

"No, he ain't been in for ages, he's away. Got two years ages ago, I don't think he's gonna be out for a while."

Holmes give him the look again. "He still living in the same place?"

The barman nodded, "What, the flats? Yeah."

I said, "What flats?"

Glad to get away from Holmes's scary eyes, he turned his attention to me. "Ashcombe House, off Devons Road."

We left him in peace then, to polish some glasses at the other end of the bar. When we were ready to leave Holmes called him over and slid three pound notes across the bar. "Have this on the twins."

I noticed everyone kept their heads down as we left the pub.

Outside, Holmes stopped a couple of people to ask for directions and soon found the way to a public library. I didn't go in with him, but sat on the bonnet of the car, in case any young ladies might come along and think it was mine, but that never happened.

It didn't take Holmes long to find out what he wanted; he came over to the car holding a piece of paper, which I noticed was covered in scribble. "Shorthand," he said this and gave a little smile that seemed to say to me. 'But you're too thick to understand it.'

We didn't talk much on the way home cos I was still brooding over what he'd said, although he hadn't actually said it, but he'd thought it. Or at least, that's what I thought he was thinking. Then out of the blue, he said, "Are you alright John, you seem a bit quiet."

That was typical of him, he knew what I had the hump about when he said "Shorthand" and smiled. But I could see some easy money coming, so I let it go and we both went home.

It was one of those ancient Greeks who said something like, "When a body is immersed in water a messenger will call." And that's what happened to me, and it wasn't the first time. I dragged myself out of the bath and into the hall, where I had a phone on the wall. It was Holmes. "John. I've got some bad news."

I said, "Yeah what's happened?"

"I can't tell you over the phone, can I call round later, about seven?".

This is what he's got me out of a nice warm bath for. I grunted, "Yeah", and hung up.

At three minutes to seven, I watched Holmes pull up outside in his Jag. He sat there for a while, and then, at a minute to seven, he got out of the car and walked up to the front door. I counted the seconds on my watch, and exactly on the hour, the bell rang.

We went into the front room, and I turned off the music.

"So what's happened?" I asked him.

He started pulling faces then, like he was trying to look upset. "Adrian's parents received a letter in the post today."

I wanted to say, "So did a fucking million other people, so what," but I didn't, I just looked round the room like I was bored.

He went on, "That bastard Teddy Kray, or whatever his name is, sent the photos to them. Adrian is absolutely distraught."

The unpleasant thought of having to give Adrian his money back made me feel absolutely distraught. "So what do you want to do?"

"Well, I know where the Krays will be tonight, I intend to beard them in their den. Are you up for it?"

That's the sort of nonsense he used to come out with "Beard them in their den". Why not "go and talk to them?" But that's Sherlock Holmes. Somehow, he'd found out that the twins would be at Esmeralda's Barn that night; the place that led to Adrian's fall from grace. There was no way I could really get out of it, plus there was a day's money owing, so I said OK. Suited and booted fit for the West End, I slapped on some aftershave, and we left.

Holmes knew the way there; he seemed to know London like a cab driver. In Wilton Place, we parked up by a grimy old church and went over to the club. There was no one on the door so we went straight up. Inside, you only had to look around to see the place was on its way out.

I remembered it as it used to be a couple of years ago. It was buzzing in those days, mostly with well-to-do people and women with lots of real jewelry. How does a place go from that to this in such a short time? A couple of the tables were operating for just a few punters. Most of the action was at the bar, where the cream of Bethnal Green were behaving like they were still in their East End local.

Holmes spotted Ron sitting at a table away from the bar, with two young men. He'd probably seen us as we came through the door, cos he whispered something, and the two fellows got up and slipped away from his table. Keeping their faces away from us, they wandered round the edge of the room and out the door. It was too late; I twigged one of them as the geezer in the photos, the one who Holmes pointed out as Teddy Kray the blackmailer. Holmes hadn't noticed him and went right over to Ron, "Hello Ron."

We sat in the seats that his two friends had just vacated and Ron was all smiles. "Hello John, Hello Hershel, what you doing over here?" Holmes took an envelope from his pocket and passed it to him.

"That report you wanted. Donaghue."

Ron was looking round now as he read the report like he didn't want our conversation to be overheard. "Yeah that's nice, very nice, only thing is I've got no cash on me right now. Can I pay you tomorrow?"

Holmes nodded. "Of course, whenever it suits you. There is just one other thing Ron."

"Yeah, what's that?"

"That blackmail business. The little shit who was using your family name has sent the photos to Adrian's parents."

Ron took a sip of his drink, leaned back in his chair, and pulled the same face that Holmesy did, trying to look upset. He said all indignant, "Well, I can't believe it, the little bastard."

Holmes went on, "I know it's not your fault, but when you said you'd sort it I thought that would be the end of the matter. And now it looks like costing me a lot of money."

Ron was nodding in sympathy. "Yeah, I know. It's a shame ennit. Mind you, I did only say I'd try to sort it, and that's what I did. I barred him from the club, and I warned him there'd be serious consequences if he carried on with it. I suppose he's done this out of spite." Then he cheered up a bit. "Well, perhaps it's all for the best. Once it's out in the open it'll soon die down. It's like lancing a boil."

This little bit of philosophy brightened him up and he took us over to the bar to meet the gang. I already knew Tommy and Bill, the Scotch fellow, but we were introduced to another Tommy, a Mick, Connie,

Alfie, Dick, two more Bills, and others whose names I can't remember. This was the firm, or part of it.

They were an ill-assorted bunch, all different shapes and sizes, with ages ranging from twenties to mid-forties. A couple of 'em had the appearance of having been boxers at some time. You could usually spot 'em by the puffed eyes, the flattened nose, and occasionally, the displaced knuckles. They seemed friendly enough.

Ron ordered drinks for us, a light ale and a gin and tonic. It made me think, how did he know that without asking?

Someone in the crowd said, "Look who's here."

Leslie Bishop and the fellow who'd been with him when we followed them had just entered the club. Ron called them over and introduced us. "Here Les, I want you to meet a couple of good friends of ours." He watched as we shook hands with Bishop and Freddie Davies, his beady eyes looking for any sign of recognition, but there wasn't any.

Ron was called over to the bar, and he left us with Bishop and Freddie. I hadn't got a good look at Les Bishop on the day we followed them. But now seeing him up close, he was a bit of a lump, just over 6 feet tall and broad-shouldered. You could tell, just by looking that him and Freddie were a different class to the rest of the firm. And the way they spoke was a bit posh, but not quite kosher. Not like Holmes.

When I noticed Holmes looking Freddie Davies up and down, I suspected the worst, and I wasn't disappointed. He stood bang in front of him, looking down, cos he was much taller. "Gets pretty cold in the desert at night, doesn't it?"

Well, Freddie took a step back, looking at Les Bishop, then at me, he looked worried. "What?"

Holmes was giving him his creepy stare. "In Egypt. You were in Egypt, weren't you?"

"No, I wasn't. I've no idea what you're talking about."

Holmes could have shut up then, but he never knew when to stop. "You're wearing an East Surrey regimental tie, and the East Surreys were in Egypt when you were doing your national service. So where were you, AWOL?"

Freddie looked relieved now. "Oh, the tie, it's not mine. I spilled some soup on mine and Les lent me this one."

Holmes now turned his attention to Les Bishop. "Mud's a fucker in the mountains when it rains isn't it."

Les looked a bit shocked. "What?"

"1944, Monte Cassino, the Italian campaign, you must have been there if that's your tie. Less you were AWOL too."

Les Bishop looked at him, shaking his head. "What are you, the East Surreys fucking historian? Come on." He nodded to Freddie, and they went to the other end of the bar.

We took our drinks then and went over and listened to Ron; he was saying what a nice fellow Stephen Ward was. Ward had just been fitted up and nicked for living off the immoral earnings of Christine Keeler.

79

The case caused a major political scandal at the time and was a diabolical miscarriage of justice.

Ron had warned him about her and Mandy Rice Davis, but he wouldn't listen. And as for them two, Keeler and Davis, they had no integrity, no honour, no morals at all. Unlike all his mates at the bar, who were listening and nodding in agreement. I looked at them and guessed that any one of 'em would jump into bed with the girls Ron was slagging; but then, seeing the company that Ron kept, I may have been wrong.

After getting another drink, I went to find Holmes and one of the Bills discussing Henry Cooper's fight with Cassius Clay. I was ready to go by now. Ron had been bearded in his den, and I still hadn't got my money. What I really wanted, was to tell Holmes about Ron sitting with the dirty Teddy Kray and marking his card as soon as he saw us.

While I was waiting for an opportunity to pull Holmes aside, Ron came over and invited us all to a party. He seemed genuinely disappointed when I said, "No, cos I had to be up in the morning, things to do."

You could have knocked me over with a feather though, when I heard Holmes say, "Yeah lovely, plenty of tarts there Ron?"

Les Bishop offered me a lift home, but Holmes insisted I take his car and he'd pick it up another time. When I left, Holmes was back at the bar, drinking and laughing with the rest of the gang.

I think those old Jags must have been like the last of the real motor cars; the interior woodwork and the smell of the leather, they smelled like a motor car. I started her up and sat for a while, listening to the purring engine, before I drove off. It took me some time to find a bridge over the river, but I finally hit Waterloo, and once on the other side I was home in no time.

Holmes usually phoned before he came round, but this time he didn't. As soon as I opened the door, I could sense something different about him. He walked through into the kitchen and sat shaking his head. "There were sodomites John, a whole roomful of them, a party of bloody sodomites."

He sat there like the sole survivor of an Indian attack in a John Ford movie, obviously still in shock. I tried to stop myself from laughing, but I couldn't.

He went on, "I thought it was funny, no girls at the party, but plenty of young men. And then someone asked me if I was an iron, which I took to mean a tough person, hard as iron. When I said yes, I was, he said, 'So am I', and tried to make love to me."

I was laughing now and had to hold on to the table to stop myself from falling over. When I finally stopped, I said to him "Iron. Iron hoof, poof, it's slang. You told him you was a poof. Your superior cockney tutor didn't teach you everything did he? So, what happened then?"

He looked pale and distraught, I guessed that's how poor Adrian had looked. "Well, I wrestled myself free and made for the door. Ron was rather upset to see me go and told me I didn't know what I was missing. God knows why he thought I'd be interested in that sort of thing."

I said to him, "Well to be honest I always thought you might be into a bit of poofery."

He looked up at me indignant, with his scary eyes wide open. "Oh did you John, did you really? I think you'll find that's what they call projecting."

I always thought projecting was throwing things about, but I didn't want to argue, cos perhaps I shouldn't have said what I did. I made him a coffee the way he liked it and got down to business.

When I told him about Teddy Kray sitting at the table with Ron when we came into the club his face changed; he was staring straight at me, and he did look sinister. "Are you sure it was him?" The way he was staring was freaking me out, so I got up and filled the kettle.

"Yeah, I'm positive. Didn't you see the way they both kept their faces hidden when they moved away from the table?" He had noticed that, and he'd also noticed that Ron had known what we were drinking in the Black Swan.

He got up, went to the window, and carried on talking, looking out to the garden. "D'you know John, I think we've been had. I don't think the Kray twins are the clean-cut young men they're made out to be."

He may have been had, but I wasn't. I had no doubt about 'em when I was handcuffed to a table and the chubby one wanted to cut my ears off. He was in the mood for talking now, still looking out of the window, "I'm not going to forgive them for what they did to Adrian and his family. No John, they're going to suffer."

"What are you going to do then?"

He spun round now with an evil grin on his face. "I'm going to take them down."

That kind of talk don't impress me. 'I'm going to take 'em down'. What's he going to take down? His trousers? Is he going to take the Kray twins down the Co-Op, down the library, down the high street?

I said, "What do you mean? Forget about taking 'em down; what are you actually going to do?"

"I'm going to ruin them financially," he said. "Are you with me?"

I had to think about that. I wasn't a great fan of Adrian and I didn't know his family. And I remembered some of the things I'd heard, "They're fuckin dangerous." And I remembered Ron's beady eyes when he held his knife to my ear. Then I thought of how dull my life had been lately, so I said, "Is there money in it?"

Holmes laughed, and it was nice to see the tension gone from his face, "Yes John, I'll make sure of it, lots of money, you mercenary bugger."

CHAPTER 7

Mugged in the Borough market

Holmes had arranged to meet the twins in The George Tavern, Commercial Road, to pick up our money. We took my car, and I drove while he gave directions.

When we got there Ron was on his own. The pub was a step up from the Horns and the Black Swan, but with the same dark-stained furniture and fake leather seating. He was sat at the bar on a stool and ordered our drinks, a gin and tonic for me and a light ale for Holmes. Winking at me, he said to Holmes

"You should have stayed last night Hershel; you missed all the fun."

Holmes gave a weak smile. "It's really not my thing Ron,"

Two fellows had come into the pub, they looked us over and moved further up the bar. Ron half-turned to look at them, "That wasn't old bill was it?"

I said, "Nah I don't think so, but you never can tell nowadays, they come in all shapes and sizes."

Nodding, Ron said, "Yeah. Reg'll be here soon with your money, and we'll go somewhere else." He hadn't finished talking when Reg came in and pulled up a stool. I got a round in, and as I'm paying the barmaid, there's a loud braying laugh coming from one of the two geezers at the other end of the bar. It was one of those laughs that is irritating and makes everyone look. Ron didn't look round, but his mouth twitched, and he began to scowl.

Reg seemed quite happy, he said to Holmes, "So you didn't fancy the party last night then?"

There was another roar of laughter at the end of the bar. Holmes gave his weak grin again. "No Reg, it's not for me. I don't want to offend anyone, but I'm just not homosexual."

Ron leaned forward on his stool and said, "I'm not homosexual you know, I'm bisexual. But I do prefer boys to girls."

There was a bit of an awkward silence, then, "Ha ha ha ha ha," much louder than before. Ron was off his stool in a flash, and charged up to the two laughing geezers, shouting in his high-pitched voice; "You think it's funny?"

They both got off their stools and one of them fronted Ron, "Fucking hell mate we're...".

He didn't get any farther than that. Ron head-butted him and followed up with a perfect left hook which spun the fellow's head round, spraying blood all over the bar, and the barmaid who'd come to see what was going on and who's now crying like a water cart.

Holmes went to go over to the action, but Reg stopped him. "Leave him, I'll deal with it."

By now Ron has done the other fellow as well, and they're both on the floor with Ron kicking them, and at the same time, he's screaming at 'em, "You don't swear in front of women, and you don't fuckin laugh at me either."

Reg and Holmes between them pulled him off and dragged him away and out of the door. I followed them out, and once we were outside Reg gave me a handful of five-pound notes and told me to go and straighten the two geezers out, and they'd meet me at the Carpenters, Cheshire Street.

I waited while him and Holmes pushed Ron into a big American car and drove off. Back in the pub, the two victims were being helped to their feet by the barmaid and another fellow who'd sat and watched it all happen. They were both marked up a bit and one of 'em definitely had a broken nose, which was still dripping blood.

While the barmaid went to get some towels, I sat on a stool next to them. "What was all that about?"

The one with the busted hooter said, "You ought to know? You was drinking with him."

I shook my head and tried to look puzzled. "I've never seen the man before in my life. I came in with my mate and he insisted on buying us a drink, said his wife had just left him."

The other one said, "Don't you know who that was?"

"No, I just told you. Why, who was it?"

The barmaid had come back with a couple of towels and started wiping the blood from their faces. "That was Ronnie Kray."

Things seemed to go quiet for a moment. I said, "So who's he. Who's Ronnie Kray?"

The barmaid, wiping some of the blood from her face, said, "He's one of the twins from Bethnal Green, and he's very dangerous."

I got off the stool. "Wow, we'd better phone the police."

One of the two victims said, "You're fuckin joking ain't you. You phone the police on them, and you wind up dead and buried in Epping Forest. No, the best thing is to forget about it. It never happened."

The barmaid was nodding in agreement, looking a bit vampirish, where she'd smeared blood over her face with a towel. "Yeah, we don't really want the police round here either."

I offered to buy 'em a drink then, but they didn't want one, and they didn't want a lift home either. I guessed they were worried about Ron Kray and the Epping Forest gravediggers finding out where they lived. After they'd tidied up and got back what composure they may have had, I followed discreetly when they left the pub. They didn't see me watching them get on a bus bound for Barking.

Once I was satisfied they were on their way, I walked round the corner to my car. Before I drove off, I counted the money Reg had given me, £85. I sat for a while, thinking about what had gone on; Ron's strange reasoning that a fellow shouldn't swear in front of a barmaid, but it was ok for him to spray her with that man's blood and then swear himself. It made me smile thinking about it, I believe that's what Holmes and his mates call ironic.

When I got to the Carpenters Arms the twins and the gang were all there, though they liked to call themselves the firm. Ron and Reg sat at the end of the bar, like proud parents, watching their kids at a party, while Holmes entertained the chaps with conjuring tricks. "Go on, do another one", somebody shouted as I pushed past Holmes to get to the bar.

He patted me on the shoulder. "What would you like to drink John?".

I had a tonic water with lemon. Someone shouted, "Go on, do one more."

Holmes held his hand up, "Alright, the last one. Bill, give me a cigarette."

Bill, standing next to him, reached in his pocket, nothing, he patted all his pockets. "Me fags have gone."

Holmes turned to me. "John, give me a cigarette."

I said, "I don't smoke, and you know it."

It was quiet now, and all eyes were on Holmes, who was smirking, cos he loved it. "If you don't smoke then what are you doing with Bill's cigarettes in your pocket?"

I felt in my right-hand pocket, and sure enough, there was Bill's fags. Holmes tried to make out he was all modest and it was nothing much, but he'd definitely impressed 'em.

Reg called us over then, and I told him how I'd straightened the other two out. I told him how they'd wanted to call the police, but I stopped them. When I gave Reg his £85 back Ron said, "So how did you stop 'em phoning the police?"

I shrugged my shoulders and said, very nonchalant; "I persuaded them, Ron".

Reg had counted and pocketed the money. He seemed pleased and was smiling. "Nice one." then casually, "You could have kept some of that and I wouldn't have known."

Looking him straight in the eyes, I said, "I never nick off people I know Reg."

That seemed to please 'em. They didn't say anything but exchanged a quick look. Me and Holmes still hadn't got our bit of money for the Albert Donaghue thing, but Reg assured us that they were owed some money; so, if we went to the Borough Market on the way home, and went to see a certain trader there, he would give us two hundred pounds, a hundred for us and the same for the twins. Before we left, Holmes went over to say goodbye to his mates at the bar; he was now on first name terms with most of 'em. He was almost like one of the firm.

The traffic wasn't too heavy, and we soon found the address Reg that gave us. It was a potato merchants, set in a railway arch, and a tall skinny geezer was pulling a roller blind down as we arrived. We parked up and he invited us inside. There were sacks of potatoes all piled up on one side of the building. As soon as we were in there, I recognized the smell, and it took me back to when I was a kid, and a barn in Cambridgeshire, where I was evacuated during the war.

I told him Reg had sent us. He didn't say anything, just looked at Holmes, then at me and took an envelope from under some sacks. "It's all there, two hundred."

I took it off him and pushed it into my inside pocket. Holmes was giving him his gangster stare, but I don't think he noticed cos he was looking over my shoulder at the street like he was expecting someone.

Before we got to the car a big old Humber pulled up and three geezers jumped out and looked like they meant business. One of 'em, about six foot, blond and slim, wearing a blazer of all things, said, "I think you've got some money for me."

My hands started sweating and I could feel the hairs on the back of my head beginning to stand up, when Holmes pushed me out of the way and said to the fellow, in his posh accent,

"Mate, do yourself a favour and fuck off. D'you know who I am?"

One of the others stepped forward half laughing, "If you don't know who you are, ask your mate. How the fuck should we know. Now, that's Charlie Dickson's money, so givvus it or you're gonna get hurt."

Holmes was smiling now, not a nice smile, but a bit sinister. "Alright, you don't know who I am. Do you know what this is?"

And he's picked up the pole with a hook on it, the one that the potato man had used to pull the shutter down. With that, the blond fellow shook his sleeve and a long rubber cosh slid into his hand.

Another one reached in his coat and pulled out a knife. Holmes was grinning now, horribly. "This is a quarterstaff."

Suddenly he's jabbed it like a bayonet into the blond geezer's belly, pulled it back, and then done him straight between the eyes. Wallop. Then he swung it round like a rifle butt and done the fellow with the knife on the temple. The last one of 'em was standing there mesmerized, till Holmes had swung the pole down on his knee, and I heard it crack. In just a few seconds there was three of 'em on the floor, two of them probably concussed. Holmes went over to the conscious one, who was trying to pull off a knuckleduster in order to attend to his knee. Leaning over him, he whispered, "You'll know me next time, won't you? I'm Hershel Coombs."

I was tempted to go over and give him a couple of slaps, but I didn't really want him to know me next time.

Driving back to mine, we talked about what had gone on, Ron's nutty outburst, and the little firm waiting to rob us. I didn't tell Holmes that I'd been quite ready to give them the money; but that was before I saw what he was capable of.

We were both of the opinion that Ron and Reg had set us up. They'd have got back the £100 they paid us, plus we'd have to give them £100 of their money, that we lost; except, cos of Holmes and his quarterstaff, we didn't lose it.

He was really pleased with himself. "You know John," he was smiling, "I know it's wrong, and I probably shouldn't say it, but I really enjoyed thrashing those thugs."

"Course you enjoyed it," I said, "Everyone enjoys bashing someone up in the right circumstances. They was bullies and they got bullied. That's good."

I remembered then, that when we were kids, Holmes hadn't always been so keen to deal with a bully.

I was ten years old at the time, and it was on a hot sunny July day, during the summer holidays of 1947. Perhaps because he had no friends of his own, he used to come down to Penge and hang about with me and my mates; going where we went, and doing the things we did, but with less enthusiasm. He was always reluctant to loot the bombed-out houses with us, even if it was just for firewood.

There was a kid called Freddie Britzman who used to hang about with us; and probably because we'd just come out of six years of war with Germany, he used to get a lot of stick about his name. He was a bit younger and smaller than me, but game as a pebble; one of them you see now and then, who never give up. My nan knew his grandfather, and she said their family was more English than a lot of them in Penge. But that still didn't stop the kids from having a go at him.

And it happened on this particular day, me, Holmesy, and Freddie ran into Horace Mundy in Oakfield Road, and he wasn't alone. At that time, Horace Mundy was the kid everyone was scared of; he was the local bully. Horace was a year older than us, but about two sizes bigger, and everything that a young bully should be, with a podgy, rosy-cheeked face, and bulging watery blue eyes under straw-colored lashes.

Like most bullies, he had a following, and this day there were two ratty-looking kids with him, and it was one of them who'd directed him over to us.

"Hello," he said,"where are you off to?"

I said, "nowhere, we're just going home, we've been up the park."

"Oh," said Horace, "that's where we're going. Hello Freddie, I didn't see you there, Heil Hitler." Freddie didn't say anything, just gave him a look, and we went to carry on walking, but Horace stood in the way. "Freddie, I said Heil Hitler, you have to say it back, go on."

Again, Freddie didn't say anything, just tried to walk past, but Horace blocked his path again. "Go on, you're a German, say Heil Hitler."

Freddie said, "No. Why don't you fuck off?"

Horace looked at his ratty mates, "Did he just call my mother a fat cow."

They both nodded like we all knew they would. I said, "No he didn't, you know he didn't."

Horace's horrible bulgy eyes turned to me. "Nobody asked for your opinion." Then he said to Freddie," Are you gonna say it or not."

"No I ain't," Freddie said, "so you can fuck off."

With that, Horace grabbed him by his shirt and punched him about three or four times in the face. As much as Freddie tried to fight back, he just couldn't reach Horace's snarling face. It might have been the sight of blood flowing from Freddie's nose and onto his own hand, that frightened Horace, because he let go of Freddie's shirt, and the three of them ran off laughing, towards the High Street.

I'll say that for Freddie, he was obviously upset, but he didn't cry; that's the sort of kid he was. Taking the handkerchief that Holmes gave him, he held it to his nose, at the same time, feeling his eye, which was swelling even as we looked at it. We walked him round to his house in Franklin Road, and as we got nearer Holmes put his arm round him, supporting him as if he was going to fall over without it.

I rang the doorbell, and when Freddie's mum answered it I watched Holmes eagerly studying her face, waiting for a reaction; and it wasn't a long time coming. "Oh fucking hell," she said, "Who did that to you?" And she's looking at me and Holmes like we did it.

Holmes soon put her right about that. "Horace Mundy did it because Freddie wouldn't say Heil Hitler,"

"Oh, did he? I'll give him fucking Heil Hitler, where does he live?"

"I don't know, I don't live here, John knows where he lives."

And he's not just sticking my name up, he's pointing at me, just in case there's another John standing in the hallway. We followed her and Freddie down to the kitchen, where she sat him on a chair and got a bowl and a wet tea towel to wipe away the blood that was caked on his face. While she was doing that, his dad had come in through the back door. "Hello," he said, "what's going on here?"

"Horace Mundy punched him in the face," Holmes said this, looking intently into Freddie's dad's face for a reaction.

"Oh did he, let's have a look. 'And he's turning Freddie's nose from side to side, "Well it's not broken." Then he's prodding and pulling the puffiness on Freddie's eye. "That's alright, you'll probably have a bit of a shiner tomorrow. Who's this Horace Mundy then?"

"He's a horrible little bastard," Freddie's mum said, "I remember him kicking little Albert Durling. I'm going round there later, have a word with his mother."

Holmes sprung off the stool he was sitting on. "We'll come with you; John knows where they live."

There was no way in the world I was going to take anyone round the Mundy house. Holmes didn't know, cos he didn't live round there; but in those days, and when you're ten years old, all the kids in Penge knew about the Mundy family, and the Mundy dog. Everyone knew that Horace Mundy's dog, which was a cross between a bulldog and a chow, although no-one could recollect ever seeing it. But everyone knew it had a poisonous bite, and it had grabbed a postman's fingers through the letterbox, dragged them through, and bitten off his whole hand and ate it. Everyone knew that. And when a policeman went round to see about it, Mrs. Mundy bashed him up and knocked him out. So they sent two policemen round there, and she did the same to them.

In the end, even the police were too scared to go round to the Mundy house; and Holmes wanted me to take Freddie's mum round there.

Luckily it never came to that, when Freddie's dad said, "No, you ain't going round there. He don't need you to fight his battles, do you son?"

Freddie didn't answer, just shook his head. His dad went on, " Are you frightened of him Fred?"

Freddie shook his head again, "No."

"No, course you ain't. How old is he, this Horace Mundy?"

I said, " He's eleven, but he's a big kid."

"Fred," he said, "how many arms has he got?"

Freddy looked up, a bit puzzled, "Two."

"What about legs, two of them?"

"Yeah."

"I suppose then, he's only got one head?"

Freddie smiled a bit then. "Yeah, he's only got one head."

"So he's only a human being then, but he's just a bit bigger. Is that what you're saying?"

Freddie must have known he was walking into a trap, but he nodded, "Yeah"

"Well, you can beat him, Fred, if you want to that is. Do you want to?"

Freddie sprung the trap for himself when he said, "Yeah, I do."

We didn't see much of Freddie for a while; he was in training. Sometimes we might see him running in the park, but he never stopped to talk; and if we tried to run alongside, we soon found that we couldn't keep up, and let him go on alone.

One time we called round his house and his mum showed us into the back garden. There was Freddie, halfway down the garden, with his dad and uncle George, chucking tennis balls at his head, and chucking them hard. Freddie was either ducking the balls, blocking them with his hands, or moving his head to the side and letting them fly past his ear. I'd never seen anything like it.

The training period must have come to an end, and Freddie started coming out again. He didn't go looking for Horace Munday, because he wasn't that type of kid. We just did the usual things; up the Palace Park, rummaging about in bombed buildings, knocking down ginger. Then one day the inevitable happened, we ran into Horace Mundy and his two rat-faced mates. It was outside a sweetshop in Maple Road, and Holmesy had just bought us an ice cream.

They must have seen us going in there, cos when we came out, they were waiting. Horace addressed us all, "I didn't get any pocket money this week, can you lend me enough to get one of those ice creams."

I put it on Holmes, pointing to him, I said, "You'll have to ask him, he bought 'em."

"Well it's no use asking me," Holmes said, "because I have no more money."

Horace's bulgy eyes latched on to Holmes and his sneer made him more horrible. "Oh, don't you?" he mimicked Holmes's posh accent. "Then I'll have a lick of yours." Snatching the cornet from Holmes he licked it vigorously before giving it back. Then, taking mine, "Let's try this one." Not content with slurping over it himself he passed it to his rat friends to sample.

Before I could throw it away, he was already reaching for Freddie's. He didn't get to take it though because Freddie rammed it straight into his face.

One of the rat boys grunted, "urghh," as if it had happened to him. Horace was in shock, not believing what had happened. He was wiping the vanilla ice cream from his chin when suddenly Freddie was punching his face. Not just punching it but doing it with unbelievable speed and accuracy. He only stopped when blood spurted from Horace's nose.

Me, Holmes, and the two ratty-faced kids couldn't believe what we were seeing. I think even Freddie was surprised that it had been so easy, but it wasn't over.

After recovering from the initial shock, and wiping the blood with his sleeve, Horace started punching his fist into the open palm of his other hand and looking round at his mates for backup. "You've done it now." he growled at Freddie, "Now I'm really gonna lose my temper."

Poor Horace. Before he had a chance to really lose his temper, Freddie was at him again, and every punch he landed sent more blood spurting from his nose. One eye was already closing, and Horace was desperately swinging his chubby arms, but he couldn't get near Freddie. His mates must have twigged they were on the losing side when they started backing away, till they got to a safe distance, turned and walked off. Horace tried to turn his back on Freddie, but that didn't work, there was no escape. In the end, he just sat down in the kerb and started crying like a baby.

The first thing Holmes did was to pick up what was left of the ice cream I'd thrown away, creep up behind Horace, stick it on his head, slap him, and jump back as the tear-stained snotty, bloody face turned towards him.

Freddie had spots of blood on his face and hands, so we went back to his to wash it off. His dad was just leaving the house as we got there; looking at Freddie he said, "Hello what have you been up to?"

Before anyone else could answer, Holmes piped up, "We've just bashed up Horace Mundy."

Well, Freddie looked at Holmes, and his dad looked at him, and there was something like disgust in his voice, "What, three of you." And he walked off down the road, shaking his head.

That was the nearest I ever saw Freddie get to crying. He didn't cry though, but he was obviously upset, and Holmes was his next victim. Before his dad was out of sight, he was beating Holmes all round his front garden, till he stopped for a breather, and Holmes ran out through the gate and legged it back to Norwood.

It didn't seem possible that that cowardly little posh kid could do what I'd seen today. But I guessed that was Hershel Coombs I'd seen in action, and not Sherlock Holmes.

The thing about Charlie Dickson though, had got me thinking. When I got home, I phoned a mate of mine, Tony, who knew Charlie well, and all the people round him. He couldn't place the three I described, as having anything to do with Charlie. And he couldn't believe that someone would go on a bit of work like that wearing a blazer. The only thing he was sure of was that Charlie wouldn't like it. And that meant trouble for someone.

CHAPTER 8

Charlie Dickson

They were waiting for us in the Carpenters when we got there. None of the others were with them, which was unusual. I paid Reg their hundred pounds and told them what had happened; they obviously knew already, but they listened just the same.

Ron was mumbling and cursing the Dicksons. Then we had to listen to the pair of 'em go into their rants about Eddie and Charlie Dickson, how they'd served together in the army. The favours they'd done the Dicksons over the years, and this is the thanks they get. Did we know that the Dicksons had had an old blind man beaten up just for looking at them the wrong way? "What!"

And then trying to have us robbed in the Borough yesterday; what sort of people did that? It wasn't easy listening to all this, knowing that they were lying, but that's what we did. To sound convincing and in agreement, I stuck in a couple of "Fucking rats" here and there.

Holmes went a bit further; "What are you going to do? Are you going to take them out?"

Reg looked a bit surprised, his eyebrows flicked up. "What do you mean? Take 'em out where?"

I interrupted, "He means, are you gonna do the pair of 'em?"

Ron had stopped mumbling and was paying attention now, "Yes we are, when the time is right. That's where you come in."

Their plan was, for me and Holmes to find out the addresses and all relevant details of Eddie and Charlie Dickson and Frankie Dexter, plus any of their firm. They wanted detailed reports like we did on Bishop and Donoghue, and we'd be well paid. Except they didn't mention a figure. I wasn't bothered cos I never intended to do it anyway. Holmes assured them it could be done but might take a while. I wondered then if it was because we came from south of the river, they thought we were dopey or did they treat everyone like that.

It was still early afternoon when I got back to mine; the phone in the hall was ringing. It was Tony, Charlie's mate. Charlie wanted to see me, he wanted to know about the fellows who'd stuck his name up. I didn't really want to go out, but after assurances that I could trust Charlie 100%, I agreed to meet him later at the Alleyn's Head in West Dulwich.

Compared to the East End pubs I'd been in lately the Alleyn's Head was a palace. There was carpet on the floor, wall lights, fabric upholstery on the chairs, and people who paid income tax drinking at the bar.

Right on time, Charlie came in. He didn't look very different from when I'd last seen him at the snooker hall in Lewisham. About 30 years old now, 5' 10", slightly receding brown hair, and powerful looking, with blue-grey eyes. It might even have been the same suit he was wearing; he certainly didn't dress as sharp as the twins. Either he recognized me from before, or else what Tony had told him, cos he came over and I bought him a drink.

We took a table away from the bar and I told him the whole story. Every now and then he interrupted me to ask questions, like what pubs did they use. He already had the Vallance Road address. Holmes turned up as I was into the story, and after the introductions, he sat and listened, sniffing occasionally. Charlie perked up when I talked about Bishop and the Westminster Arms. He knew Les Bishop and Freddie Davies . "Slippery, the pair of 'em. Long firm merchants."

Holmes stopped sniffing. "Does the name Enugu mean anything to you?"

Charlie looked down at the table, smiling, then he looked up. "Yeah, Enugu, it's a pisshole of a place in Nigeria. Les Bishop and John Manning's boy have been trying to raise funds to build a new town out there."

Holmes said, "I don't think he's mentioned it to the Krays. Why would that be?"

"Cos he don't want to share the dough with 'em, that's obvious. But there wouldn't be any money to share anyway, cos it's all a swindle by the locals out there." He poured the remainder of the beer into his glass, and carried on, "I went out there last year to look at it. Con men the lot of 'em, from the mayor down to the waiters in the hotel. I sussed 'em in two minutes. You know they're better at the fraud game than we are over here, don't you?"

Me and Holmes both nodded, although we didn't know anything at all about Enugu's waiters or mayors.

I carried on with the story, and when I got to the end and told him the twins were planning to kill him and his brother and Frank Dexter, he didn't seem surprised or particularly worried about it. He said, "If I told Eddie this, he'd take Frank over there and do the pair of 'em tonight. So don't mention this to anyone else," We were happy about that. "They're a couple of moronic fucking psychopaths, you know that don't you?" He was getting a bit worked up now. "Fucking do me in? Pair of fucking mugs. All they're good at is bullying shopkeepers and car dealers. You know that, don't you?" We didn't know it but I thought it best to agree with him. He got hold of my arm. "I'm personally gonna drive 'em fucking mad. Next time you go over there, tell 'em you've found out we've got something big going on. You understand?"

Holmes said, "And is there?"

"No, but they won't know that. I know how their minds work. That'll drive 'em fucking nutty. They get very jealous. You must know that yourself." We didn't know it but we nodded anyway.

We left it for a couple of days before returning to the East End. Holmes had made an appointment and we met the twins at Vallance Road. Instead of Mrs. Kray or one of the twins, the door was opened by a tall blond young lady. She was certainly something to look at, a bit more than pretty, and a bit more than stunning. There's not a word for it, but she was exceptional.

"Hello," she said, "I'm Maureen, the twins are upstairs, they'll be down in a minute."

We followed her down to the kitchen, where Mrs. Kray sat with bits of silver paper in her hair. "Hello boys, you've met Maureen haven't you, she's just doing my hair. And this is Frances, Reg's young lady."

She indicated a pretty dark-haired girl with huge brown eyes sitting in the chair where Mr. Kray usually sat reading his paper.

I knew this would be too much for Holmes to ignore, and I was right. He went into his full theatrical mode. "Good God, this looks like the final of the Miss Bethnal Green Beauty Pageant. And I've got to judge the winner of the three finalists. What do you say John?"

Shaking my head, I said, "I'll leave it all to you."

"Right," he said, "Ladies and gentlemen, the panel has deliberated, and we declare the winner to be the vivacious Mrs. Violet Kray, and a dead heat for second place with the fabulous Frances with the brown eyes, and the magnificent Maureen. Congratulations ladies." Mrs. Kray and Maureen were laughing at Holmes' performance, but Frances looked at them both before she allowed herself a shy smile.

Just then, Reg poked his head round the door, "You ready?" We went up to the front room where Ron was waiting for us. This was the first time I'd seen Ron without a jacket, and frankly, he looked a bit of a slob, with his braces, and shirt open down the front. We soon got down to business.

Ron spoke first, "So, did you find out anything?" Holmes produced some sheets of notepaper that Charlie had dictated to him, Charlie and Eddie's and a few other addresses and phone numbers, and the address of an empty flat in Camberwell, where Frank Dexter was supposed to be living.

Ron was ecstatic, rubbing his hands. "Nice, very nice."

"There's something else" said Holmes, "they've got something big going on."

That got Reg's interest. "Something big?"

"Yes"

"But you don't know what?"

"No, it seems only Dexter and the other two know. I spoke to a fellow from their scrapyard, and all he knew was something was going on, and it was something big."

Ron got to his feet, knocking an ashtray to the floor. "The fucking greedy bastards." He punched the wall, making a picture rattle. It was getting uncomfortable being in the room. Ron was talking to himself now, gibbering. "I'll put a fucking bullet in all of 'em. They ain't fucking bigger than us. Fucking rag and bone men."

I said, "We'd better go now, see if we can find out anything else." Holmes was already up and halfway out the door.

"Go on, fuck off then. I'll fucking shoot 'em myself." Ron was now talking to a mirror on the wall.

Reg took us out into the street and passed some money to Holmes. "There's a oner there, let me know when you need more."

This was on a Wednesday afternoon. The next day, the 8th of August, something big happened.

THE GREAT TRAIN ROBBERY.

It had been on the news for about ten minutes when Reg came on the phone. "Get over their yard right now. Find out what's going on. Call me back in the Carpenters." I didn't like the way he thought he could boss us around, but I was curious anyway, so I phoned Holmes' number and left a message.

We met in the Anchor and Hope, just up the road from Charlie's yard in Camberwell. Old bill was everywhere. As we had a drink at the bar, one of 'em came and stood next to us, pretending to read a newspaper. He looked like proper old school C.I.D., about forty, cheap blue suit, and you could almost see his ears moving as he tried to listen to our conversation. There were police in cars too. One was parked opposite the scrapyard, with three coppers in it. We'd left the pub, and walked down past the yard; and there was Charlie and Eddie Dickson, unloading scrap metal off the back of a lorry. They didn't look to me like two men who'd just done the biggest robbery in British history.

I phoned Reg from mine, while Holmes made coffee. He wasn't surprised that the others were working in their yard. "Yeah, they're carrying on like normal. That's what we'd do. Let us know when you find out anything."

The Great Train Robbery affected the whole country, certainly the criminal community. House burglars, shoplifters, pickpockets, bank robbers, car boot thieves, as well as some normal members of the public, all felt an affinity with the train robbers. It was seen as government money, and in stealing it, we'd got one over on them. It gave us a boost, similar to the boost the British public had after the victory at El Alamein in WW2. The 8th army did the fighting, but we all shared the victory. It was like that.

And everyone had an opinion, and most of 'em started with: 'they reckon'. "They reckon it's the same mob that was doing it on the Brighton line a few years ago - I've got a good idea who done that. I won't say anything on the phone, I'll tell you when I see you - They reckon Billy Hill organized it, along with M.I.5."

Later, everyone knew someone, who knew someone, who knew someone who was on it and never got caught. But it was definitely a coincidence when Charlie said something big was going on.

I had a couple of phone calls saying don't bother going out, Old Bill's everywhere; they're stopping cars, and going in all the pubs, looking for the usual suspects. Later in the evening, Charlie rang. He was well pleased when I told him the other two believed he was behind it. His laugh was not a happy one, but the laugh when somebody you don't like falls over. "That must be doing' their heads in. Heh, heh heh. Now, here's what I want you to do." Holmes took notes, as I dictated to him Charlie's plan to aggravate the twins.

A couple of days later, all I told Ron on the phone at the Carpenters, was, "I've got something.". Ron gave us directions to meet at the Regency Club in Amhurst Road.

We found the place alright and got signed in by a fellow named Mick. He was tall, about the same size as Holmes, good looking, and he seemed to be a cut above the others. His suits were smarter for one thing, and he didn't seem so servile round the twins as the rest of the firm. Ronnie and Reg were at the bar, and straightaway left their drinks and took us into the office. Making sure the door was closed, Ron said, 'So, what have you found out?"

I told 'em the story we'd rehearsed with Charlie; "Last night I drove down to check on the scrapyard, to see if there was anything going on, but there wasn't. Walking back to my car I found this tart crying outside the Anchor and Hope. I talked her into coming in the pub and having a drink, to calm her down.

Her name was Irene. She told me her boyfriend, who worked for the Dicksons, had dumped her and gone back to his wife. Previously, he had told her that the Dicksons had planned the train robbery to get money for what they called the Enugu project. They planned to take over a country called Enugu, build a town and get diamonds from somebody called Cameroon. When I asked her boyfriend's name she clammed up, probably thought I was Old Bill. Wouldn't have a lift home, said she'd get a cab on the corner. And that was about it."

It was quiet in the room, we all had different thoughts. Finally, Reg said, "Where's Enugu?"

Holmes stood up and addressed us like he was a schoolteacher, "It's not a country Reg, it's a state in Eastern Nigeria, and the Cameroon she referred to, is probably not a person, but a country, Cameroon, which borders Nigeria. If you remember, your friend, Mr.Bishop, was discussing Enugu with the chap in the Westminster Arms. It's in the report we gave you."

Ron was growling now, "What a greedy bastard, He's got a fuckin gold mine in South Africa, now he wants to run Nigeria too."

Reg said, 'Funny Bishop never mentioned it 'ennit. Wonder why that was."

Ron was getting angry now, glaring at Reg, and his eyebrows were coming together. "I never did trust that slippery fucker. He's your fucking mate. You'd better have a word with him. If I get hold of him, I'll fuckin cut him. "

"Oh, will ya? You fucking won't. He's the only one earning us any money; what you're spending on your boyfriends, and them lot of fucking deadbeats out there."

There was tension in the air, like watching two dogs getting ready to fight, but it didn't bother Holmes. "Listen chaps, I think we'd better be going, still got lots to do you know."

That seemed to change the atmosphere and Ron got all apologetic," Take no notice of us, that's just a family discussion. Come outside, let me buy you a drink." laughing, "Don't make me have to persuade you."

It was about two minutes after that when Les Bishop and Freddie Davies walked in. Reg said, "D'you want to leave us for a minute." And as we moved away, "Oy Les, we wanna have a word with you."

Those words must have meant something to the people in there, cos it went deathly quiet and everyone was sneaking glances to see the outcome. We were near enough to hear bits of the conversation. Les, "No Reg, I told you about it a couple of weeks ago. I didn't think you were interested. Don't you remember?"

Ron said, "Well I don't fuckin remember. What's going on?"

"You might not remember Ron, cos you were a bit pissed that day. But I definitely did tell you."

I'll say this for Les Bishop, he kept his nerve, and I think, by the time me and Holmes slipped away, he'd convinced the twins that he had told 'em about Enugu. He was right in one thing; they were often too drunk to remember things, which was handy to know.

Charlie was well pleased when I phoned and told him what had happened. "Heh, heh, heh, lovely. D'you know what, if I had the time to fuck about, I could take all their money off of 'em. I'll tell you what I will do though, I'm going to send 'em out to fuckin Enugu."

I was curious. "How are you gonna do that?"

"I don't know yet, but it shouldn't be hard. Leave it with me and let me know if you hear anything."

CHAPTER 9

Phone Bugging

August was nice that year; it was still warm, and there was some rain, but not too much, just enough. And it was nice to get in the park first thing, when the gates were opened. That's when everything was fresh, and you could actually smell the pine trees. I liked to walk up past the marble gorilla and round the lake. There would be boats tied up at the water's edge, swaying, waiting for later. Then I'd walk round past the rockeries, and over the little wooden bridge to where the dinosaurs were. It didn't matter how many times I'd seen 'em, they still fascinated me, and made me stop to look again. Sometimes a carp would swim up to the surface of the lake to watch as you went past. Up toward Anerley, there was another gate, and I used to go out through there and walk back down to mine.

It wasn't that long after the robbery, that the police found the farm where the gang had counted out the money. That was the day that Ron rang, and asked me to meet him on my own that afternoon at the Regency. I wasn't ecstatic about the thought of that and rang Holmes. He said not to worry about it, go to the meeting, and he'd be there, but I wouldn't see him.

Ron and Reg were waiting for me, and we went into the office. Ron seemed a bit excited. "We've got a little job for you."

"Oh yeah, what's that?"

"It shouldn't be too hard."

"Yeah, what is it then?"

"Break into Charlie Dickson's yard, well, into the office. You could do that, couldn't you?"

They were staring at me as I was thinking of what they were asking. I said, "I've got two questions. What do you want me to get, and what's in it for me?"

"That's reasonable." Reg said. "All we want is you to make an entry and lock up afterwards. £100, what do you think?"

I said, "Yeah, sounds alright. I'll go and have a look at it tonight when they shut. Shouldn't be too hard."

They were pleased with that and said I didn't need to tell Holmes; then I wouldn't have to split the dough with him. That's how they worked, the old divide and conquer game.

As we left the Regency an old dosser, in a greasy old overcoat and a trilby hat, walked by, he ignored the others and said to me, "Got the price of a cup of tea guv."

Before I could say no, Ron shoved a couple of notes into his hand. "Here you are, go and get yourself a bit of grub."

He touched the grimy hat and really grovelled, "God bless you, guvnor, you're a toff, sir." Then he shuffled off up Amhurst Road.

Driving home, I stopped at a set of lights in Great Dover Street, and who should pull up next to me, driving his taxi cab, Holmes, still wearing the trilby hat. He winked, gave me a thumbs-up, and roared away when the lights changed. That was the first time I thought my nan might have been wrong when she said not to trust him.

I drove down to Camberwell, parked up some distance away, and met Charlie in his yard. Up in his office, I told him what the twins had asked me to do. He didn't seem bothered about it at all, I'd have to say he was more amused. "That's not a problem," he said. "D'you think you'll be able to do it?"

"Yeah, I can, but it would be much easier if I could see the keys."

He opened a desk drawer and pulled out some keys on a ring. There were two mortice keys, an E and a Y, and an old padlock key. I'd clocked the padlock on the way in; it was an old Squire 440, and they were easy, plus I had some mortice skeleton keys that Holmes had given me. I said, "there's no alarms or anything?"

"No." He gave his mirthless laugh, "heh, there's nothing to nick. The only thing that's valuable is the metal in the yard, and nobody's gonna nick that."

"So what do they want me to break in for?"

He smiled. "They'll probably tell you when they're ready. But don't worry about it. Just do what they say, it's not a problem."

That night, I met the twins again in the Regency. They had another fellow with them, who they introduced as Bob. He was short, about five seven, wearing a donkey jacket and a trilby hat which he never took off. He hardly spoke when we were introduced, just sort of grunted. After that, I ignored him and just spoke to the twins. I told them that I'd cased the place, and it should be easy. "What about tomorrow night then?"

"Suits me." I said, "So, what's going to happen?"

They explained that I was to unlock the main gate at 10.30, and Bob would be there to meet me. Then I was to unlock the office, and any other interior doors, and let him in. At 11.30, I was to come back, lock up and leave everything as it was before. It sounded easy enough, but as I was about to leave Ron said, "John. Don't mention this to anyone, will you."

"Course not."

Holmes came round early the next day. We were having coffee in the kitchen and the radio was playing, "And here are the Crystals with Da Doo Ron Ron." Holmes turned it off, "D'you mind?"

I did mind, but I didn't tell him, instead I said, "Tell the truth, would you do Ron Ron?"

He looked at me, shaking his head like I was a naughty kid. "Do you really think that's funny John?" It was no use telling him that it was funny, so I told him about the plans for tonight. He started pacing

116

round the room again. "Have you considered the fact that they may be planting a bomb in there?"

I hadn't thought about that, so I phoned Charlie to tell him. "That's alright," he said, "Just do what they say, and I'll take care of it this end."

Holmes was sitting down now, sipping his coffee. "There's more to this than meets the eye, John. Ask yourself, would you be comfortable, knowing that someone might plant a bomb in your office?"

I didn't have to think about it, I said, "I can't really answer that, cos I ain't got an office."

Holmes agreed with me, he gave a little smile. "No, you haven't, John, have you."

It was dark and had just stopped raining when I parked up in Addington Square. I checked my watch, 10.25. The streets were quiet, no one walking, just the occasional car going by, quietly on the wet road. Bang on 10.30 I undid the padlock and suddenly out of nowhere, Bob's standing next to me. In less than five minutes, I'd opened the main door and two office doors and was out of there, leaving Bob to do what he had to do.

With an hour to wait, I thought about driving up to the West End, just to drive about and kill some time; but suppose I broke down or got a puncture. There was a little drinking club in one of the old houses in the square, so I parked up opposite with my lights off. Anyone going by might think I was Old Bill, or else a private cab waiting for a punter.

The time dragged, but 11.20 came at last, and I strolled round to the yard. The padlock was just as I'd left it, everything was. I locked up inside, secured the padlock, and walked back to the square, pleased with myself.

Driving home, it was pretty quiet on the roads. I did get one of the old Triumph Herald police cars tail me up for a while on Denmark Hill, then he turned off, and it was quiet all the way home.

The next day everyone was happy, and no one had been blown up. Charlie was happy, the twins were happy, and I was happy. I felt unique; I was the only one who had made the Kray twins and Charlie Dickson happy at the same time, and about the same thing. Holmes was not so easily pleased, "There's something odd about this. We're not being told the whole story."

The whole story, or part of it, became clear to us later, when Ron summoned us to Vallance Road. We arrived to find Charlie Kray and the twins fiddling with a Grundig tape recorder, wired up to the telephone. Ron was giggling, "Listen to this."

Reg pressed a button, there was a buzz from the tape recorder, then voices, "What do you want 'em to do with that zinc Charlie?"

"Put it out by the front, they're coming to collect it later."

118

Then the sound of an engine, firing up, chugging, like a diesel. Ron turned down the sound on the tape recorder.

I said, "What was that?"

They were all smiling, and I don't think Ron had ever been happier in his life. He was almost dancing. "That is Charlie Dickson in his office, in his scrapyard."

Holmes sounded impressed, "Good God, how did you manage that?"

Reg pointed at me, "He did it. Sorry, we couldn't tell you at the time, but you know how it is."

Holmes nodded, "Yes, of course." then to me, " I didn't know you could bug phones, John; you should have told me."

They were all looking at me now, and Ron came to my rescue. "No, he didn't bug it, he just opened the gaff up and locked up after. Next time we might put a bomb in there, but we need to get some information first."

Mrs. Kray came in then, with tea and sandwiches. While we ate, Ron told us how Tom had met this crooked telephone engineer in the Grave Maurice. They'd tested him out, and he'd bugged the phone in the Widow's pub, while they timed him. It took him just about 40 minutes, and it worked perfectly. Holmes gave me a look, and I think we both knew then why Charlie Dickson had been so relaxed about it all.

That night was party night, and Ron persuaded me and Holmes to meet him later at the Regency. The firm were all there when we arrived, and we were greeted like members of the gang. The booze was flowing free, but I didn't see anyone paying for the drinks. I understood then, why Reg had called them a load of 'fucking deadbeats.' Ron was a bit more laid-back about it, he did, at least, have a sense of humour. He called 'em his 'assistant spenders'.

I wasn't too impressed with any of 'em, apart from Mick. He was about my age, tall and smart, and he stood out from the rest. To me they weren't criminals as such, they were just bullies, pimps, and ponces.

I'd known criminals for most of my adult life, and the ones I knew, had some sort of trade, or skill. Regardless of what they were, burglars, pickpockets, bank robbers, long firm merchants, hijackers, even petty con men. You might not like what they did, but they had some expertise; they could do what other people couldn't, or at least, do it better.

But this little mob. They gave the proper East End villains a bad name. How hard is it to go and bully a shopkeeper, or a car dealer, or a club owner, especially if there's enough of you? What do they tell their wives or kids, when they came home from work? "Had a nice day today, Luv, beat up a geezer who owns a café. Now he's got to pay us ten quid every week."

These weren't people you could respect. The best thing was, when one of 'em said in the Carpenters one day, "Yeah, but we never harm women or kids."

And he said this like it made him something special. Like he was one of the knights of the round table upholding the tradition of chivalry in Bethnal Green. What normal person in their right mind *does* harm women and kids?

But we don't harm women and kids.

Except perhaps, when their dad comes home from the hospital, and they don't recognize him cos his eyes are black and blue, and so swollen he can hardly see out of them. And his broken jaw's wired up so he can only be fed through a straw. And he's terrified when the doorbell rings.

Don't that harm them?

And what about the publican's wife, when they've had a bad week, but the firm still wants money off of them. And she's terrified all the time, they're going to get their pub smashed up. And the girlfriend who opens her door to find her boyfriend dumped outside with his face slashed open and pumping blood.

What about the old lady, who hears in the market that her son's been shot, and is in hospital?

No, we don't harm women and kids. Well, we do, but not directly. We're gentlemen.

But that didn't stop me enjoying myself for a while. There were women there, and it struck me, that this was the first time I'd seen women out with the firm. They were wives and girlfriends and a few spares, probably mates of the wives and girlfriends.

It was getting to be an enjoyable night till, all of a sudden, the place went quiet. I got that feeling that you get when it suddenly kicks off, like an electric charge goes through the room.

Then crash, a chair went over. Then a scream, "Aaaagh. What's that for?"

And there's a geezer holding his face with blood oozing through his fingers. Then Ron pushed him face down over a table, and one of the goons is holding him there, while Ron is slashing at his arse with a sheath knife. Now as well as the geezer screaming, the girl he was with was screaming her head off, and bashing Ron, till he finally stopped and walked away, shouting, "Get them out of here.''

I'd been talking to Mick when this happened. He gave a little smile, "Well, that's the floor show for tonight."

I was shocked. "Does this happen often?"

He nodded, "Often enough, that it don't bother people anymore. Look around."

And he was right. Everyone was carrying on as if nothing had happened. Except you've just witnessed something horrible, and you've still got to avoid slipping on the patches of blood on the floor.

Ron got on the microphone, and it echoed in the room, "I'm very sorry about that incident. I hope it won't spoil your evening. Thank you."

A couple of the slimeballs even managed to clap him for that. I'd come to realise that they were all terrified of him. There wasn't any fun or humour in 'em; they only dared to laugh when he was in a good mood. And the more you got to know him the scarier he got.

Mick's glass was empty, so we wandered up to the bar, where Holmes was entertaining his fans with card tricks. There was an excited scream as a big busted, trollopy-looking tart pulled a card out of her bra. "How the fuck did that get in there?"

Holmes was smirking as usual. "And is it the king of diamonds?"

"Yeah, it is."

He nodded. "Have a look, do you know why he has only one eye?"

She held up the card and the others crowded round to see it. "No. Go on."

"Because you're too beautiful for two eyes to absorb. So he plucked the other one out."

Perhaps no one had ever complimented her before, I don't know. But she got a bit emotional. "Ooh, that's lovely, come here."

And she's grabbed hold of Holmes and planted a big slobbering kiss bang on his lips. That would have been the high point of my evening, except I heard, "Oh ain't that nice. …. He's gorgeous ain't he.... why can't you say nice things like that to me?..... Ooh, I could take him home with me".

123

And these stupid wives and girlfriends were gazing at Holmes like he was some sort of fucking love god; for talking about someone digging their own eye out.

Charlie rang the next day to invite me and Holmes round to the yard. He had something to show us. He was amused when we arrived, dressed up in painter's overalls; but he knew as well as we did, the consequences of the twins finding out.

We were introduced to a fellow in the office as Jack, but I knew him as Bob. It was the fellow I'd met with the twins yesterday, the one I'd opened up Charlie's office for. Then another one came in, John. I remembered him from before at Lewisham. After more introductions, Charlie said, " Now be quiet. You ready John?"

Pressing a switch on his desk, a red light bulb on the wall started flashing. After opening and slamming the door, they went into a conversation that they'd obviously rehearsed. "No it's no use John, I'm gonna have to put off Enugu till next year."

"Are you sure Charlie? You're talking about millions of pounds here. I thought that's what you did the train for."

"Yeah, well I can't touch that money yet, the way things are. Anyway, Enugu will still be there next year, won't it."

"Yeah Charlie, but suppose someone else gets out there first. And what about the diamonds?"

Charlie gave his little laugh," Heh heh, Like who? No one else knows about it. And who else has got the money and the brains to do it? Anyway, we'd better be going."

John opened the door and slammed it shut, as Charlie switched off the flashing light. He was grinning like a Cheshire cat. "What do you think of that? Every time that light goes on it means the twins are listening in. Good ain't it?"

Holmes was impressed. "So it was you who planted the dodgy telephone engineer?"

"Yeah, course it was, that was him." pointing to Bob. "Good ennit. I'm only sorry I can't see their faces when they hear it. Still, you can do that for me, can't you."

My phone was already ringing when we walked through the door. It was another summons to Vallance road. It wasn't midday yet, and I did want to see their faces when they were fresh from listening to Charlie.

We found the twins in near enough the same position as last time, fiddling with the tape recorder. It occurred to me that Ron was more obsessed with the Dicksons than Reg was.

"Listen to this." He pressed a button, and we listened again to the conversation we'd heard first–hand, less than three hours ago. Ron didn't say anything, but was scowling, and making strange grunting sounds as he listened to the tape.

Reg said to Holmes, "tell us about Enugu again. What you know."

"As I said before, it's a state in Nigeria. They did have a coal mining industry, but I'm not sure about that. Some speak English, but the native language is Igbo."

"What about diamonds?"

Holmes shook his head. "I'm not sure that they mine diamonds in Enugu, perhaps they do. I know that diamonds are smuggled into the country from Cameroon, and then on to Europe."

Ron was taking notice now. "How do you know all this, you been there?"

Holmes smiled. "No, but I've been to Cameroon."

"Go on, what did you do there?"

"Oh, this and that, you know."

"What, diamonds?"

"Well different things. I don't really like to talk about the past."

Ron sat in his chair, lit a cigarette, leaned back, and blew a cloud of smoke toward the ceiling. Then,"How'd you like to go to Enugu? The pair of you."

I said, "What for?"

Reg had been quiet for a while, letting Ron do the talking. But now he said, "To build a town. Fuck Charlie Dickson. Never mind about no one else has got the brains or the money. We're gonna get out there before him, and we ain't just gonna build a town; we're gonna take over that part of the country. We've got inside information that them rag and bone men don't know about."

Staring at Reg, Holmes said, "We're not builders Reg. So what would you want us to do?"

"Well mainly keep an eye on the others. I think we can trust you two, but I'm not so sure about the others."

"And who's the others?"

"Bishop, Freddie Davies and Manning. Our Charlie might be coming later on, once we get things moving."

"And what's in it for us?"

"That's up to you. We can put you on a percentage or you can have a fixed price. We'll work it out."

I stood up then, and Holmes took the hint. "Give us a bit of time to think about it."

And that's more or less how it was left.

When I phoned Charlie Dickson, he wasn't at all surprised. "I knew it. Heh heh heh. And Bob Manning, what a fucking spiv. He's the brains behind this, you wait and see."

After we'd agreed that we were going to Enugu, Holmes relaxed his security a bit, as far as I was concerned. He gave me his home phone number and took me to see his house. I'd always guessed he'd been staying in the West End, and I was right.

He was living in what had once been a stable in Balfour Mews, at the back of Park Lane. It was now a very nice two-bedroomed house in a nice area with genteel neighbours, and with a garage underneath. He also had access to two other garages which he'd blagged off of some elderly neighbours who didn't drive. I couldn't help thinking it was Watson money that had put him in his present position; but as I couldn't change it, I pretended to be pleased for him.

CHAPTER 10

Kathy

You would have thought that Charlie would have been satisfied with sending the twins off to Nigeria, but he wasn't. He still kept winding Ron up with bits of false information. And you would have thought Ron would be satisfied with finding out about Enugu, but he wasn't either. He still kept listening in to Charlie's phone and getting wound up. It wasn't long before the next call came; at least it wasn't a summons to Vallance Road, well, not directly.

It was Reg, but I could hear Ron mumbling in the background. "What does Gert and Daisy mean to you?"

"It don't mean anything to me. What is it, slang or something?"

"What about Laurel and Hardy?"

I said, " Yeah, they used to be in the old black and white films, in the Saturday morning pictures. Why, what about 'em?" Ron was in the background saying fucking this and fucking that. It sounded like he was punching the wall, or kicking it.

Reg said, "Have you heard anyone mention any of those names lately?"

I guessed this was something Charlie Dickson had put in their heads. "No, I haven't. Why what's happening?"

"I'll tell you when you come over, might have a little job for you."

For the next four weeks, me and Holmes socialised with the twins and the rest of the firm and got well paid for it. Our job was to listen in on conversations, see if anyone slagged the twins off behind their backs. In particular, see if anyone mentioned Gert and Daisy. Ron wanted to know who said it and who he said it to. This wasn't the sort of thing I enjoyed doing; but as I didn't particularly like any of 'em, and I didn't expect any of 'em to slag the twins in front of me, I said,"OK."

Holmes was still interested in learning about the Gangland culture. The relationship between the bosses and the underlings, the hired help. But he wasn't getting a true picture, because I guarantee there wasn't another gang in the country that operated the way this little mob did. They lived in genuine fear that the wrong word or the wrong look could get them a right-hander, or a cutting, or a shooting. It might depend on which twin they were talking to and what mood they were in that day.

I saw Ron one day give away a gold watch. It was in the Carpenters, and two young fellows came in, looked like builders. One of 'em said to Ron," Scuse me, have you got the time?"

Ron had his glasses on, he looked at the pair of 'em. Looked 'em up and down." What's up ain't you got a watch?"

The kid said, "No, no I ain't." With that, Ron took his watch off and give it to him.

Now the other one is looking at Ron and shaking his head. "You're fuckin mad."

That got everyone's attention and the place went quiet. Someone whispered, "Oh oh," and people started moving away, so they didn't get splattered with blood.

Ron said quietly, "I know I'm mad, but I take tablets to control it. So that I don't upset anyone."

The kid must have sensed he'd said the wrong thing 'cos he started stuttering and stammering and apologizing, "I'm sorry, that's not what I meant. The reason I said it is 'cos you've given him a lovely watch and he can't even tell the time. That's why he has to ask people."

Ron smiled at him. "Well, perhaps you can teach him to tell the time. Now fuck off and let me finish my drink." And this is the geezer who a couple of weeks ago was trying to kick a man to death for laughing.

Another time, in the Regency, someone who was half a mate of theirs said the wrong thing to Reg while they were having a drink and got a right-hander. He said something else and Reg pulled out a short knife and cut the fellow's face open like it was a natural thing to do. I did notice that nearly all, if not all, of their violence, took place when they'd been drinking.

I noticed as well that they didn't seem to have a lot of mates, not real mates. They had one good friend called Laurie, although he was more Ron's pal than Reg's. They had plenty of hangers-on though, mostly people who were scared of them.

Reg said as much to me one day; it was in the morning at Vallance Road, and he was talking about the firm.

"These people ain't our friends, we know that. They pretend to respect us, but they don't. They fear us. But they know, without us they couldn't get a living. They'd be down the Bun House signing on every week."

I said, "Well Reg, my old nan always used to say, "If you want a friend, be a friend."

He thought about that for a bit, then he smiled, "Yeah, that's right. Would you say you're our friend, John?"

I tried to look as genuine as I could, nodding my head, "Well, I'd like to think so, yeah."

He smiled at that, and gave a little laugh, "Heh, well that's good."

We were spending a lot of time in the East End now, doing things for the twins. Sometimes it might be picking up some money that was owed to them or reminding someone they were late with a payment. Thank God they never asked us to beat someone up or threaten 'em, cos I think Holmes, in his gangster mode, would have done it.

A funny thing happened in the Widow's pub one afternoon. It was really the Lion, but everyone called it the Widows. We'd met Ron and a few of the firm in there and were having a drink. I had my back to the bar, talking to Holmes when someone behind me said.

"Well, I didn't think I'd ever see you again." I didn't look round 'cos I wasn't sure if she was talking to me, but I thought I recognised the

132

voice. "Oy you." I turned round, and it's the barmaid, and I knew the face, but I couldn't place it. Then she smiled, and it was Kathy, the brass, who I last saw in Soho four years ago.

"Fucking hell." That was my first reaction.

"Well, that's nice", she smiled some more. "I thought you might be pleased to see me."

"Yeah, why would you think that?"

"Well, you used to fancy me back then, didn't you?" Holmes was listening and came over to the bar.

I introduced him, "Kathy, this is Hershel"

He said, "You two know each other?"

She winked at him. "Yeah, he used to fancy me like anything, didn't you?"

There was a shout from the other end of the bar. "Oy, can we get a drink down here or what."

"Hang on I won't be long." she went to serve the fellow who'd been shouting.

The fellow in question was an obnoxious little bastard, about 5' 7", with a mop of curly hair that had run amok all over his head. He was one of those people you couldn't like, even if you wanted to. Apart from the fact he was a pimp, he had a loud mouth and was a known troublemaker. He wasn't exactly a member of the firm, but he used to hang about with them sometimes; and the only reason anyone drank with him is because he was buying the beer.

133

He was a bit self-obsessed and his usual way of starting a sentence was, "see me." I heard him one day, talking to his beer-swilling captive audience: "See me, I'm as hard as nails, and yet I'm a sucker for kids. You wouldn't think that, would you."

They wouldn't think anything about him at all once he left the pub and they had to buy their own beer. Hard as nails, and yet every time he got in trouble, he had to stick the twins' name up, and for some reason they let him get away with it.

After serving them down that end of the bar she came back and carried on where she'd left off. "So, what are you doing around here; have you come looking for me?"

"No I haven't. But it's nice to see you. What are you doing, you still with Adie Morris?"

She laughed at that. "Adie Morris, you're joking ain't you. I was never with him. Who told you that?"

"Manchester Ted".

Just then, the poison dwarf came storming up, "Oy, are you gonna serve some drinks or stand there talking to these fucking two all night?"

Before I could say anything, Holmes turned very casual from the bar. "Listen Goldilocks, keep your voice down and fuck off back down there. She'll come when she's ready."

Well, his eyes were already a bit bulgy, but they almost came out of his head. He was nearly exploding with rage. "Wha, Wha, what did you call me?"

"You know what I called you, that's why you're spluttering, so fuck off while you can."

Instead of fucking off, he picked up my gin and tried to fling it in Holmes's face, but Holmes saw it coming and moved, so it went all over me. The glass dropped from his hand as Holmes grabbed him by the shirt and slapped him. He did it like the old movie gangsters did it, left right, left right, then pushed him away.

It had gone quiet in the bar, and someone shouted,"Not in here Benny."

From under his coat, Benny had pulled a knife, but before he could bring it up Holmes grabbed his right arm and gripped his left shoulder, just below the neck. The silence in the bar was broken by the strange yelps and grunts from Benny as Holmes held him rigid. Then, as he dropped the knife, his head began to twitch and his right leg began to jerk as if he was kicking an imaginary football.

For about a minute Holmes held him like this, till in the end, he dropped him in a heap on the floor.

As poor Benny was trying to pull himself up by clinging to a chair, Holmes turned to Kathy, very casual, "Sorry about that. What were we talking about?"

Without looking up, Benny brushed the dust from his clothes and rushed out of the door. Once the little rat had gone Ron came over; he pulled us away from the bar. "You know that was Benny, one of the Morrises don't you?"

Holmes said, "No. Who are the Morrises? What are they, something special?"

"Well, they think they are." Ron said, "They've got a little firm, out Romford way. There's four brothers, Adie, Benny, Tojo, and Winston."

"Tojo?"

Holmes looked at me and we both looked at Ron, who went on to tell us about the Morris family, and Tojo.

The family had lived in Vallance Road before the war, but Mr. Morris had got involved with Oswald Mosely and the fascists. He was convinced that we would not win a war with Germany. So, when his first son was born, he named him Adolf, which was shortened to Adie so the neighbors wouldn't know. Then Benito came along, and he became Bennie. When Tojo was born the secret got out, and as we were already at war with Germany, Italy, and Japan, the family had to leave the East End. When the old man saw the way the war was going, the fourth boy, born in 1943 was Winston.

They never came back to Vallance Road, living out at Romford somewhere, but the boys used to hang about the East End and the West End.

So this was the Adie Morris that had put the frighteners on Manchester Ted, and Holmes had just been knocking his little brother about. If I'd only known, the trouble this was going to cause, I'd have left the East End then and never gone back.

Once I'd found out she wasn't with anyone, I started seeing a lot of Kathy. She had a nice little flat in a council block in Old Ford Road. From the outside it was a council flat, inside it was something different. There was carpet throughout, proper quality carpet, and genuine teak G plan furniture in the front room. It was easy to see she hadn't furnished this place on barmaid's wages.

Her having this flat was handy, cos it saved me driving or getting a cab home. And at that time in my life, she was everything I could want in a girl. She had her own drum, her own money, she was funny, streetwise, popular, attractive and she could smile. And if she didn't have any of those other things, just the smile, that would have been enough for me.

When I thought about it, she may have been right; I probably did fancy her years ago without really knowing it. She knew it, Manchester Ted knew it, and her mate, Marylin did too. Still, that was then, and this was now.

I got her to fix Holmes up with a mate of hers. a very attractive girl name Gaynor. She was a blond, not all that tall and a bit chubby, but very bubbly and easy to get on with. The only thing wrong with her was she was a bit thick. I thought this might have put Holmes off, but for some reason, it didn't; I don't know if he thought he was gonna educate her. The only other thing wrong with her was she had a kid; a little boy of about seven or eight, named Patrick, and Holmes didn't even mind that.

So me and Holmes became part-time East enders for a while, and it was a nice situation.

Kathy told me some of her story. Since I last saw her, she was still on the game in Wardour Street. Until one night, she had some aggravation with two geezers, whether it was to do with her pitch or protection, I don't know. Her mate, Marylin, intervened and got striped down her face with a razor for her trouble.

Just then, the twins and some others came out of the El Condor and saw what was happening. They cut and beat the two geezers till they were unconscious and left 'em bloody, slumped in a doorway.

Marilyn's cut wasn't all that deep, but the twins paid for her to have plastic surgery, and in the end, it hardly noticed. She went back up north, married someone she went to school with and wound up with a pub in Leeds.

The twins took a shine to Kathy, even Ron; and it was through them she stopped working the street. They got her her flat, and they got her work when she wanted it, in the pubs and clubs they used. And she was always welcome round Vallance Road for a cup of tea with Mr. and Mrs. Kray. After what she'd told me I was beginning to feel a bit guilty about plotting with Holmes to ruin the twins, and I mentioned it to him.

"Well John," he said. "What they've done for Kathy is very laudable, but let's not forget that they tried to bilk us out of our money, and Ron's covering up for the so-called Teddy Kray. However, if it makes you happy, I'm willing to forget about ruining them completely; I'm quite sure that they are going to do that for themselves. But I do intend to recoup the money, plus interest, that Adrian paid to Teddy Kray, and I'll hold the twins responsible for that."

I was finding it hard to dislike the twins; though it was easy enough to dislike what they did. They were bullies, there's no doubt about that. They got their living by bullying people and taking money off of 'em. And what made it worse, they bullied their friends and the people who worked for them. They'd never tried any of that with me and Holmes up till then, but all that changed in one night.

Kathy was doing a shift behind the bar in the Regency, and I was waiting for her to finish. Both the twins were in there drinking, but Reg seemed to be a bit hyper, like he was on speed or something. It was getting toward closing time when Tommy came and told me that Reg wanted to see me outside. When I saw him, he was pacing up and down on the pavement, grinding his jaw like he's got toffee stuck in his teeth. "John, you got your car with you?"

He knew I had, so I said, "Yeah, why's that?"

"We need you to take us somewhere, won't take long."

I went back inside and told Kathy to wait, and I'd be back soon.

With Reg and Tommy in the back seat, I drove for about ten minutes, while they directed me through the streets of the East End. Finally, Tommy said, "Pull up here," and I stopped outside a terraced house, in a street similar to Vallance Road and a hundred others in east

London. There were narrow passageways between the houses that gave access to the back gardens, and that's where Reg went. Tommy knocked on the front door, then shouted through the letterbox. "Billy, open up, Reg wants to talk to you."

No one answered, but I heard a door slam at the back of the house, then two bangs, gunshots. I started the car and began moving slowly. Tom had opened the back door and Reg came dashing from the alley, jumped in, and away we went.

As we pulled away, it was going through my mind, I'm an accessory to a murder, through this pair of fucking lunatics. I opened my window to blow away the smell of cordite that was in the car. I glanced at Reg in the rear-view mirror, and said, "have you just shot someone?"

He sounded excited. "Yeah, I have. Why, is that a problem?"

"Yeah, it is as it happens. You could have told me."

Tommy said, "Well, we could have, but we didn't. Ain't you ever shot anyone John?"

I couldn't see his face, but I knew he was sneering. I said, "Yeah, I've shot people, but not using someone else's motor though. And I did it on my own."

Reg tapped me on the shoulder. "But you don't mind taking our money, do you. You'd best fucking shut up now and just drive."

I wouldn't have wanted to argue with him at any time; but now, when he'd just shot someone, still had a loaded gun, and was in a bad mood. I took his advice and shut up.

The story soon got about and got stretched. In the new version I'd had a right go at Reg for using my car, and he'd held a gun to my head and told me to shut the fuck up, or he'd shoot me there and then. I can't remember who it was, but someone said, "You're lucky, cos Reg don't like anybody talking back to him."

At the time I didn't say anything, but I thought, "I'M LUCKY? I'm an accessory to a shooting, which I knew nothing about. And in a position where, if I say anything about it, I could get cut or shot, or worse. And that's what they call lucky in Bethnal Green.

CHAPTER 11

Sonny Liston

It was around this time I was thinking of leaving the East End altogether and going back to South London. The only problem with that would be Kathy; would she want to leave her flat and the mates she had in the area?

The thought though, of putting some distance between me and the twins, then phoning them up and telling 'em to go and fuck themselves, appealed to me, which was a shame really, cos I liked chatting to Ron. When he was in the right mood and had taken his medication, Ron could be a very funny fellow and better company than all his hangers-on.

He was certainly better company than Reg, whose main preoccupation was getting hold of money and hurting people.

I would guess that during the time me and Holmes spent around Bethnal Green, there was probably one or two cases a week where somebody would be cut or bashed or shot. And if you didn't witness it yourself, you heard about it from someone.

And when people talk about women gossiping in the hairdressers, they could not beat your East End gangster for it. They might be tight-lipped around strangers, but once you were in that circle, you heard it all. Except for, that is, Teddy Kray. The twins must have marked their card about him cos as far as anyone in the East End knew, he didn't exist and never had done.

Their friends, though, weren't under the same cloak of secrecy that Teddy was:

"You know why he eats out all the time dontcha. She couldn't boil a fucking egg, sloppy prat."

Another one. "She fuckin hates him. You wouldn't think it, would you? When they're out, they're all smiles and what have yer. They ain't slept in the same bed since he came out the last time."

"How about Mickey West. That was him put a brick through the barber's window. Did you know that?"

"What cos of that haircut he's got. I'd have burnt the fucking place down."

And I knew, if they talked about each other like that, they'd be talking about Holmes and me.

Holmes had got to hear about the incident with Reg, and he turned up at Kathy's one afternoon while she was out shopping. "I heard about what happened, John. Are you alright?"

He wasn't fooling me with his phony concern, and I could almost guess what was coming. I said, "Yeah, 'course I'm alright, why wouldn't I be?"

"Well, I heard that Reg put a gun to your head and told you to shut up. You must have been terrified."

I shook my head. "No, he didn't put a gun to my head, and I wasn't terrified. And I've had guns pointed at me before."

"But being told to shut up, that must have been humiliating for you."

I could see he was enjoying this; he was trying hard not to smile, so I said, "Why don't you shut the fuck up. How's that. Do you feel humiliated?"

He laughed," No, John, I don't, because I know you don't mean it."

I made coffee while he rambled on about Gaynor and her kid, comparing him to a border collie he once had. We sat down in the front room, and the conversation went back to the twins.

"I'm guessing that you don't feel so warm-hearted towards brother Reg right now, John."

"No, I don't, and that goes for Ron as well. I know he's got half an excuse cos he's mad as a hatter, but you can't separate 'em. Pity really, but I've had enough of this little lot. I'm thinking of going back to Penge."

He was shocked. "What, and let them go unpunished for humiliating you, for trying to steal our money, for trying to make fools of us. I thought you had more backbone than that." He went quiet for a bit, then. "Listen, John, if you're absolutely serious about this, packing it in. Would you mind if I made a play for Kathy?"

I couldn't believe this. I knew he was weird, but fucking hell.

"Yes, I fucking would mind. There's something wrong with you. What's up with the one you've got?"

144

"Oh, calm down, John. When you said you were packing it all in, I naturally thought you weren't interested anymore. I'm sorry if I got the wrong end of the stick. It's nothing carnal, John, you must know that. It's just that I think she'd be such an interesting subject for my research."

I said, "Yeah, well right now, she's an interesting subject for my research, so put that right out of your head.

We left it at that, and he talked me into staying on until after Enugu. That's when he told me about an old saying that he'd heard once in Sicily. "Keep your friends close, but your enemies closer."

He was still there when Kathy came back from shopping. So I brought her into the front room and asked her, "Did you know he fancies you?"

She laughed and winked at Holmes, "Course I did. Why, didn't you?"

For once in his life, Holmes was stuck for words; he was stuttering, "Here, here, here. Hold on. Let's get this straight. Kathy, as lovely as you are, there's no getting away from it; you've a nice smile. You're a funny girl, and you're intelligent. I suspect you have an excellent body, but I'm not interested in that. My interest in you is clinical rather than physical if you know what I mean. I've got too much respect for you and John for it to be anything other than that."

All the time he was talking, Kathy was nodding and smiling to herself. The same smile she'd had years ago in Doris's café. When he'd finished, she said, "That's lovely, Hershel. So, what you're saying is, you'd rather dissect me than have sex with me. I think that's really nice."

I was still laughing while Holmes tried to explain what he meant.

He hadn't been gone long when the phone rang; it was Ron. "Hello John, been trying to get hold of you for ages. We're opening a new club tomorrow, place called New Malden. Everyone's invited, so bring whatsername with you. Tell Hershel to bring his young lady. Gonna be a nice night; Sonny Liston's opening it for us. I'll send a car round to pick you up about half eight."

And that was it. It was like we were being instructed to attend. I did think of ringing back and saying 'sorry, but we're busy.' It was only the thought of a free night out, free booze, free cab, and a chance to meet Sonny Liston that made it seem acceptable. I gave Holmes half an hour to get to Gaynor's and rang to tell him about the invite. He was pleased with the prospect of seeing Sonny Liston up close, and I guess, studying the firm in different surroundings.

The Cambridge Arms, or Cambridge Rooms, was a big old pub on a junction just off the Portsmouth Road. We got there sometime after nine and were met by Reg at the door, the perfect host in his evening suit. "Hello, John, Hershel, evening girls, glad you could come. Go through; everyone's in there."

He was right, everyone was there, all the usual faces, and a few we hadn't seen before. There was a long buffet table in the main room containing everything an East Ender might want to eat; there was chicken, turkey sandwiches, salmon, rollmops, jellied eels, cockles, prawns, bread rolls, and much more.

We grabbed a table, and while the girls went to load up with food, and I went to the bar for drinks, Holmes wandered off to see the main attraction, Sonny Liston. After sitting with the girls for a while, I took my drink and went to find Holmes. I was surprised to see Freddie Foreman there and he gave me a nod. I'd met him once or twice at Tommy McGovern's. Then I saw Sonny Liston. He was seated at a long table, looking thoroughly pissed off, with Ron on one side, his manager on the other, and surrounded by fans and admirers. Ron would only allow a certain few to shake his hand, but others were patting him on the back or draping their arms round him, posing for photographs.

A lot of the firm's wives and girlfriends were out with them for the night. Mr. Kray was there, which wasn't usual for him, and so was Charlie, with Dolly, his wife, and she looked very pretty. I found Holmes and brought him back to the table. We sat chatting for a while about nothing in particular, when Reg came over, pulled up a chair, and sat down.

"Everything alright? Is the food ok? Nice place ennit, we should do well here."

Kathy said, "It's lovely, Reg, very classy."

He leaned over to me with his head close to mine, "Sorry about the other night, John, I was a little bit drunk."

I shook my head." No need to apologise, Reg, I've forgot about it already."

He was talking very quiet, "No, I was out of order. It won't happen again. Next time I'll definitely let you know what's happening."

Looking him in the eye, I said, "No, I don't think there'll be a next time Reg."

I'm not sure that he liked that. "No? We'll see." Then he got up and said to Holmes, "What about you, Hershel? Do you want to meet Sonny Liston?"

"I'd love to, later on, Reg; I think he's a bit too crowded right now."

Reg gave him a nod and said, "I'll sort it."

Holmes got up to get us some more drinks, and Gaynor went with him, clinging to his arm. As soon as they were gone, Kathy put her hand on mine. "You shouldn't upset Reg, John; you don't know what he's like."

Well, since I'd driven him to shoot someone, seen him bashing people up for no reason. Seen him cut a man's face with a knife; I think I've got a pretty good idea what he's like. Holmes and Gaynor came back with the drinks, and I noticed she kept kissing him every chance she got. I guess he was pleased when Ron came over to our table with his sinister smile. "Everyone enjoying theirselves? Nice here ennit." He put his hand on my shoulder, "Here, come and meet some people. You'll be alright girls wontcha."

He steered Holmes and me to a corner of the bar, where Reg, Charlie, Mick, Liston's manager, and a couple of others were jealously guarding Sonny Liston. First of all, we were introduced to Terry Spinks, who won gold at the 1956 Olympics and went on to become British bantamweight champion. A very nice fellow. Then I put my hand in Sonny Liston's gigantic paw. Looking at his face as we shook hands, he looked sad. I could see him thinking: ' What the fuck am I doing this for.'

Ron introduced Holmesy, "Sonny, this is Hershel, a good friend of ours."

Holmes got the sad stare and handshake, then he said, "Not like Ellie Mae's Sonny, is it?"

Well, Liston's head came up like he'd had an electric shock. He was suddenly awake, staring into Holmes' eyes. "You know Ellie Mae's?"

Holmes smiled at him, nodding, "Yeah, Ellie Mae's on South 4th Street. I was in there the night you fought Bert Whitehurst at the Arena, about 1958. Good times, and what a loving woman Ellie Mae was, but I suppose you know that."

Liston still had hold of Holmes's hand, but he let it go and poked him in the chest with a giant finger. He was grinning now, "Don't tell me you're the skinny little white motherfucker she fell in love with back then. Was that you?"

149

Everyone was listening to this, and Holmes was loving it. He tried to look modest, "Yeah, I'm afraid it was."

"If that was you, what was the thing she kept beside her bed?"

Holmes was grinning now, the centre of attention, "You mean Otis. A stuffed possum. She had him as a reminder that she'd never have to eat possum again. Am I right?"

Well, Sonny Liston was grinning, and I've seen photos of him, but he never looked so happy as he did that night. "Come here." And he grabbed Holmes in a bear hug and he put his arm round him like they were best mates. Then, turning to his manager, he said, "Ella Mae used to call him her 'dynamic cracker'." And they both burst out laughing, and so did all the others.

Holmes wasn't so amused, "Did she? I didn't know that."

Sonny said, "Perhaps you didn't, but everyone else on South 4th Street did." Then he laughed again, and it was nice to see him happy.

Holmes got serious then and got close to Liston. "Sonny, would you be offended if I gave you some advice?"

Looking a bit puzzled, Liston said, "Well, that's the only thing anyone ever gave me for free; go on."

"If you do get to fight Cassius Clay, don't chase him; make him come to you."

Liston and his manager exchanged looks, and the manager slid in front of Holmes and sort of edged him out of the way.

"Yeah, well, thanks for that. Come and see us again when you get your trainer's licence."

Then they all closed in around Sonny and made it plain that conversation was over.

We spent some time wandering about in there, chatting to different people. I didn't really want to, but I suppose it was the price we had to pay for the free booze and food. We passed the girls on the way back to our table; Kathy seemed to know everyone there, so we left them chatting to some of the wives and girlfriends. Other members of the firm were at the bar, getting as much free booze into them as they could before the night ended.

Sat at the table, I asked Holmes, "What were you doing in America in 1958? I thought you was in the army."

He wasn't looking at me but sort of staring into the distance, remembering. "I was in the army, John. A few of us had been sent over to train with the Yanks at a base called Fort Leonard Wood. It was out in the backwoods of Missouri. One night I went down to St. Louis with two black soldiers to see Liston fight at the Arena there. Then, after that, we went drinking in downtown St Louis and wound up in Ella Mae's place. You know the rest."

"So what was Ella Mae, was she a brass?

He shook his head." No, not when I knew her; she may have been before, I don't know. She had a bar. I suppose you could call it a club; they called it a joint. You could buy drinks, marijuana, cocaine, anything you wanted. There was gambling there, cards and dice, there was music. Oh, and there were girls in the rooms upstairs, so I suppose you could call it a brothel."

I wanted to ask him some more, but then Kathy and Gaynor came back with some more drinks. Kathy leaned back in her chair and looked round the room. "They're starting to leave."

Gaynor looked round too. "I don't want to be too late back, mum's got Patrick."

Just then, Liston loomed up to our table, followed by his manager and Reg. He tapped Holmes on the shoulder, making him look round. "Hey, Hershel."

Holmes pushed his chair back and stood up, "You alright, champ?"

"We're leaving now. Been nice to meet you. If I see Ella Mae, I'll tell her that I met you and you was looking good." He laughed at that, and they shook hands.

"Been a pleasure meeting you, champ, and good luck to you in the future."

Liston tapped me on the shoulder and leaned over the table to say goodnight to the girls. And if you saw the way he smiled, you wouldn't believe it was the same face that growled at the camera in so many pictures.

When we left, I gave the driver a tenner and got him to drop me and Kathy off at my place before he took Holmes and Gaynor back to the East End.

On the way back, I'd been trying to get my head around the thought of Holmes, 'the dynamic cracker,' stirring the passion of Ella Mae in a St. Louis brothel. I know he'd told me some stuff about him and Hitler having some mysterious power over women and dogs, but I never really believed it. Dogs, perhaps.

I'd always thought of Holmes as being a bit more Martha than Arthur. Now I had to look at him a bit different; what with the way he did Benny Morris, and then the other three geezers he done with a quarterstaff. I was beginning to see him as something special.

My cleaner had been in while I'd been away, and she'd left everything spick and span, which was nice. She'd put clean sheets and pillowcases on the bed and fresh milk in the fridge.

We were talking in the front room before turning in, when out of the blue, Kathy said, "Do you love me, John?"

Well, I've got three good suits of mine in her wardrobe: shirts, a couple of pairs of shoes, and my car's parked outside hers. What did she think I was gonna say? "Of course I do. I don't know why you need to ask that."

She held my hand, and I got the impression she was trying to feel my pulse. "Are you sure, John, this is important?"

153

Trying to sound as convincing as I could, I said, "Course I'm sure Kath, I love you more than anything. What's this all about?"

She didn't answer right away but sat there thinking, like she was trying to make up her mind, then she said, "It's the twins. They ain't your friends John."

I already knew this well enough, but I didn't let on. "Go on, why do you say that?"

"They've asked me to spy on you. They want to know how you get your money; how much you've got. And the same with Hershel, and they want to know where he lives."

I pulled my hand away, "And is that the reason you're with me?"

"Of course not, you fucking idiot. I've always wanted to be with you, ever since I used to see you in the West End."

Her saying that made me feel good. It had been a good night, good booze, good grub, and I think I really did love her at that time. And there were nice clean sheets on the bed.

The next morning, when we got up, it was nice. I pulled the curtains back and the sun was shining through the bedroom window warming the whole room. Instead of making breakfast, I said I'd take her to the Chinese man's café in Maple Road, and we might see the cat.

It was a pleasant walk down the top of the High Street on a warm September morning. There was a freshness in the air that you didn't get in Bethnal green. We walked down past the Red House, under the railway bridge, past the laundry on the corner of Oakfield, past the Queen Adelaide, and into Maple Road.

There was a tall wall on the other side of the road facing the café, where on sunny days, when it was warm, the cat would lie on the top of it, with one front leg hanging over the side. Perhaps it wasn't warm enough 'cos there was no cat there when we went in the café. "Hello, John. You want the usual?"

"Hello Mr. Lee, yes please, and...." Kathy had two slices of toast and a cup of tea.

The usual for me was a mushroom omelette and toast. And it didn't seem reasonable that this Chinaman could make a mushroom omelette better than anyone else in the world, but he could.

It was pretty busy, but we found a table by the window, and I looked out and saw the cat. He had just arrived, jumping up from a lower wall. He stretched and yawned, then spread himself out in his usual position. I tapped Kathy's hand and nodded in his direction. "He's here."

She looked at the cat, squinting a bit, then at me, smiling. "It's a fucking cat on a wall, John. I've seen a similar thing before."

She might have thought she had, but she hadn't. She hadn't seen a cat like this one before cos it was unique; well, if it wasn't unique, it was unusual.

The first time I saw it in action was one day in the summer, the year before. It was a lunchtime, and I'd just come out of The Dewdrop with

Joey Johnson when he pointed out Bobby Fetterman and his dog, Kong, walking down on the other side of the road.

Bobby Fetterman was ugly, his whole family was, so I suppose it was only natural that he'd have an ugly dog. He claimed it was an English Bull Terrier, but it would be easy to believe there was a pig somewhere in his pedigree. It was pure white, with little piggy eyes, like Fetterman's, and at one time or another, it had bit nearly everyone in Penge, except for me and Fetterman.

All the time you were stroking it, he was good as gold. He would wag his silly little tail and stare at you with his little piggy eyes, daring you to stop. And if you did stop and walk away, he would bite you. He was more spiteful than vicious, insomuch as he wouldn't try to make you bleed, just rip the bottom of your trousers or puncture the back of your shoe.

The reason he never did it to me is because I'd twigged what his problem was. He didn't handle rejection very well. So, if ever I had the misfortune to come across him, I would stroke him and talk to him at the same time.

"Who's a good boy, Kong. Who's got a lovely little face? You have, haven't you? Yes, you have." Then I would back away from him, like those people do with royalty, but still talking. It was embarrassing sometimes, but at least I never got bit. When I was far enough away that I knew he wouldn't catch me, or there was a shop I could dive into, I'd say, "Gertchyou ugly little bastard."

This particular day the cat was on the wall spread out with his front leg hanging down. Joe nudged me, and nodded to where the cat was, "Watch this." As Fetterman and Kong came level with the cat on the wall, Kong suddenly stopped. His fur stood up, and he started shaking. Slowly he turned and stared at me and Joe, then he turned some more and looked up the road where he'd come from.

Joe said, "Watch the cat."

The cat had leaned his head over the wall, and his mouth was moving, but we couldn't hear the sound. Kong spun back round, and his head was jerking like he was listening for someone calling his name. Finally, he looked up and saw the cat, which was looking down at him, sort of bored. Kong was close to the wall and straining his neck to look up. He took a couple of steps back and started snarling, showing his teeth and turning his head so everyone could see he meant business. The cat nodded his head, lifted his front leg onto the wall, and let his tail hang down, swinging like a pendulum. I don't know if that's some sort of insult in the cat and dog world, but that's how Kong saw it. He stopped growling and began a horrible piercing, yelping sound like you've never heard before. Then he started jumping up at the wall, sometimes falling over, but he'd get up and try again. People were stopping now and watching his performance; some were laughing, and I think that embarrassed Fetterman and Kong. With all his jumps, Kong never got within two feet of the cat, who, in the end, got up slowly and went back the way he'd come. When Kong realised his tormentor had

157

gone, he stopped the yelping sound and went back to a high-pitched growling and began head butting the wall in temper. He'd probably be doing it now if Bobby Fetterman hadn't dragged him away. That was the first time I saw the cat in action, but over the summer months, I watched him repeat his act with lots of dogs.

I saw a Yorkshire terrier leaping up the wall, a collie, a greyhound, various mongrels, and it always started in the same way. They would stop, and their fur would go up, then they'd look round like someone was calling them. And the best of 'em never got within two feet of the cat.

Kong was never fooled again. One day, I saw him stop underneath where the cat was, then he looked on the ground like he was interested in something on the pavement, wagged his tail, and walked on. No dogs came along while we were there, so there was no action, but I knew she'd never seen a cat like that before.

Giving her my keys, I told her I'd meet her back at mine, as I had to see someone about a bit of business. The truth was, I was going up to my parents' house, and if I'm honest, I was ashamed of the fact that she'd been a brass.

It's not as if Kathy would have said, "Oh, by the way, I used to be a prostitute in the West End when I met your son." And there's no reason they would have known. But I had it in my head that my nan would have guessed somehow. She was a very wise old woman, and she was nearly always right in weighing people up.

Anyway, I had a short visit with my family, which I didn't enjoy much, cos I felt like a coward over Kathy. That's one thing I'll say about the EastEnders I'd met; they were much more open-minded about people's previous occupations, or even their present ones.

Back at mine, she'd tidied up, made the bed, had a bath, and was pleased to see me. I couldn't have been home more than five minutes before the phone rang. It was Reg, and he didn't sound very happy. Could I get hold of Hershel? Somebody wants to see him at the Carpenters. When I phoned Holmes, he was of the same opinion as me. It sounded like trouble.

CHAPTER 12

The Fight

Kathy was still wearing the dress she'd come out in the night before, so I took her into Bromley and gave her a few quid to buy some clothes. After taking her to a good clothes shop, I arranged to meet her in the Greyhound when she'd finished.

It was over an hour later before she came back. I'd read the Daily Mirror from cover to cover and was now trying to do the crossword, so I was glad of the chance to put my pen down.

Fucking hell! She looked like a fashion model, or a film star, or a millionaire's wife, or even a super high-class top-of-the-range brass. That must have been the best few quid I ever spent. She'd bought a suit in what looked like some sort of tweed material, a sort of bronze, brown colour, and shoes to match.

I can't describe it, other than to say I'd never believed that someone from up north, who'd been a brass, could look so classy. That don't make me sound very classy, I know, but that's the way I thought in those days, and not just me. She could see I was impressed. "D'you like it?"

I said," You look stunning."

She was smiling at me, or smiling to herself, and nodding he head again like she knew a secret.

We got a cab back to hers, then I got my car and went to Gaynor's to pick up Holmes. He was curious to know what it was all about, and so was I. We soon found out when we got to The Carpenters.

A few of the firm were at the bar, and in the middle of them was a fellow called Harry Chambers. He wasn't one of the firm but used to hang about sometimes, and he was at the Cambridge Rooms last night. I guessed this was something to do with him by the looks he kept directing at us.

About ten minutes after we got there, Reg came in. I assumed someone had phoned him to say we were there. He came straight over to us.

"Hey Hershel, I think you've upset someone last night; he wants a word with you."

He turned to the bar, nodded, and this Harry came over. He was a big lump, about as tall as Holmes, but bigger built and had the look of a fighter with the puffed eyelids, and slightly flattened nose.

Holmes looked at him very casual, "Yeah, what's your problem?"

"You're my fucking problem. Where'd you fucking get off, telling Sonny Liston how to fight."

He said this very belligerent, nearly pushing Reg out of the way to get closer to Holmes. Holmes smiled at him. That's what he was like; he liked to wind people up.

"I asked Sonny if he wanted some advice, and he said he did, so I told him. I happen to know that he's not at his best with defensive fighters, like Clay, like Eddie Machin, Bert Whitehurst, Johnny Summerlin. I only hope he takes my advice. What's wrong with that?"

Some of the others had drifted over, and it seemed to boost Harry up a bit more. He was sneering now. "So what are you, a fucking boxing expert?"

"I suppose I am really," Holmes said, nodding, "yes, I suppose that's what I am."

"Have you ever actually put a pair of gloves on and been in the ring?"

I saw Reg taking a bit of notice then.

"Oh yeah," says Holmes. "I modelled myself on Panama Al Brown from years ago."

Harry looked round at the others for support, shaking his head. "Yeah, and what was you fighting, fucking girl guides?"

That got a couple of sniggers till Holmes said, "No, generally loud-mouthed mugs who got a bit too saucy."

Well, it went quiet as the grave in there, then someone in the crowd, "Oh Oh." Harry had gone red and was sweating.

"You talking about me?"

Holmes pushed me slightly to one side. "Well, if you think you're a loud-mouthed mug who's a bit too saucy, I suppose I am."

Someone in the crowd found this funny and burst out laughing, but Harry wasn't amused.

'Right, me and you in the ring. You skinny bastard, I'll give you Panama fucking Al Brown."

Holmes was grinning at him now like he thought it was amusing. "No, I don't think so. Why should I want to fight with you? What's the point of that?"

The grinning was making Harry angrier. "You might not want to, but I'm gonna have a fight with you. Or else you'd better fuck off and don't come round here anymore."

Shrugging his shoulders, Holmes turned to Reg. "What do you think, Reg? What do you think I should do?"

Reg stepped between the two of them. "Well, if you want my opinion, you've both insulted each other. I think you should sort it out in the ring."

And so it was arranged that they'd fight the next day at a gym down in Aldgate.

I drove Holmes back to Gaynor's, and we talked about what had gone on. We both reckoned that Reg was behind it. Holmes had noticed that Reg didn't look too pleased about him being friendly with Sonny Liston the night before. There was that. And also, the nutty way they liked to test people before being enlisted to the firm; though that usually entailed a striping or a gunshot to your leg.

I tried to talk Holmes into not turning up for the fight, cos to be honest, I didn't fancy his chances. I'd heard people talking, and when it came to fighting, Harry was on a par with the twins, but he wouldn't have any of it. He wasn't bothered at all.

"Let them play their silly games; we'll beat them in the end, John."

He said cheerio to Gaynor and, after arranging to meet me at Aldgate the next day, drove back to his own place.

The Gym was in a building that had probably been a warehouse in a previous life. Once you were through the main door off the street, you were in a corridor, and a door on the right took you into the Gym itself. The first thing you noticed was the smell; the usual combination of leather, sweat, and liniment. Low benches lined the walls on two sides of the room, and at the far end was a bank of metal lockers. A couple of speedballs were suspended from brackets, and three heavy bags hung from the ceiling rafters. What looked to be a full-size ring, about 20 ft., stood in the center of the room.

When I arrived, Holmes was already there, sitting on a bench by himself. His shoes were under the bench, and he was lacing up a pair of white gym shoes. Word must have got about because there was a lot more people than had been in the Carpenters. I could see Harry on the other side of the room; he had on a vest underneath his jacket, had his trousers tucked into his socks, and was wearing what looked like a well-worn pair of boxing boots. Holmes called me in close and put some money in my hand.

"There's a hundred pounds. See if you can find someone to have a bet."

I felt embarrassed asking, but I did anyway, "Er, who on, you or Harry?"

Perhaps I should have expected it when he said, "On me, you fucking idiot."

I soon found out that on the other side of the room, Sammy was already taking bets on the fight. But the only betting was on how long it would take Harry to knock Holmes spark out. I asked Mick, who was standing by him, "What's the price on Hershel to win? I've got a oner."

"There ain't one," he said, then shouted to Sammy, "What price Hershel?"

Someone behind him shouted, "How much?"

"Hundred pounds."

Sammy said, "I'll give you five to one."

I nodded to Mick, and he took the money off me, saying to Sammy, "A oner at five to one."

"You've got it."

Straightaway, there were people trying to buy the bet off Sammy, "I'll give you eleven to two on that, Sam."

"I'll give you six to one."

The way they were so quick to write Holmes off didn't seem right to me. It was disrespectful. And if they were disrespecting him, I felt, in a way, they were disrespecting me too. I counted the money in my pocket, seventy-three quid. Mick was still where I'd left him. I gave him the seventy, "See if you can get me six to one on this."

He counted it and shouted, "Who'll give me six to one Hershel for seventy quid?"

There was a clamour to take the bet till Tommy stuck four hundred and twenty pounds in Mick's hand. "You've got it."

I was glad it was him; he was the sneery mug who'd been with Reg the night I drove 'em to shoot that geezer.

I'd long come to realise that confidence was nine-tenths of winning a fight, and Holmes was extremely confident, and now so was I. He'd had plenty of opportunity to get out of this, in fact, he didn't even have to cause it, so I guessed he had a motive.

Some of my confidence had rubbed off onto Mick; he was now holding up his own money, or was it the money he'd just taken off Tommy, "Who'll give me ten to one Hershel for twenty pounds?"

He soon found a taker.

Sitting on the bench with Holmes, I looked up when the room went quiet, to see the twins had arrived with Bobby Ramsey, who was to be the ref. Bobby was an ex-fighter who had the marks of his trade on his face, plus some more that he'd picked up out of working hours. I liked him and found him easy to get on with.

Ron came over to speak to Holmes while Reg stood talking to Harry and the others. After looking Holmes up and down, noticing his gym shoes, Ron said, "You don't have to go through with this, Hershel, if you don't want to."

"Thanks Ron, but I think I have to now. I've just bet a hundred pounds on myself to win."

Ron looked at him, a bit puzzled, to see if he was joking." Are you serious?"

I said," A oner at five to one with Sammy, and I could have got six to one."

It was the first time I'd seen Ron smile when he didn't look sinister. Ruffling Holmes' hair, he looked really happy. "Good luck to ya, Hershel. I'll have a few quid on you myself."

And he strutted off to the other side of the room, chuckling to himself.

Somewhere near the ring, a bell rang, and with that, Holmes got up, took off his jacket and shirt, folded them, and laid them on the bench. "Don't let anyone steal them."

Bobby Ramsey came over. "Hello son, you alright. Are you his second?" I nodded, and he pointed over to the ring. "That's your corner there. You'll find a bucket, a sponge, and a stool. It's three-minute rounds with a minute in between. The fight ends with either a knockout or someone concedes, right." I nodded again, and he said, "Good, if you're ready then, let's go,"

Harry was already in the ring in the far corner. We watched as Ramsey went over to speak to him, then Holmes climbed into the ring.

I say climbed, but it was more like stepped, as the ring was only about a foot off of the floor. Holmes had on a white tee-shirt, and it was funny, but he looked bigger in that than when he was wearing a suit. He seemed absolutely relaxed and gave a little grin, then winked at me as Bobby called them both to the centre of the ring.

"I want a clean fight, no biting, gouging..." He stopped then cos Holmes was leaning to one side, looking at Harry's boots and laughing, not just giggling, but laughing out loud. Now Harry was looking down at his boots, a bit puzzled, cos he couldn't see anything funny about them. Bobby Ramsey wasn't amused,

"What'choo fucking find so funny? You're here to have a fight ain'tcha?"

Holmes apologised, and he carried on where he'd left off,

"No biting, no gouging, no kicking, and break when I tell you to. Now, good luck, touch gloves."

He stepped back, and as soon as he did, Harry swung a big right, but Holmes had backed away, still looking at Harry's boots and smiling. Now Harry had his guard up, with his right hand protecting his face, throwing out his left. But Holmes was always out of range. Harry tracked him round the ring, throwing punches that didn't land. Twice he got Holmes in a corner and tried to open up, but each time Holmes ducked under his punches, turned him, and flicked him, sort of with contempt, on the nose. This went on for the first half of the round.

Holmes was holding his hands low, with no attempt at defence, just relying on his foot movement.

Harry's swings were getting wilder, and every punch he threw was either too late or too short. Now Holmes started to throw some serious punches, they were random punches, thrown from unorthodox angles, and all the time skipping round the ring like a dancer. I could hear moans from the crowd, "This ain't fighting." "Come on, Harry."

Towards the end of the round, Holmes stood for a moment face on to Harry, then stepped aside and threw a long right hand that broke Harry's nose. I could hear it from where I was standing, and the groan that went up told me the others had heard it too or seen it. The bell rang for the end of the round.

Holmes came to the corner and waved the stool aside. "Don't bother with that. Well, what do you think? D'you think Panama Al Brown would approve?"

" I'm sure he would," I said, " but be careful, he's a powerful geezer."

Holmes leaned over the ropes grinning," He couldn't hit me if I nailed my feet to the floor."

In the other corner, Harry was sitting, not too happy, with his vest the raspberry colour of watered-down blood. The bell rang, and they came to the centre of the ring. Harry was serious now, he threw two sharp left hands, but Holmes stepped to the side with a loping right uppercut, followed by a left to the temple, that shook Harry. After that, it was Holmes all the way. Harry did manage to land a couple of blows, but each time Holmes was moving away, so they didn't bother him. Now Holmes was landing two punch combinations at will, left-right, and they were powerful punches and accurate. Then halfway through the round, Holmes landed a vicious right hook under the heart, and Harry dropped like a sack of spuds. Bobby gave him a few seconds before he started counting; and with a slow count, Harry got up at eight. Holmes immediately steamed into him and was hitting his head at will for about half a minute, with vicious left and right hooks, till Harry dropped to the canvas again and someone threw in the towel. He was sparko, and they had to leave him there and chuck water on him till he came round. Then they yanked him to his corner and hoisted him onto a stool, where he sat looking at the floor, despondent.

While Holmes was dressing, I went round to collect our winnings. It was funny to see the floor on that side was littered with discarded tickets, the broken dreams of Harry's disillusioned fan club. I found Mick arguing with Sammy, who was demanding a stewards inquiry. "Hold on, let's not rush things. The fight wasn't officially over cos there was no count, was there? The ref never officially counted him out."

Mick grabbed him by his tie, "Give me my money, you fucking little rat, or I'll open you up."

Tommy came over, "He's right, you know. That should be called a no contest. There wasn't a count. I think I want my money back, case there's a rematch."

Mick let go of Sammy, "You can want what you fucking like. You had a bet and lost, so shut up."

I pushed my way through the crowd, "You might want to ask Ron if it's official or not. He had money on Hershel."

Sammy didn't need to hear anymore; he was pushing the money into Mick's hand. "Perhaps you're right. He wasn't in any condition to carry on."

Mick turned to Tommy, " Go and tell Ron he ain't getting paid, and if he stands for it, I'll give you your money back."

I don't know if it was because I was smiling, but Tommy scowled at me and walked away muttering to himself. Holmes had come over by now, and I could see people looking at him with new respect. The best part was when Mick paid us our money six hundred for Holmes and four hundred and ninety for me, and he wouldn't take a drink out of it, cos he'd had a nice little earner himself. It was like us three were the only happy ones in the crowd, then Ron came over, smiling, "Hershel, you was great. Where'd you learn to fight like that?"

Holmes put on his modest face, "I don't know Ron, I just picked it up. Mind you, let's be honest, it wasn't hard, was it. I don't know whoever told that Harry he could fight."

That little bit of work in the Aldgate gym put Holmes on a bit of a pedestal within the firm, and the story soon spread. Everyone wanted to buy him a drink wherever he went, and naturally, I got included. For a

171

while, he wasn't Hershel anymore; he was 'Champ.' "Hello champ, what are you having? Marge, give the champ and his mate a drink."

The Bethnal Green gossip machine soon got to work. Kathy would tell me stuff she'd hear when she was working. 'Hershel was a good mate of Sonny Liston--- Sonny Liston and Hershel used to drink in a nightclub in St Louis--- Hershel and his girlfriend used to run a brothel in St Louis--- Hershel was trained to fight by an old black man in Panama and boxed under the name, Al Brown.'

Somehow, I got included too. I was supposed to have killed someone in my car. Kathy asked me, ''Is it true John? Is that what the twins want you for, to kill people?

"No, I haven't fucking killed anyone," I said, "and Hershel didn't know Sonny Liston in the states, and he wasn't trained to fight by an old black man, and he's never been to Panama. So don't believe anything them fucking morons in the pub say about us."

I don't know if that convinced her or not, but she continued to tell me bits and pieces that she'd heard. One other thing that she mentioned was that Adie Morris had phoned her in the Lion and told her he'd be meeting her fucking skinny boyfriend soon. And no-one could have guessed the trouble that was going to cause.

CHAPTER 13

Adolf Morris

A few weeks after the fight, we'd been invited down to Vallance Road to tell Ron more about Enugu and Cameroon. We parked up a few doors away and walked down to 178. Holmes noticed, on the other side of the road, a black Austin Westminster with the rear window wound down. Ron had answered the door, and as soon as we were inside, I mentioned the car to him.

"Probably old bill," he said. As he pulled the curtain aside to look out, the car shot away from the kerb and out of our sight. Ron said to Holmes, "Did you recognise the fellow in the back? That was fucking Adie Morris. What's he doing parking up near our house? I'm gonna fucking have a word with him."

It was then I remembered the phone call Kathy had got. I guessed Adie might have the idea she was seeing Holmes and not me as it was him who scragged his brother.

He laughed when I told him about the phone call. "If he had any guts he would come and see me himself, not make threats on the telephone. He sounds to me, like the type of fellow who would let down your tyres or scratch your paintwork. Cowardly." We didn't know then that Adie Morris was a bit more serious than that.

After leaving Vallance Road we drove over to Holmes's, taking all the precautions to make sure we weren't followed. We jumped at least two sets of lights and did a couple of U turns.

The reason for that, was that I'd seen the very same motor parked up near my flat. Knowing they couldn't have tailed me there, it had to be that someone had given them my address; and to my knowledge, the only ones who knew it were Tommy, Dick, the Scotch geezer Billy, and the twins. Five of 'em, and I'd put my money on Tommy. Holmes was certain he'd seen the same car as well, but he couldn't think where.

Fortunately, he'd clocked the registration outside Ron's, and he had a contact in the relevant offices who could give him the name and address of the owner. It took about ten minutes to find out that the car was registered to Miss Louise Rutherford at an address in Radnor Mews, London W2.

Back in his flat, while we were waiting for it to get dark, Holmes cooked me a nice meal of spaghetti. I'd never ever eaten it before, and never wanted to, simply because it reminded me of worms.

Anyway, he persuaded me, and I watched him while he cooked it. He soon found a bit of opera on the radio and went to chopping the mushrooms and onions. While they were cooking, he was splashing in white wine, and cream from the fridge, and different herbs. In less than half hour we were sitting at the table eating, and the operatic girl was warbling away. If I'm honest I'd have to say that in that flat, at that time, in that atmosphere, and with the wine, it was one of the best meals I've ever had. And it even made Madam Butterfly bearable.

After we'd eaten and cleared up, Holmes went into his dressing room to get changed. A fucking dressing-room. I thought my flat was nice, but compared to this it was a rat-infested slum. He came out wearing his beatnik gear, corduroy strides, roll-neck jumper, and a duffel coat. On his head, he had on what might have once been a trilby, with the brim turned down all the way round. He got his mini cooper out of one of the garages and we set off for Radnor Mews.

The traffic wasn't bad for that time of night, and we drove up to the Edgeware Road and turned into Sussex Gardens. Further on, turning into Radnor Place, I spotted the car, and Holmes confirmed the number plate. It was parked up near the entrance to the mews, pointing down toward Gloucester square. We drove down a bit, parked up and walked round into the mews. The address we had was a white painted two storey lot with a garage on the ground floor.

There was an ornamental flowerpot by the front door, and Holmes, bending down to tie his shoelace, gave it a nudge. Walking down to the end of the mews took us into Sussex place, then round the block and back to his car.

I didn't go back into Holmes' but picked up my car and drove to Kathy's. Without saying what had gone on, I asked her to tell me everything she knew about the Morris brothers; and it was an interesting tale.

Adie, Tojo, and Benny were pimps and had four or five girls working for them in the West End. Adie lived up around Sussex Gardens somewhere with Leicester Lou, a brass. And every night about eight or nine o'clock he'd drop her off in Park Lane where she'd ply her trade.

Benny, Tojo, and Winston lived out at Romford somewhere. While Adie was dropping Lou off, Bennie and Tojo would round up the other girls and take them to their pitches. Apart from the fact they lived at Romford, and sometimes used the pubs and clubs of the East and West End, there wasn't much she could say about the other two. The only problem in my mind was, who was Adie interested in, me, Holmes, the twins, or all of us?

I decided to settle that matter the next day with a phone call to Charlie Dickson. After listening to what I had to say, he said, "Leave it to me. You might want to expect a call from the other two later on. Let me know what happens. Heh heh heh."

Sure enough within the hour there was a phone call from Ron, "John, is Hershel with you?"

I said, "No, what's up?"

He sounded excited. "I won't say on the phone. Try and get hold of Hershel and come round home. Don't drive, get a cab, and keep your eyes open for that black car."

It was late afternoon before I could get in touch with Holmes; he'd been doing some research on the Morris family. He picked me up from Kathy's and we went down to Vallance Road. Reg let us in, and as soon as we were in the front room Ron was at the curtains looking for the black car. The tape recorder was where we'd last seen it, attached to the telephone.

"Listen to this." Ron twiddled the knobs and Charlie Dickson's voice came through loud and clear. "Did Adie Morris ring yet Jack?"

Then another voice, "Yeah, he's got the twins under obbo. He reckons by this time next year him and Benny will have them two out of the West End, and Big Frank and Bernie Silver as well. Then we can do some business."

Ron's eyes were bulging and his hair, which was normally neat, was waving about on his head. He had a look somewhere between distraught and crazy. His voice had gone up a notch,

"Did you hear that?" Then he was shouting, ranting. "Did you fucking hear that? Adie Morris is going to get us out of the West End. That fucking two bob fucking pimp and his fucking brothers. And they're gonna do business with the Dicksons. I'll wipe the fucking lot of 'em out."

This outburst seemed to have tired him out a bit and he flopped into an armchair. Reg patted his arm. "Slow down Ron. We've got the advantage here. He don't know that we're on to 'em. We can do 'em in our own time. What do you think Hershel?"

177

Holmes nodded, like he was thinking, which he probably was, "I think you're right Reg. Who are Big Frank, and Bernie Silver, do you know them?"

"Yeah, they're friends of ours," Ron was at the curtains again, "They're not going to be too pleased when they hear about this."

I had to give Charlie Dickson credit; with one moody phone call he'd given poor Adie Morris about twenty enemies he didn't even know about. But somehow, he did get to know about it, cos someone tipped him off.

It may have been a week after that meeting; Kathy was thinking about going back home, up north for Christmas, and we were talking about it when there was a knock at the door. It was Ron with a question.

We went into the front room, and I shut the door and turned on the radio, so no-one could hear. Sitting opposite me Ron was giving me his creepy stare. "Reg said you told him you shot someone, is that right?"

I remembered shooting someone, but I didn't remember telling Reg about it. Perhaps that's where the stories came from. "Yeah, I shot and killed three men and a boy, in the hills in Aden. Why do you ask Ron?"

He had taken off his glasses and wiped them, "Oh, so you was in the army then."

I said, "Yeah, why did you want to know about that?"

Without answering, he said, "What about Hershel, has he killed anyone?"

I almost laughed at that, but then I remembered, and told Ron the story of Mrs. Greenacre and her son, Henry. Henry was a market trader, and somehow, he'd upset Holmes's mother. I can't remember what it was about, but he got a bit uptight over it and demanded Henry apologise. Well, he got the response any cocky, snobby, fifteen-year-old would get off a market trader; 'Fuck off.'

Naturally he wasn't satisfied with that, so he schemed and plotted to get his revenge. He found out that Mr. and Mrs. Greenacre were big fans of Max Bygraves, the comedian. Saving his money, he bought two tickets for a show Max Bygraves was in. With a moody letter, saying they'd won a competition, he sent the tickets to the Greenacres, and they stood for it and went to see the show.

That night while they were out, laughing at Max Bygraves, he got into their house and stuck broken bits of razor blades in Mrs. Greenacre's toothbrush. Then he walked the streets waiting for them to come home. Once they were back indoors, he hung about outside, watching the lights gradually being turned off.

The bathrooms in those houses were at the back, so he didn't know if his plan had worked, till he heard the screams. He was still there when the ambulance came to take her to hospital, blood pumping out of her mouth.

Ron stopped me there, his face was pale, and I'm not sure if there wasn't tears in his eyes. He looked distraught.

"Are you saying he did that to someone's mum? That's 'orrible."

179

"Well, that was his reasoning at the time," I said, "He was only fifteen. That geezer had upset Hershel's mother, so he'd upset his mother and see how he liked it."

"What about the feller, the market trader, why didn't he do something to him?"

"He was going to," I said, "but the poor fellow died before he got round to it."

Ron was scowling a bit, thinking, "What did he die of?"

I know I shouldn't have laughed, but I always found it funny when I thought about it. "Blood poisoning. He trod on a rusty nail outside of his front door, and then he trod on another one right by his van. They reckon the nails was infected in some way, probably rats or foxes wee'd on em. I always thought he'd put 'em there, but he just laughed and said 'prove it'."

As soon as he left, I phoned Holmes and told him about the conversation, and Ron's questions. It didn't take a lot of working out, and we both knew he wanted us to get rid of Adie Morris.

It was a few days after Ron's visit, I was in the kitchen round Kathy's when I heard, "Oh fucking hell."

I went into the front room and found her sitting on the sofa with tears rolling down her face.

"What's the matter?" I said, " Are you alright?"

Between her sobs she managed to get out, " Somebody's shot Jack Kennedy."

I couldn't get my head around what she was saying till I heard and recognised the serious tone of the news reader on the tv. Someone had shot and killed the president of the United States in Dallas Texas, that afternoon. I sat down next to her and felt a loss, like it was a good friend, someone close, who'd been murdered.

The phone rang, it was Holmes; have we heard the news. He must have heard Kathy sobbing in the background cos he hung up without saying anything else. I don't know what it was about Kennedy that made us take his death personally. None of us had ever met him, or ever would. He was like a relatively new acquaintance, who'd come into our lives through the tv and the newspapers and yet, without knowing him, we believed in him. Perhaps it was because he was young and good looking, or the way he spoke, whatever it was, he made you think he was going to make the world a better place. And now he was gone.

The next day we got the news that the police had arrested a suspect for the shooting, and a couple of days later he'd been shot dead too, in Dallas police headquarters. A week later Kennedy had been buried, there was a new president, and twenty-five shopping days till Christmas.

CHAPTER 14

We're at war

It was a week after Kennedy got shot that they tried to shoot Holmes. And it was Tommy who set him up.

I'd arranged to pick up Kathy when she finished her shift in the Lion, but by the time I got there, she'd gone. Madge told me that Ron had phoned and said could she help out in the Carpenters cos one of the barmaids hadn't turned up. It wasn't too busy, so Madge called her a cab, and she'd left.

There was a few of the firm in there, and I was surprised when Tommy bought me a drink. "Here you go, John. What have you been up to? We ain't seen you about lately. How's the champ?"

I didn't even like looking at the slimy bastard, but I didn't let on. I raised my glass to him. "Good luck Tom. Yeah, he's OK. He should be in here soon."

Madge came over with a message, Kathy had rung, and could I pick her up at the Carpenters. I finished my drink, bought a round for Tommy and the others, and said to tell Hershel when he arrived; I'd be in the Carpenters.

Nearly an hour had gone by since I got to the Carpenters, and I was at the bar talking to Mick when Holmes came in with the twins. He pulled me to one side, and we sat at a table out of earshot. "I think we're at war, John."

He then told me how he'd got to the Lion not long after I'd left. Straightaway, Tommy had bought him a drink and told him I'd popped out but would be back later. After a few drinks with Tommy and the others, Holmes sensed something wasn't right and got the impression that Tommy was trying to keep him there.

As soon as he was sure, he left the pub a bit lively; but as he turned right to go down the road, a grey car spun out of the street opposite. The sound of accelerating wheels was enough for Holmes, and he ducked down behind a parked car as he heard two loud bangs, and two bullets hit the wall where he'd been standing.

While the car sped off down Tapp Street, Holmes slipped back into the alley next to the Lion, climbed a fence, and got up onto the railway bank. He walked along by the line till he could find a place to drop off near the arches at Vallance Road and made his way to 178.

Reg came over with a couple of large gin and tonics and pulled up a chair. He said, "I've just phoned Tommy at the Lion and told him to come down here, but he didn't sound too happy. Anyway, Billy's going to bring some things over soon, case they have another go."

Soon came sooner than I expected, cos in a few minutes, Billy was sitting at our table, holding a carrier bag with Christmas wrapping paper sticking out of the top. I'd seen a few Bills and Billys with the firm, but I'd never seen this one before. He was an older man, about fifty, short, fair-haired, and very smart in his navy overcoat. After Reg gave him the OK, he reached into the bag and gave me something wrapped in a yellow duster. I could feel it was a medium-sized automatic pistol.

It had always been a rule of mine not to be involved with firearms, but if these crazy bastards were going to have shootouts in the street, I felt, yeah fuck 'em, we'll fight fire with fire. Holmes was given a similar package. He slipped the gun into his pocket, folded the duster, and put that into another pocket. Billy said, "They're wolfers, and they're both full up. Don't worry if you have to get rid of 'em."

Reg gave him a look and a nod, and Billy got up and left the pub as discreetly as he'd come in. Ron came over then with a drink for Reg, sitting down, he said," Who d'you think's just phoned me? Adie Morris."

Reg's eyebrows went up, "How did he know you were here?"

"Exactly," Ron said, "And that's what I asked him, but he wouldn't say who told him. He said someone's been feeding us false information, and he's got no intention of pushing us out of the West End." He was scowling a bit now, but he went on, "I told him to come down here, and we'd talk about it. What do you reckon he said?"

"What?"

"He said he didn't think that was a good idea right now, but he'll see us another time."

Reg sat back in his chair. "Oh, he'll see us alright, but it might be for the last time."

That made Ron laugh and lightened the mood a bit." What about you, Hershel," he said, "are you OK? You don't get shot at every day, do you."

Holmes gave him a slight smile, his heroic smile, "I'm fine, thanks, Ron. Incidentally, I've been shot at by far finer marksmen than those today, and I'm still here. So, cheers everybody."

He lifted his glass, and we all did the same.

I spoke to Kathy and told her I wouldn't be able to see her for a while till this was sorted. She seemed to know all about it, or at least enough to understand. "Just be careful, and make sure you phone me." I wiped away a tear that was slowly running down her cheek, and she smiled, just a bit. Then we left.

With the twins following in another car, Mickey drove us in my car to Liverpool Street station; he said he'd put it in his lockup till we got back. After watching them pull away, we took a cab to Tottenham Court Road, then, crossing the road, we got another one to the Dorchester. It was just a short walk from there to Holmes's place in Balfour Mews.

Once we were indoors, Holmes asked me for my pistol. I was reluctant to part with it cos there's no doubt about it. They do make you feel confident. After wiping the pair of 'em down with something he'd

185

taken from under his kitchen sink, he wrapped them in a tea towel and vanished out of his front door. It wasn't long before he came back and told me that he'd hidden them in one of the garages that he rented from a neighbour. He assured me that the garage owner was an old lady, and the police would never have any reason to search her garage; even if they did, it would be doubtful that she'd be charged and convicted. But if that did happen, a spell in prison might do her good because she was a nasty old bitch.

I was laughing at this cos he didn't often joke about things; then I realised he wasn't kidding; he meant it.

I was getting hungry by now, and so was Holmes, so he took me round the corner to a restaurant in Mount Street. Well, I thought I'd been in some classy places, but this topped the lot. As soon as you walked through the door, you could smell money. Obviously, you couldn't literally smell money; it was a restaurant. But there was an air of luxury.

They all knew Holmes in there, not just the waiters, but some of the punters too, and he acted very polite and condescending. Finally, the head waiter, or manager, I don't know what he was, but he seemed like the top dog, came sliding through the thick carpet, "Good evening Mr. Holmes, we've missed you. Your usual table?"

Holmes gave him his brittle smile, "Thank you, Michael, that would be nice."

His usual table was halfway down the room, which gave a good view of all the exits and entrances. Holmes ordered Bannockburn rib steak and some poncey vegetables, and I had deep-fried haddock with chips and mushy peas. It was nice, but I have to say, a posh restaurant in the heart of Mayfair couldn't cook fish and chips as good as my local chip shop round the corner from the Crooked Billet in Penge.

While I was eating, thoughts came into my mind; thoughts that wouldn't go away. What the fuck was I doing here, sitting in a posh West End restaurant, eating fish and chips, when all my clothes, apart from what I had on, were at Penge or at Kathy's; and I'm some sort of fucking fugitive. It occurred to me that the whole thing started when Holmes had scragged dopey Benny Morris in the Lion. Actually, it had really started when he came round mine whining about his mate Adrian and getting us involved with the Krays. All this was his fault.

But getting back to Benny Morris, it was Holmes who chose to shake him like a ragdoll, no-one asked him to, certainly not me. The more I thought about it, the more I came to realise this was Holmes's problem, not mine. When I'd seen the Morris's car plotted up near my flat, no-one tried to shoot me. And numerous times when I'd been round Kathy's, I would have been an easy target, but no-one tried to shoot me. It must have been Holmes they were waiting for. By being with him, we were giving them two targets to aim for now instead of one.

187

"Is the fish OK," Holmes interrupted my thoughts. He was staring at me like he knew what I'd been thinking, but there's no way he could have known that, could he.

"Yeah, it's nice; the chips are nice too."

"You seem to have something on your mind, John. Are you alright?"

"Yeah, course I am. I was just thinking I'm gonna need some clothes if we're gonna be banged up in yours for a time."

As much as I tried to sound convincing, you could never be sure that Holmes was convinced.

"It's not going to be a very long time, John. I'm going to put an end to this soon."

He said this as he's calling the waiter over for the bill.

Back at his, I thought we'd be in for a night of watching the television. Instead of that, he went and got dolled up in his hippie gear with the duffel coat. "I wonder if Adolf will be taking his young lady to work tonight. Shall we go and have a look."

Down in the street, he pulled the mini out of one of the garages, and we drove over to Radnor Place. The Austin was in the same place as when we last saw it; seems like that was his regular parking spot. Holmes stopped outside a block of flats where we had a good view of Adie's car and the entrance to the mews. Luckily there weren't many streetlights, and what there were were pretty dim. A grey car pulled up on the other side of the road, just past the entrance to the mews. Holmes had wound his window down and was listening.

"Can you hear that engine, John? That's a GT version Ford Cortina. That's the car they used this morning."

If he had any doubts about it, he soon lost 'em when Adie Morris got out of the back of the car.

Even with the dim lighting, we could see the resemblance to Benny, except this one, was bigger, about six feet, and a bit beefy with it. The similarity was a mop of fair curly hair, that looked like a load of light brown springs waving about on top of his head. He must have liked looking like a fucking idiot, cos any normal person would have got a haircut. As he leaned forward at the front window, he took something from the driver and put it in his back pocket.

"That's a gun," said Holmes, "and probably the one they used to shoot at me."

I slumped down in my seat when he said that cos if they'd have looked round and twigged us, we'd have to drive past 'em. And I guessed they'd have more than one gun with them. But that didn't happen. Adie had a few more words with the driver and walked round into the mews.

"Listen," Holmes said, as the grey car reversed a couple of yards, then the engine revved up, the tyres screeched, and it went away like a rocket toward Gloucester Square.

It was getting cold sitting in that mini, and you could almost feel the damp from outside where there was a mist coming down. I began to envy Holmes in his duffel coat. While I was considering whether or not I'd wear one, Holmes nudged me. "Tally Ho. The game's afoot."

That's the sort of idiotic comments he used to come out with, but he was right in one respect.

Adie had emerged into the street with a tall blond girl wearing what looked like a fur jacket, ankle boots, and a very short skirt. He had changed into a chunky cardigan, so we knew he wasn't going to be out for the night. They got in their car and cruised slowly down to turn left into Somers Crescent.

Making no attempt to follow them cos we knew where they were going, Holmes took a different route to the top of Park Lane. One or two girls were out on the street, already touting for business. Just a few yards from the Dorchester, Leicester Lou was getting out of the car as we went by. As soon as we passed them, Holmes put his foot down. Halfway down the road, he swung a right, into the opposite lane and sped up toward Marble Arch.

We took the route we expected Adie to take, Edgeware Road, Sussex Gardens, and into Radnor Place from the top. This time we drove down past the mews and pulled up on the other side of the road. It wasn't long before I saw Adie's car in the rear-view mirror slide into his usual parking spot. We watched him lock the car door, looking up and down the street before he crossed the road and disappeared into the mews.

Back at Holmes's, he'd put the car away, got out of his hippy gear, and put on what looked like a silk smoking jacket. From a cabinet, he'd taken a bottle of bourbon which I'd given him for a Christmas present a couple of years ago. It was warm in the room now and nice to relax after all that had gone on. Holmes must have felt it more than I did. Putting his glass down on a side table, he suddenly leaned forward. "All this could have been avoided, you know, John. If he'd only had the guts to confront me, we could have had this out man to man."

I thought,' Yeah, if you hadn't got hold of his brother and started squeezing his neck, he wouldn't have had to confront you,' but I didn't say anything, just nodded.

"But it's too late now John; the die is cast. They mean business, and I can't ignore it."

I poured myself another drink, and the room was getting warmer, or was it me. "So, what are you going to do? You gonna take 'em out?" This was the gangster language he liked to use now and then.

"Well, I didn't want to." he said; "We'll have to see what happens. I will say this though, John, I can't think of anyone I'd rather have at my side right now, and I mean that."

I thought, 'Yes, you fuckin liar.'

I bet there were a thousand people he'd rather have at his side right now, but they weren't here, and I was. I didn't let on though, I said, "Well, thanks Sherlock, that means a lot to me."

191

There were paintings on the wall of the guest room, not prints, but proper oil paintings and watercolours. And if you couldn't have sold them, the frames must have been worth a nice few quid. There was a Chinese rug on top of the maroon wall to wall Wilton carpet, and on the bed were pale blue silk sheets under a patchwork quilt. Within a minute of climbing into that bed, I'd forgotten all that had gone on during the day and nodded off.

There's something about cold frosty mornings that makes me want to stay in bed, and this was one of 'em. I did eventually ease myself out of the warm sheets and into the shower. Then I dressed in the clothes I'd had on the day before and went downstairs to the kitchen. The smell of frying bacon had drifted to the top of the stairs, and Holmes was lifting it from the pan with a fork. "I thought you might like a fry up, John," he said as he took two plates from the oven.

It was a fry-up like I hadn't seen since I lived at home when my nan used to do it, sausages, bacon, mushrooms, and two fried eggs. Then he had to spoil it by telling me that the eggs came up from Sussex every day, the sausages from Lincolnshire, and the bacon from Norfolk. The fact that he didn't mention the mushrooms, I guessed he picked 'em himself in Hyde Park that morning.

He may not have meant anything by it, but it seemed like he was saying, 'this bit of grub's better than anything you've been used to'; perhaps he was right, but he didn't have to say it, although he never actually did say it, but he implied it, and I wouldn't have done that.

That's the sort of condescending arrogance that's come down to him through the generations since the original smarmy bastard, Sherlock Holmes.

It was probably being surrounded by the luxury in Holmes's little house that made me feel resentful, thinking that all this was bought by money initially generated by my great grandfather, Dr. John Watson. We finished the meal, and I helped him wash and dry up the breakfast things, something he'd never done round my house. Back upstairs, Holmes disappeared into his dressing room. He opened the door slightly, "I have a few things to do today, John, so you'll have the run of the place. There's food in the kitchen, drinks in the cabinet, the radio, records, use the phone if you want."

He came out of the room looking like what you'd think of as a guards officer in civvies, cos I guessed that's what he'd been. I'd never seen a Crombie overcoat with a velvet collar before, but he had one; draping it over his shoulders, he went to the top of the stairs and said, "To quote Lawrence Oates, 'I am just going outside and may be some time'."

I could hear him chuckling to himself as he went downstairs. I don't know if Lawrence Oates was a real person or one of his imaginary friends, but he didn't have to quote anyone. He could have just said, "see you later." But that's Sherlock Holmes.

While he was gone, I took the opportunity to look around. He'd made me promise to stay out of his bedroom, which I did. I know there's nothing in my bedroom I'd be ashamed of someone seeing, but then again, I didn't go to Eton.

There was one room downstairs at the back of the house that was interesting. It was a small workshop with three of its walls lined with shelves. On the shelves were bottles and jars, tins and boxes, all labelled with what looked like Arabic writing; probably shorthand, cos Holmes was fond of that. On a bench was a hand-operated printing press, and next to it, boxes of lead type. After looking round, and making sure that nothing was disturbed, I shut the door, confident that Holmes would know I'd been in there.

Holmes had told me that the Norfolk bacon, Sussex eggs, etc., came to him via a grocer's shop round the corner in South Audley Street, and as there was no ham to be found in the kitchen, I went round there. When Holmes said a grocer's shop, he understated it. This shop was fat kid's heaven. There were sausages of all shapes, colours, makes, and sizes hanging from the ceiling, big round whole cheeses on a slab behind the counter, whole hams, and fresh loaves and rolls.

And there were smells; apart from the smell of the fresh ground coffee, there were smells that I recognised, that I remembered but couldn't identify.

The staff all wore a sort of uniform, a navy striped apron, a stiff white shirt, and a striped tie. Looking at them, and some of the punters in the shop, made me realise I hadn't changed for a couple of days, so I bought some Wiltshire ham and a couple of rolls and left.

Back at Holmes's, the first thing I did was phone the Widow's pub. Kathy was working, and she gave me all the latest news. Tommy never turned up at the Carpenters and hadn't been seen since. Reg and Mickey went round his flat, but there was no sign of him.

This morning before she went to work, she'd seen a grey car parked opposite the flats, then it passed her as she walked down to the shops, and Tojo Morris was driving. She'd told Mickey, and he'd told the twins.

We talked for a while, and I suggested that she might want to leave London and go up north early to spend Christmas with her family. That made her laugh, and she said she wouldn't go anywhere till she'd seen me. She'd already told Gaynor that she wouldn't be seeing Hershel for a while; it was too dangerous for her and her boy. I waited while she called Mick to the phone, he had something to tell me. "Hello John, you alright?"

I said, "Yeah, we're fine; what's happening?"

I could hear the pub noises in the background, glasses clinking, and muffled conversation. "We're all tooled up here. We've found out, the grey car is Tojo's, and him and Benny share a house somewhere over in Romford. We're still trying to find out the exact address. And Adie is somewhere in Bayswater with a girl named Lou. Oh, and someone said our friends in the West End have put a £1000 price on Adie's head. That's about all we've got so far; the twins might be able to tell you more."

Putting the phone down, I almost felt sorry for Adie. What had started off as a joke call from Charlie Dickson had now got out of hand and put a price on his head. Then thinking about it, they had tried to shoot Holmes, and they were pimps, who, Kathy said, really used to beat the girls who worked for them. So fuck Adie, and the other two as well, they should have chose a different line of work.

After finishing my ham rolls and a nice cup of tea, I loafed about all day. Holmes' collection of vinyl records surprised me; they weren't all classical. There was jazz: Brubeck, Errol Garner, Chet Baker, even some traditional jazz records. There was Churchill's speeches, folk music from Scotland, Ireland, United States, but none from England, and definitely no pop music. Along one wall was a bookcase, and nearly all the books were to do with crime. I guessed he kept the Playboys and porno stuff in his bedroom, and that's why he didn't want me to go in there.

He had the complete hardback set of the Newgate Calendar, The Knights of Bushido and Scourge of the Swastika, about war crimes. And naturally, all the books about his ancestor, most of which weren't true.

It was about six o'clock and dark outside when Holmes came back. He was loaded out with parcels and carrier bags, a couple of which he gave to me. There were socks and ties, underpants, and shirts, all quality gear from Simpsons and Austin Reed. "I wouldn't presume to buy you a suit or jacket," he said. "But never mind, you'll be home soon and wearing your own. I've ordered some food, John. It's simple fare, but nourishing."

He'd no sooner said that; there was a ring on the doorbell. We went downstairs, and through the front door, I could see a green van with gold lettering; then a geezer appeared, very smart in a black jacket and bow tie. He passed a tray to Holmes, and then, with a bit of bowing and scraping and, "Thank you so much, Mr. Holmes, thank you very much," he backed away from the door.

The simple fare Holmes had mentioned wasn't simple fare at all. Perhaps it was to him. A large fillet steak, with chips and peas, and a vegetable I'd never seen before, all in a delicious light brown gravy. The mysterious vegetable, Holmes said, was broccoli, and very good for you. And all this on the finest Wedgewood bone-china plates.

While I was telling him what Mick had told me, Holmes had taken a bottle of red wine from a rack in the corner of the kitchen and poured a couple of glasses. "I've been doing some work of my own, John," he said, "I think that Tojo and Benito are using a nice semi-detached property in Tudor Avenue, Romford. It's registered in the name of Mrs. June Pottersby, probably one of their employees. Young Winston and the parents have a not so salubrious place near the town centre. I have all their phone numbers and car registrations. It's really not very nice to think I that might have to spoil their Christmas."

We took the wine upstairs, and Holmes explained to me that he had to go out again, alone. There were one or two things he had to do that he could do better on his own, and he hoped I didn't mind. Well, as much as I was fed up with being banged up, given a choice between wandering about outside without an overcoat on a cold December night, and sitting in Holmes's warm front room drinking wine, I chose the second one.

While I sat watching TV, Holmes had gone into his bedroom, and I guess his dressing room, cos he came out wearing a chunky dark grey wool cardigan, the same as Adie had worn, and under his arm, he had one of the parcels he'd brought in. I had to look twice, cos I don't know what he'd done, but his hair was waving about on his head, like a load of coiled springs, like Adie's.

He ruffled my hair as he went out to the top of the stairs. It was unusual to see him looking so happy; he was really grinning. "You know John," he said, "nothing pleases me more than to go out on a dark winter night, looking like someone else."

Perhaps I should have been more curious about why he was dressed like that, and where he was going, but I wasn't. Maybe it was the fact that he wanted to do it on his own, or perhaps it was the red Shiraz wine, that was so easy to drink.

I was asleep on his sofa when he came home and woke me up. Sitting upright, I waited for my head to clear, "How'd you get on?" I asked him.

Not so boisterous now, he was looking at me with his starey eyes and his grim smile, "Quite well, I think John, you'll probably be able to go home soon."

After phoning round their house and a few of the pubs, he finally got hold of the twins at the Regency. "Hello Reg, it's Hershel. Just thought I'd let you know, you can tell your friends in the West End, that problem will be all over in the next few days. I won't say any more on the phone, but I'll tell you when we meet up."

He poured himself a drink from the cabinet and sat next to me on the sofa, sipping it. His eyes were closed, and he sat sort of dreaming with a smile on his face. I guessed he was going over the events of the night. Now I was curious. I said, "Are you going to tell me what happened? That's made you sit there grinning like a Cheshire cat?"

He got serious then, "No, John, not right now. I don't want you to take this personally, but you'll have to trust me. It's best I don't tell you right now."

There was nothing at all in his manner, that would have told me he'd just killed someone.

CHAPTER 15

Leicester Louise

By the time I got up the next morning, Holmes was up and about and ready to go out. "John," he said," I've just remembered, I didn't go out last night after all. Can you play cribbage?"

I said, "Yeah, I can play crib; why d'you ask?"

"Because, if anyone wants to know, that's what we were doing last night; you and I, playing cribbage and listening to music."

I nodded. "Yeah, alright."

"Good," he winked at me, "I've one or two things to attend to this morning, but I'll be back soon. I've bought some nice mushrooms for you and some fresh bread. There are eggs in the cupboard, and coffee on the stove, so eat, drink and be merry for tomorrow..." he paused, then, "Who knows what tomorrow will bring?" As he went down the stairs, I heard him laughing to himself; not a pleasant laugh, but, 'heh heh heh,' like Charlie Dickson. Then he was out of the door and gone.

The mushrooms were excellent, and together with some of the ham I'd bought yesterday, I made myself an omelette. It was warm in the kitchen, and what with that and the smell of coffee bubbling on the stove, I felt really comfortable. There was no cream to be found anywhere, so I had my coffee black the way Holmes did. As I was finishing it, I could hear the phone ringing upstairs. And it did what I expected it to do when I was halfway up there; it stopped. Standing on the stairs, I knew that if I went back down, it would start again, so I tricked it and carried on up. Sure enough, it rang again. I could hear breathing, then a posh voice, like Holmes's, but a woman. "Hello Sherlock."

I said, "He's not here at the moment, can......."

That's as far as I got before the rotten trollop hung up on me. That's the sort of manners these people have got. And they look down on us, call us Riff Raff and the Hoi Polloi. I bet you could find better manners even in Bethnal Green. While I was sitting on the sofa, waiting to see if she'd ring back, and thinking how I'd like to kick her up the arse with a pair of Dr. Martens, I heard someone moving about in the kitchen. Guessing Holmes had come back already, I went back down.

How do you think I felt, when, instead of Holmes, I'm confronted by a big Amazon type of woman pointing a carving knife at me? And apart from the knife in her hand, she was quite attractive. I guessed her age at late thirties, too young for her clothes, an oatmeal woolen twinset with a matching skirt and pearls. While I was trying to figure out what was happening, instinctively, at the same time, I was wondering if, in different circumstances, I would give her one. That would be a yes. She was tall, about five nine and well built; shoulder-length reddish-brown hair framed her face, and her eyes were a shade of green I'd never seen before. "Don't come any closer."

Her voice was clear and confident; probably cos she was the one holding the knife. "I've killed three men already, so one more won't bother me."

There was no sign of blood on her hands or clothes, so I assumed she wasn't talking about this morning, but some time previous. Weighing up the situation, I decided to apply the same tactics I used on Bobby Fetterman's dog, Kong. Keeping my voice low and steady, I looked her in the eyes and started backing away from her, up the stairs."Good girl.... who's a good girl.... who's a pretty girl.... you are aren't you.... yes you are."

It must have worked because she was frowning, similar to what Kong used to do, like she was confused. Once I felt safe, I dashed up the stairs and locked myself in my bedroom.

It wasn't long before the door handle started moving to and fro, and she was banging on the door. Not entirely confident that she couldn't get in, I opened the window, case I had to go out that way, and shouted, "Gertchoo crazy bastard. If you don't fuck off, I'm going to phone the police."

"Oh no you won't," she said, "there's no telephone in that room. You're going to stay in there till Mr. Holmes returns."

As soon as she said Holmes's name, I realised what must have happened. She obviously knew him, and the layout of the place, cos she knew there was no phone in this room. I guessed she must have come in; maybe the front door was open, seen me, and thought I was a burglar. I tapped on the door, "Are you still there?"

"Yes, I'm still here," she said, "and I still have the knife in my hand. So don't think of trying anything rash."

Standing close to the door, I said, "I think there's been some sort of mix up here. I'm John Watson, a friend of Sherlock's. I've been staying for a couple of days."

"Oh, that's good," she said, the dopey daft pratt. "You won't mind staying a little longer then, will you, until he gets back and decides what to do with you."

"Yeah, bollocks," was the only answer I could think of, and I flopped on the bed.

It might have been half an hour later when I heard Holmes's voice, "Jane, what on earth are you doing, sitting there with that knife?"

"I've caught an intruder for you, Sherlock."

They must have gone back down to the kitchen, cos when I opened the door, from the top of the stairs, I could hear Holmes laughing. Other times I'd heard him sort of gurgling to himself. I'd heard him chuckling, sniggering, but I'd never heard him laugh like this. It was as if he'd just been told the funniest thing he'd ever heard in his life. "Come down," he called out, "come and meet Jane." I went downstairs.

"We've already met," I said, "Although she didn't introduce herself, only pointed a knife at me and said she'd just killed three men." She was laughing now, and she was lovely,

"I'm sorry, John, I must have frightened the life out of you, waving that thing about. But I really did think you were a burglar."

I could see Holmes was really enjoying all this; he had that piss-taking smile on his face. "You must have been terrified, John, seeing Jane with that knife. Are you alright now?"

I said, "No, I wasn't terrified at all. I've seen enough crazy people round Penge. I was more worried about you, in case you wandered in unawares."

"So you locked yourself in a bedroom." He said this with a sneer on his lips and rolling his eyes to the ceiling. I imagine they were trained to do that at his boarding school.

She piped up then, "He said some very nice things to me, didn't you, John. He said I was a good girl, a pretty girl, lovely things like that; until he scampered up the stairs and locked himself in the bedroom. Then he called me a crazy bastard."

That totally amused the pair of 'em, and while they sat at the table looking at each other and giggling like a pair of school kids I remembered I had things to do upstairs, so I left 'em to it.

Jane must have left, cos I heard the front door slam, and Holmes came upstairs to tell me all about her. She was a neighbour, an old war-time friend of his father's, who sometimes came in to tidy up for him; that's why she had a key. It was her on the phone, who'd hung up on me when she thought she'd heard a burglar, the sloppy pratt. I was going to ask about the three men she said she killed, but I wasn't really that interested.

What I was interested in was phoning Kathy to see what was happening in the East End. There was plenty going on, but it was nearer to us than to her. She had a friend, Maggie, who was a good friend of Leicester Lou, and who was giving her the lowdown on Adie. He was in St. Marys Hospital.

Lou had found him in bed when she got home last night. He'd trod on a drawing pin getting into bed, and then his leg had swollen up alarming. Lou had called an ambulance, and they whisked him off to hospital. Overnight, he'd taken a turn for the worse and was now in a coma and might not come out of it.

Lou thought there was something funny about it cos she'd found drawing pins and a box of Christmas decorations in the room. And Adie hated Christmas. He hated it so much that he wouldn't drive up Regent Street if the Christmas lights were on. He would heat up pennies in the oven and throw them out of the window for carol singers to pick up. So what had changed his mind?

Holmes didn't seem at all surprised when I told him the news. "Oh dear," he said, "I hope they don't try to pin this on me." Then he started chuckling and gurgling the way he did. I thought back then, to Harry Greenacre. It was treading on a tack of some sort that had killed him. Suddenly Holmes put down his newspaper. "John," he said, "I know Adie Morris, and I had our differences, but I'd like to think he finally got my point." He then went into a fit of giggling, which, if I'm honest, was a bit scary.

I'd made up my mind now to go back to Kathy's. Apart from needing a change of clothes, I wanted to see her again. If it was going to kick off, I thought, it might as well be in the East End; get it over and done with once and for all. So, putting on a pair of gloves, Holmes went and retrieved one of the pistols from the old tart's garage. With that in my pocket and the clothes that Holmes had bought for me, in a holdall, I walked down to the corner and got a cab to Bethnal Green.

I wouldn't have thought, after the Mayfair experience, that I'd be glad to be back in the East End, but I was. The West End is nice, to go shopping, when you've got a few quid, in Regent Street or Oxford Street; but it ain't really me. Neither is Bethnal Green, come to that, but it's more me than Mayfair is.

Kathy had gone to work, but I had a key to her flat, so I let myself in and changed my clothes. The phone rang and it was Tony, Charlie Dickson's mate, he must have heard about Adie.

"Hello, mate." He said, " I've got a message for you. A certain person said get rid of his phone number and forget you ever had it. You never met, never spoke, he don't know you and you don't know him."

I was happy enough with that cos I'd already been wishing we hadn't got Charlie involved. But if the twins hadn't tried to make out it was Charlie's gang mugging us in the Borough Market he wouldn't have been involved at all. It was their fault.

When I got to the Lion, it was like the old song, 'Hail, hail, the gang's all here'. And the gang was all there, well not all, but most of 'em; all except Tommy. It was weird, I'd only been away a couple of days, but it seemed like ages. The twins were there, and Ron was shaking my hand, in one of his happy moods. "Have you heard the news? Adie died an hour ago."

Reg came and patted me on the shoulder, "He won't be hanging about outside our house anymore."

That was like Adie's obituary; I heard a couple more. Kathy: "Well, he won't be knocking Louise about anymore," and later on from Holmes,

"He's not going to be shooting bullets at me anymore."

Reg had hold of my arm. "Here, come upstairs; we can talk up there."

I grabbed my drink and went upstairs into a room at the front, looking out on the street. It was a nice furnished room that they used sometimes for private conversations. They obviously wanted to know what we'd been up to, but I never mentioned Holmes's place. I told 'em we'd taken rooms in a hotel in Bayswater, not too far from where Adie lived. "So, how did you get him to tread on a tin tack?" Ron asked.

I didn't answer straight away, trying to look serious, I said, "Ron, if we had got him to tread on a tin tack, and if that had been what killed him, that would be murder. Remember I said if. But if that was the case, and I told you, I'd be making you an accessory to murder. And I wouldn't do that. I prefer to think he was putting up his Christmas decorations, spilt the tacks on the floor, and trod on one by accident."

Reg was smiling now, which wasn't all that usual for him, "That's what I think too. Anyway, he's gone. What about the others, Benny and Tojo?"

"I don't think they're going to be a problem for much longer," I said.

I was just quoting Holmes. I had no idea what was happening with Benny and Tojo.

We went down to the bar, and people were buying me drinks like I was the prodigal son just come back, and I'd only been gone two days. Without anyone saying it, I got the impression they thought I'd done away with Adie Morris. And no one respects a killer more than your East End gangster.

It occurred to me that anyone in that pub could have been a police informer, and if the police came to the conclusion that Adie had been bumped off, then I could become what they called a 'person of interest.' And what might be worse, if I wasn't already, I might become a person of interest to Benny and Tojo as well. I moved away from the bar and sat by myself, thinking.

This sequence of events, which wasn't over yet, started when Holmes called Benny Morris, Goldilocks. Now Adie Morris was dead, and there could be more bodies to come, and all cos someone called someone Goldilocks. And we're involved, all cos Holmes's silly mate, who means nothing to me, went and got himself pumped up by a friend of Ronnie Kray.

Kathy had finished her shift and came and sat at the table, "You alright love, you look fed up? What's the matter? Come on, let's go home and have a nice cup of tea."

Like a nice cup of tea is gonna solve anything. Being back with Kathy made me realise how much I'd missed her these last couple of days; her fuck 'em attitude, her smile, and even her Yorkshire accent. Since Adie had gone, she'd got Lou's number from their mutual friend, so I got her to ring up and find out what was new, while I went out and got us some fish and chips.

It was cold and damp out, so I put on an overcoat, which made it easier to carry the pistol. It hadn't occurred to me before how heavy a gun would be, and how it would pull your coat out of shape; I guess that's why they wear shoulder holsters.

What I'd only just found out, is that Kathy and Leicester Lou had been pals before she'd got iked up with Adie Morris. It was only the fact that he kept trying to pull Kathy that caused a bit of friction between them. And what always happens happened, Lou blamed the object of his attention instead of blaming him. As time went by, she got to disliking Adie almost as much as Kathy did, but for some reason, only she knew, she stayed with him.

We'd finished our fish and chips and opened a bottle of wine, and Kathy told me the story that Lou had told her. Most of it, I'd already heard. But what I hadn't heard is that Lou had told Maggie to tell Kathy that the Morrises were out to kill her boyfriend. That would be me. I guessed when Holmes had slapped Benny for getting flash with Kathy, he must have thought that Holmes was her boyfriend. All I had to worry about now was Tommy whispering in their ear, and then I might become an additional target.

Another thing I hadn't heard about was the neighbour in Radnor Mews. She'd seen Adie and Lou go out on that night at the usual time. Then shortly afterwards, what she thought was Adie, but was really Holmes, came back into the mews carrying a shopping bag. He was only in the house for about five minutes, and this time he left the mews by the bottom entrance, which was something he never did. He came back again about ten minutes later in his usual way.

Lou knew something wasn't right. She'd found the Christmas decorations in a bag under the bed, and the tin of drawing pins spilled on the floor on Adie's side. Knowing how Adie felt about Christmas, it didn't add up. But now he was dead. She was on her own, and every cloud has a silver lining. She now had Adie's money, thirty grand in readies.

Worried about the police coming round, she'd left the cash with someone she trusted, one of her regular punters, who happened to be a well-known TV personality. This was what Holmes would call ironic, cos a lot of the money was what this fellow had paid her for her services over the years.

And how about the other two, Benny and Tojo. As soon as Adie died, before he was even cold, they'd phoned her up, saying she worked for them now, and what about his money. Naturally, she told 'em to go and fuck themselves, and she was going to talk to Big Frank and Bernie Silver and get them to sort it.

Kathy had finished telling me all this, and I sat thinking about the thirty grand. That was a nice bit of money to have saved in just a few years. I was wondering how much she had put away somewhere. Then suddenly she said, "I know what you're thinking,".

My heart missed a beat, and my mind was racing. I said, "Do you?"

"You're thinking of helping Louise, aren't you. With the Morrises"

"I was, as it happens." I said, trying to look surprised, "How did you know that?"

She was smiling and nodding her head, the way she'd done before, "I know what you're like, John. You've got a good heart."

That's how much she knew. I was thinking that apart from everyone looking down on you, and losing your own self-respect, was the life of a pimp such a bad one. Half of the Kray's firm were into it at one time or another. Then I remembered, I was better than them.

The phone rang, and it was Holmes. He was just leaving the Carpenters, and could he come round. Ten minutes later, Kathy had left us alone in the front room, and I was telling him all that Lou had said. He'd already heard a lot of it in the Carpenters, but he hadn't heard about the thirty grand. He was impressed, the same way I had been. Then he got onto the Morrises. "I think we can forget about them now, John. My guess, is that now Adie's out of the game, they're a spent force. Cut off the head of a snake, and the body dies."

"That's all very well," I told him, "but we're not dealing with snakes, we're dealing with people, and from what I've heard, Tojo is worse than the other two put together."

He was looking at me and smiling his silly condescending smile, "Alright, John, we'll see. Supposing we talk to the twins, and if they're agreeable, I'll tell the Morrises they can call it quits and no hard feelings."

We didn't know then, that the Morrises weren't agreeable at all. They didn't want to call it quits, and they had lots of hard feelings. But we were soon going to find out.

CHAPTER 16

Heroic Holmes

Holmes turned up the following day driving his taxi cab. He'd arranged for us to meet Ron at Pellicci's to discuss a ceasefire with the Morrises. Kathy had a shift at the Lion, so we dropped her off and drove down to meet Ron. Hague Street was empty, so we parked up and walked around the corner to the café.

Ron arrived just as we were ordering; he'd come from his weekly visit to Mr. Edmunds, who sent his regards. We got talking, and Ron wasn't ecstatic about the thought of letting the Morrises off the hook. But Holmes persuaded him. With a ceasefire, and them off their guard, he could do them in his own time if he still wanted to. Once we were all in agreement about that, Ron said what I expected him to say, "Right, let's go and have a drink."

Walking out of the café, I thought I saw the grey Cortina parked up on the road opposite, but it was behind another car, so I couldn't be certain. Holmes and Ron were already turning the corner when it pulled out and roared straight across the main road, following them into Hague Street. I ran to the corner in time to see Holmes grab Ron and push him into an alley as the car mounted the pavement. While I was trying to pull the gun from my pocket, the grey Cortina was backing up, then trying to follow them into the alley. My gun was caught up in the lining of my pocket, but I heard gunshots, three of 'em, and saw glass flying off the car's windscreen. Then it reversed and raced off up the road with the tyres smoking.

Holmes was picking up cartridge cases from the floor when I reached them.

"You ok?" I asked him.

He was grinning, "Yes, we're fine," then sniffing, "I love the smell of cordite, don't you? I think we'd better get out of here."

Reg was in the Lion when we got there, along with a few of the others. In no time at all, they were gathered round Ron while he told 'em how Hershel had saved his life. As usual, Holmes was acting all modest, but I knew he was loving it. He didn't bother to mention, though, he was saving his own life at the same time.

"As soon as it started up," I heard him say, "I knew it was Tojo's grey Cortina, and without looking round, I knew it was approaching us at speed."

Someone said, "Well, you must have fucking good ears then."

"I'm training my ears," he said, looking round to make sure he had everyone's attention, "to be as acute as those of the mouse-tailed bat."

I know I shouldn't have said anything, but I couldn't resist it. "What for, so you can catch moths and eat 'em."

He'd been about to take a drink, but he put his glass down, "No John," he said, "so that I don't have to rely on anyone behind me to shout a warning when I'm about to be run over."

That was another thing he'd inherited from his great grandfather, fucking sarcasm.

Ron said, "He was like fuckin James Bond. Tell 'em how you shot their windscreen out."

"Well, as soon as I heard that car, I knew it meant trouble, so I pulled Ron into the alley and got in front of him. I fully expected them to come alongside the alley and fire from the back window, in which case I was prepared to take out the shooter and let the driver make off. But they didn't do that. Instead, they tried to drive into the alley, expecting us to run. So I fired a couple of shots into the windscreen, enough to frighten them, and off they went. Quite entertaining, really."

Reg said, "Why didn't you just shoot the driver?"

"If I'd done that, we'd have had a dead man in a car. John would have probably shot the fellow in the back. So we'd have two dead bodies with gunshot wounds in broad daylight just around the corner from Pellicci's. I think it would have got a lot of police attention, don't you."

"He's right." Ron said. "Once we find out where they are, we'll do 'em on their own manor."

Even Reg agreed with that. "Yeah, you're right. Good work, Hershel, now let's have a drink."

And it was party time again.

We didn't stay too long; Holmes had advised me not to drink too much as we might have a long night ahead of us. Driving back to his, he took all the usual precautions, U-turns, sudden lefts, and jumped one set of lights. There's no way in the world anyone could have followed us. Back at Holmes's, it looked as if Jane had been in and had a bit of a clean-up. Sitting in the kitchen, drinking coffee, I asked Holmes, "Are you giving her one?"

"Am I giving who one?" he answered, a bit irritable.

I said, "Jane, the one who tidies up in here, the killer."

I got the starey eyes treatment then. "I don't answer questions like that, John. And I'd like to say I'm surprised that you asked, but I'm not."

"You're not what?" I said, "You're not giving her one, or you're not surprised that I asked if you was?"

I could see by his face that he wasn't amused, and he confirmed it. "You're beginning to get on my nerves now. It might be best if we ended this conversation, and I'd rather you didn't speak about that lady again."

He'd never spoke to me like that before, so serious. Knowing what he was capable of and the fact he'd already answered my question, I thought it best to shut up.

After finishing our coffee, we went upstairs, and he vanished into his dressing room. I'd switched on the radio and was listening to a girl called, The Singing Nun, when he came out dressed all in black and looking a bit sinister. "What do you say we end this tonight, John. Finish it once and for all."

Have you ever done something you shouldn't have, or been in a place where you shouldn't have been, and all of a sudden it hits you, and you think, 'what the fuck am I doing?' That's how I felt just then. I said, "What do you mean, end it? How are we going to do that?"

"Well, there's only one way left now, isn't there."

"You mean top 'em, is that what you're talking about."

"Can you think of another way, John, after what they did today?"

"Yeah," I said, "forget about 'em. Forget about the Krays. Let them sort it out between themselves. Nobody knows where you live, and I'm quite prepared to move."

He sat down next to me on the sofa, shaking his head, "And what about Kathy, John, and your parents? Are they going to have to move, and how many times? Remember what we're dealing with. These are scum; they beat up women. They'd have no qualms about hurting Kathy if they couldn't get to you, or your mother or your nan. Could you live with that, John?"

Thinking about it, I knew he was right. They knew where Kathy lived, and they knew where I lived, and all down to that rat Tommy. "Alright," I said, "what do you want to do?"

"We'll give it a few hours, wait till it's dark, and we'll take a ride out to Romford."

While I was sitting there worrying, Holmes had taken a book for his bookshelf and sat in an armchair reading.

"Ain't you worried," I asked him, "having three deaths on your conscience?"

He put the book down, leaned his head back for a moment, thinking; then he turned to me and said," Mencken had a theory about conscience, John; he said, 'Conscience is that inner voice that warns us that somebody may be looking.' And I go along with that. As far as I'm concerned, if nobody sees me do something, then I never did it. It's as simple as that."

Mencken! He's taking advice from a fucking film character out of The Wizard of Oz, when we're talking about killing people.

A few years ago, I killed three men and a young boy on a moonlit night in Aden; and I never forgot it. We'd set up an ambush on a footpath up in the hills, waiting for insurgents. Long before they came into view, we could hear their footsteps on the gravel. The ground must have been soft as they came closer because we didn't hear their approach, till suddenly, they were in front of us, lit up by the moon and right in the sights of my Bren gun. All at once, I was ice cold, my hands were sweating, and it was only the corporal kicking my leg, saying, "Pull the fucking trigger." that made me do it. I squeezed the trigger and swung the barrel in an arc, watching the four of them being knocked to the ground. A flare had gone up, and some of the squad ran over and pumped shots into one of the bodies that was still moving. I went to look at the people I'd shot, not because I wanted to, but because I knew I'd be talked about if I didn't. One of them, the one that I've never been able to forget, was a boy of about sixteen. He was laying on his back, his chest soaked in blood, and his eyes wide open, staring at the thin clouds that drifted over the moon. My only consolation in this was that they were all armed and mostly with British weapons; old Lee Enfield rifles, a Sten gun, and a couple of hand grenades. So they would have killed us if they could.

My thoughts at the time weren't with them so much as their families, especially the young boy. He had a mother somewhere, sisters, brothers, waiting for him to come home, and now they were never going to see him again.

That's what we were going to do to Benny and Tojo's family, who'd already lost Adie. Those two might be the worst, scummiest slags in the world, but to Mrs. Morris, they were her sons, and brothers to Winston. And because one of her sons had been rude to a barmaid, she was going to lose three of them.

Every now and again, Holmes would say something, but I didn't answer because I wasn't really listening; I was thinking. I was thinking about the same things I'd thought about before; how this all started, before it got out of hand. Holmes had slapped poor dopey Benny and shook him up a bit. No blood, no broken bones, just a bit of humiliation, and that could have been put right. I knew a fellow in a similar situation got mugged off by a bully in a pub. He went straight home, came back with a gun, and shot the geezer in the leg. That's what Benny could have done and kept his respect, but he didn't. He went crying to his brother Adie. Now Adie, if he had any guts, could have come and fronted Holmes, but he didn't; instead, they tried to shoot him from a moving car. And now I've got to go and be a party to a double murder, for what is essentially nonsense.

"Are you ready to go?"

Holmes took me away from my thoughts. I hadn't heard him go downstairs and come back. "We'll take the Jag," he said, "it's warmer."

The car was outside ticking over, and soon we were on our way to Romford. Once we had passed Picadilly Circus and Shaftsbury Avenue, I had no idea where we were, but Holmes seemed to know where he was going.

Christmas carols were playing on the radio. Lovely, the season of goodwill to all men, and we were going out to kill two of them. I got to thinking again, and said to Holmes, "Supposing we just shot 'em in the legs, give 'em a warning. Don't you think that might be enough?"

"It might, John," he said, "or it might not. Do you want to take that chance? A wounded animal can be much more dangerous, you know."

Now he's talking about animals again. There's certain people, not just him, who can't talk about human behaviour without relating it to animals. A leopard can't change its spots. Who said it can't? Who's ever counted them? An elephant never forgets. How the fuck would anyone know that.

We didn't talk much after that, just listened to the radio; until the Beatles sang, 'I wanna hold your hand.' and Holmes switched it off. "How about, I wanna hold your throat." He said that without smiling, like he really meant it.

Once we got to Romford, we swapped seats, and Homes had no trouble directing me to the road and then the house. It was a nice house, semi-detached, with a porch sheltering the front door and a driveway onto the road. And parked at an angle on the drive was Adie's Austin Westminster. "Looks like they've got a visitor," I said, remembering the car was in Lou's name.

Holmes shook his head. "If you mean Louise Rutherford, I don't think so. I don't think anyone would park their own car like that. My guess is they've repossessed it."

We'd passed the house by now, so I drove round the block and stopped near the corner, where we had a view of it. Just as Holmes was about to get out of the car, Benny left the house. He got in the Westminster, backed out, and went off in the opposite direction. I looked at Holmes, "What now?"

"Pick me up on the other side of the road in fifteen minutes."

Then he was out of the car and walking up toward the house. I'd noticed a pub called the Unicorn on the main road, so I drove up there and pulled into the car park. After twelve minutes of looking at people leaving and entering the pub, and watching the traffic go by, I drove slowly back into Tudor Avenue and picked up Holmes.

"Not quite what I was hoping for." he said as he got in the car. "Let's go home."

Just before the A 12, we changed seats, and Holmes drove us into London, telling what he'd seen through the kitchen window. It was nothing much really; apart from Tojo, he assumed it was Tojo, drinking scotch from a bottle while he counted a pile of gold coins.

So, all in all, it was a wasted night.

CHAPTER 17

Murder by suicide

Having heard all about what had gone on this morning and Holmes's heroics, Kathy was confident nothing bad could happen to me while I was with Hershel. No, of course not, nothing bad, apart from a good chance of being hung for murder; but I couldn't tell her that.

One thing that was worrying her, and a couple of her mates, was Leicester Lou. No one had seen or heard from her or been able to get in touch. Of course, there was the possibility that she'd gone back home to Leicester, but surely, she would have let someone know.

At the time, I had too much on my mind to think about Leicester Lou, let alone worry about her. Perhaps she had gone back home and left everything, and that's why the other two had Adie's car. Some of these questions were answered the following day. We'd had breakfast, and Kathy was washing up, when the phone rang. It was Maggie, wanting to speak to Kathy.

After listening for a few seconds, she said, "Oh no, fucking hell." Sitting on the sofa and biting her lip, I could tell it was serious. She looked up at me, "Lou's dead. Murdered."

I went and finished the washing up while she carried on talking to Maggie. When the conversation stopped, I went back into the room, and she was sitting, holding the silent phone, thoughtful. "That's them two evil bastards have done this," she said.

I knew by them she meant Tojo and Benny, and I guess them having Lou's car confirmed it.

She was obviously upset by what she'd heard, which surprised me. She was never a close friend of Lou's, and they'd had their ups and downs in the past, which they'd put behind them; but she was more upset than I expected her to be. It was a funny thing with these brasses. They might not get on, in fact, I've seen 'em fighting in the street, but they would band together to protect one of their own from an outsider, and an outsider generally meant a man. They were like a sisterhood, a bit frightening, really. I'd thought about it, and I guessed it was because they shared an experience that only them that had lived that life would know, and that made them special.

It took a little while for her to compose herself, then she told me what she had just heard. After getting no answer to her calls, Maggie and her boyfriend had gone round to Lou's and found the front door open. While the boyfriend waited outside, Maggie had gone in to find the place turned upside down. Worse was to come. In a bedroom, lying on the bed, was Lou, dead. She'd been badly beaten and finally strangled with a telephone cord. Not wanting to get involved, Maggie had picked up Lou's address book, then her and her boyfriend had shot off, hoping no-one had seen them hanging about in the mews.

Kathy wanted to talk about Lou, so I sat down next to her and did my best to listen. Lou was beautiful. They'd all come down from up north at about the same time—Marylin and Kathy from Yorkshire, Lou from Leicester, and Maggie from Liverpool. In the early days, they'd all worked the streets around Soho. Sometimes they'd venture up to Picadilly and Park Lane, till they found out that pitches were property; and there could be serious consequences for working on another girl's pitch.

Their friendship almost came to an end when Lou got iked up with Adie Morris. He isolated her from her pals and put her to work in Park Lane. Down in Soho, the girls heard stories now and then about the bruises, the occasional black eye; and she wasn't the same old happy Lou anymore. Now she would never have the chance to be happy again.

I was feeling sorry for her myself now. I'd never met her, only seen her once, but I was thinking about the life she'd had. There must have been something that made her leave her home and family, to come down to London and be a brass. And then to wind up with a rat bully like Adolf Morris controlling her life and knocking her about. And then to die in the way she did.

I've never been one for hitting women or strangling them; but if you're going to strangle someone, then strangle 'em. You don't have to beat them up first, especially women. That is unless you're some sort of pervert, or else you really hate them. But what reason did them two fucking Morrises have to hate Lou, who'd only ever been good to 'em. The only reason I could think of was 'cos they couldn't get hold of Adie's thirty grand. And now poor Lou was gone, and it was first come, first served as to who got that money.

I was seeing Tojo and Benny in a different light now. Perhaps they were more dangerous than I'd thought; they were certainly unpredictable. Before I left to phone Holmes, I told Kathy to lock the door after me and not open it for anyone. She went into the bedroom and came out smiling, with a small automatic pistol in her hand. "If they knock on this door, I'll shoot the fucking pair of 'em. So don't ask me not to."

I said, "suppose it's the milkman. Or the postman. Suppose you shoot them by mistake?"

"Then they'll have to get a replacement, won't they." She winked and smiled." Go on and hurry back."

I phoned Holmes from the call box down on the corner, aware of every car and every person that passed. I had no reluctance now about killing Tojo and Benny or the whole fucking family of 'em if it came to it. After speaking to Holmes, I took a cab over to Coventry Street, another one to the Dorchester, then walked round to his place.

He sat grim-faced while I told him the story. "Do you still think we should have given them another chance, John?" he said. "They're vermin."

I don't remember saying give them another chance; that was his idea. My idea was to fuck off and let them all get on with it. I was waiting, and expecting him to phone the Police, but he didn't, didn't even consider it. There was something in his face now that I'd never seen before, and perhaps it was the way he used the word 'VERMIN' that told me he was intent on killing them. "I'm going to end this today John, once and for all. Are you coming?"

As much as I wanted to say, 'No, let's concentrate on Adie's thirty grand,' I nodded. "Course I am, whenever you're ready."

He went into his dressing room, and about five minutes later, a different geezer came out. This one was about the same height as Holmes, but heavier built, and older; about forty-five years old. His face was pale, and he wore a neat military-style moustache. On his head was a peaked cap with a badge, and as a type of uniform, he wore a loose-fitting navy raincoat.

"What do you think?" It wasn't Holmes's voice, but a slight northern accent that I couldn't quite place.

I said, "What the fuck are you dressed like that for?"

"I'm a metropolitan water board inspector with authority to gain access to any habitation using water. It never fails, John."

While he was getting the Jag out of the garage, I phoned Kathy to tell her I might be a while. The voice that answered wasn't hers, "Hello, is that John?"

I said," Who's that?"

227

"I'm June, a friend of Maggie's." she said, "They've gone out looking for you; she's really worried."

I put the phone down. Now I've got all sorts of thoughts going through my head. Supposing Benny and Tojo had got in the flat and swagged her off, or strangled her, but then they wouldn't have left someone to answer the phone, would they? I told Homes about the phone call as I got in the car, and he just said, "Don't worry about it; she'll be alright."

We discussed the plan of action as I drove the car over to Romford, with Holmes giving me directions. It was pretty simple; if they were home, Holmes would persuade them to kill themselves. If they were not home, he, or we, would wait in the house till they arrived and shoot them. It was as simple as that.

"And how are you going to persuade them to kill themselves?"

I felt stupid asking the question, but he just shrugged and grinned. "Like Hitler, John, I sometimes have great powers of persuasion."

His lack of concern about the thought of killing two people was a bit troubling. And it was the second time he'd likened himself to Hitler. What with his strange power over women and dogs, and now his powers of persuasion. Funny geezer.

I pulled over as we got into Tudor Avenue to let Holmes out of the car and watched him as he walked along, with a slight limp, to where Lou's car stood on the drive. After watching him walk up the path, I gave it a couple of minutes and drove up past the house. There was no one on the doorstep, so I guessed he was in OK. Now all he had to do was persuade 'em to kill themselves.

The arrangement was, if he got in the house, I was to give him twenty minutes, then drive back in the opposite direction and pick him up from there or in the first turning on the left. First of all, I drove up to the Unicorn on the main road and had time to get a gin and tonic down my neck for a bit of Dutch courage. Twenty minutes soon went by, and I turned into Tudor Avenue and drove slowly down, looking out for Holmes.

About seventy yards in front of me, on the other side of the road, was a red car, parked outside of the house. As I came closer, I could see it was a Rover P6. "Please God," I'm thinking, "don't let it be Old Bill." Then I heard a popping sound, pop pop, and again, pop pop. Drawing level with the car I watched a tall woman, wearing a headscarf, come running down the path, she dived into the back of the Rover, and it roared off up the road. The front door was wide open, and someone was sitting on the doorstep, leaning against it. That's when I realised the popping noises I'd heard were gunshots.

There was no sign of Holmes on the road, so I turned left at the junction, and there he was, limping along with his cap tucked under his arm. Pulling alongside of him, I opened the door. "Lively," I said, "we've got to get away from here."

229

He climbed into the car, removing his moustache, and putting it in his briefcase, "Why, what's the rush? It's done. It's over. Turn right at the next junction."

I said," What exactly happened back there?"

His eyes were closed, like he was dreaming. "You should have been there, John; it was beautiful. Have you ever listened to Ralph Greaves' arrangement of Greensleeves?"

"No, I haven't."

"What about Olivier's Henry the fifth speech, on the eve of Agincourt?"

I said, "Fuck Henry the fifth, just tell me what happened."

"I'm an artist John," he said, "I've made justifiable homicide into an art form. Or should I call it pesticide."

With that, he started giggling and gurgling the way he sometimes did.

I said, "Yeah, well is there a word for fucking boring people to death? Just tell me what happened."

Then he told me. Tojo had answered the door, reluctant to let him in, but Holmes fannied him, told him it would only take a couple of minutes to test the water. The reason for the test was that a distillery in the area had leaked gin into the local water supply. In the kitchen, Holmes had taken a beaker from his briefcase and half-filled it with water from the tap. He'd tasted it and sniffed it but couldn't be sure that it contained any gin. Tojo wanted to smell it, but Holmes asked him for a cup, took some water from the tap, and passed it to him. Yes, Tojo could smell gin, and taste it. Then Benny tried it, with the same result as Tojo, definitely a slight taste of gin. Holmes assured them both that the matter was being looked into and everything would be back to normal in a few days.

What he didn't tell them was that he'd poisoned the pair of 'em, and they'd both be dead in half an hour. So, in a way, he had persuaded them to kill themselves. Except someone else might have killed them, and I had to tell him. "I don't want to piss in your cornflakes," I said, "but I don't think you killed 'em."

"What?"

The look on his face was a combination of shock, horror, and distress, and I had to feel a bit sorry for him. Then he smiled, "Oh they might not be dead right now," he looked at his watch, "but ten minutes tops, they'll be saying hello to Adie in hell."

"No," I said, "what I mean is, someone's come along and shot 'em both. A tart in a red car. I drove past as she came out of the house."

Now he's distraught again. He didn't often swear, not like the rest of us, but he did then.

"The fucking bastard. I put a lot of thought and effort into this, John. This would have been almost fucking perfect."

I knew two things about him then; one was he was a bit nutty, and two was, I was never going to get on the wrong side of him. On the way back, we stopped at a block of flats, and he got rid of his waterboard outfit and his bottle of poison gin in a communal waste bin. We didn't talk much after that; I guessed he wanted to be left alone.

CHAPTER 18

In the clear

Kathy wasn't home when I got back, and the flat seemed empty without her in it. There was a couple of pork chops and some mushrooms in the fridge, so I cooked them, buttered some bread, made a cup of tea, and switched on the radio. It soon came on the news:

"Police were called to an address in Gidea Park, Romford, this afternoon, where two men were found with gunshot wounds. Both were pronounced dead at the scene. There is now a murder investigation, and detectives are anxious to trace the female driver of a red Citroen motor car that was seen in the area. Anyone with information should contact the Police at Romford or telephone Whitehall one two one two."

Then there was some music, 'Dominique,' by The Singing Nun. It was hard to turn on the radio without hearing her, night and day. That's how crazy it was in those days; a Belgian nun singing in French was number one in the charts, in front of the Beatles.

The song was just ending when Kathy came in, wearing the same clothes she had on when she shot Benny Morris, except she'd taken off the headscarf. "Thank God you're alright,"she said, " I've been worried sick all day. When you went out and didn't come back, I thought something might have happened to you." She seemed a bit nervous, picking things up and putting them down and not looking at me when she spoke like she usually did. She went on, "I phoned everywhere, and

233

no-one had seen or heard from you. In the end, I got Maggie to come round, and we drove about, looking for you."

I gave her a little kiss on the cheek, "I didn't know Maggie had a car."

"No, it's not hers; it's her mate's. She borrowed it for the day."

I said, "What, was that before you went and shot Benny Morris and Tojo, or after."

Just for a second, she looked shocked, then she smiled. And that smile was the one when you're done bang to rights over a mistake you've made; you smile like that sometimes.

"Why do you say that, John?"

I said, "Cos I fucking saw you running out of the house. I heard the shots. And now Old Bill's looking for you, and if they find you, you can get topped. You know that don't you? They hung Ruth Ellis for shooting one geezer. You've done two."

She sat on the sofa, "Yeah, well, they'll have to catch me first, won't they."

I was seeing a side of her now that I hadn't seen before, and I didn't like it. I said, "You was gonna lie to me, wasn't you? All that nonsense about driving round with Maggie. You must think I'm as thick as these fucking morons round here."

"Didn't you lie to me?" she said, "When you killed Adie Morris, and said you was out for a meal with Hershel."

Typical fucking woman, when you accuse 'em of something, they bring up something you've done or supposed to have done.

"No-one killed Adie Morris," I said, "He had an accident. He trod on a drawing pin, and it turned septic. Anyway, who said I killed him?"

"Everyone's talking about it, in the Carpenters, in Madge's."

"Well tell them," I said, "to keep their fucking mouths shut, or the same thing might happen to them. Loada fucking mugs."

That was your so-called gangsters, telling a barmaid in a pub that her boyfriend had murdered someone. I phoned Mick Parker and asked him if he would sort out my car and bring it down the Lion. I wasn't talking loud, but she must have heard me, cos she said, "You gonna wait for me. I've had nothing to eat all day." I didn't even bother to answer, just put on my coat and walked out of the door.

It was pretty busy in the Lion. Mick was already there and gave me my car key. "Did she manage to get in touch with you?" he said, "She was phoning everyone, said you went out to make a phone call and didn't come back. She was really worried about you."

Someone must have twigged the identity of the two geezers shot in Romford from the news report, and that was the topic of conversation. But who was the lady in the red Citroen? Somebody said, "Could have been a feller in drag, you know. It's been done before."

"What about the bus conductor?" someone else said, "What was that all about?"

235

There'd been an update in the news since I heard it. A witness had come forward to say a bus conductor with a limp was seen entering and leaving the house shortly before the shots were heard. Now the Police are looking for a limping bus conductor and a lady in a red Citroen, so good luck with that.

Madge was behind the bar, and she called me over. "Did Kathy manage to get in touch with you? She was really worried about you."

"Yeah," I said, "it's sorted,"

It wasn't long before the twins arrived, looking very dapper and pleased with themselves. Reg gave me a nod, and we went upstairs to the conference room. Ron spoke first. "What was that all about, bus conductor and a tart in a red car. What happened?"

Laughing, I said, "Looks like someone shot 'em, probably one of their brasses, got brassed off."

That made Ron laugh, "Yeah, that's a good un. A brass got brassed off, so she shot them."

Reg wasn't amused; his eyebrows went up a notch. "Someone said it could have been a geezer in drag."

"Could have been." I said, "It definitely wasn't me, though."

"You won't be needing that shooter anymore, now, will you."

I took the gun from my pocket and put it on a side table. "No, thank God I never needed it, but thanks anyway."

I watched as Reg felt the weight of the gun, then dropped the magazine out and began counting the bullets. Now, that is as good as him saying, "I don't trust you." And saying it to your face. That seemed to satisfy them for now, and we went back downstairs.

I found Mick and a couple of the others talking about last week's dog racing at Walthamstow. Suddenly the noise in the bar dropped, not silent, but quiet like when something's happened. Turning round, I saw Kathy had just come through the door, and looking like a movie star. She was wearing a sheepskin coat with a check skirt and a beige jumper, and her hair looked different. I was already regretting being so rude earlier. That's one thing about the firm; they were generally very polite toward women, even when their eyes told a different story. They were used to seeing Kathy behind the bar in here, or the Carpenters, or the Regency; they hadn't seen her like this before. Neither had I. She turned down a couple of offers of drinks and went to the bar, putting some cash on the counter.

"Give everyone a drink Madge." then pointing at me, "Give fucking grumpy over there a large one, cheer him up."

That got a few laughs, and someone near to me said, "You've got a blinder there, son."

He didn't need to tell me that; I knew it. After paying for the round, she brought me a large gin and tonic," Here you are, miserable bastard."

I pulled her near, kissed her discreetly, and whispered in her ear, "Sorry."

"So you fucking should be," she said, "I did that for you, you know."

That wasn't the place to talk about it, so we joined Mick and the twins at the bar, and I tried to forget about the day's events. But as much as I wanted to forget about them, I couldn't. It seemed that Kathy could, and I found that a bit disturbing. A few hours ago, she'd shot and killed two people, don't matter they were a pair of slags. And now she's laughing and joking like nothing's happened. She must have said something funny, cos even the twins were laughing. And when they were happy, everyone was happy.

We left before closing time, and it was nice to be in my own car again. Driving back through the dark streets, you could see that the East End was gearing up for Christmas. Where the curtains weren't drawn in the houses, you could see the paper decorations on the walls and ceilings, and the occasional Christmas tree lit up. Wreaths of holly and ivy hung on some of the doors. You could feel Christmas in the air, and today there's two more bodies in the morgue.

Before we went to bed, I got Kathy to tell me the whole story, or as much of it as she was prepared to. When I left this morning, she'd thought I was coming straight back, although I hadn't said I would. Anyway, when I didn't, she rang round everyone we knew. Obviously, no one had seen me cos I was with Holmes. Somehow, she got it in her head I'd been swagged off or done in by the Morrises, so she phoned Maggie and told her what had happened. Maggie wanted to do the Morrises for what they'd done to Lou. Now Kathy did too. All they needed was to find out where they were, and Maggie knew the answer to that as well.

June, one of their girls, whose house they'd taken over, was staying with a mate of Maggie's till she could get her house back. So Maggie borrowed a car from another mate who was out of the country, got hold of June, and brought her to Kathy's. And that's when and where they made plans to do away with Tojo and Benny. June had to be out of the way cos it was her house they were in, so after they left, she got a cab to Euston station and was on her way to Glasgow when the Morrises got it.

Maggie knew the address and how to get there cos she'd visited in happier times before June got mixed up with Benny Morris. They must have arrived at the house at about the same time I was leaving the Unicorn. Maggie waited in the car while Kathy went and knocked on the door. Benny answered, looking like he was drunk or drugged.

"Well, look who's here,"

They were his very last words before she shot him twice in the chest. As he was sliding down against the door, she went into the house and found Tojo asleep, sitting at the kitchen table, so she shot him twice in the back of his head. She hadn't noticed me coming down the road as she ran from the house and jumped in the car.

On the way back, she'd dismantled the gun, took out the magazine, and threw the pieces in different parts of the canal. I asked her, "How'd you know how to take a gun to bits?"

"Someone taught me." she said, "Taught me how to shoot it, clean it. He knew all about guns."

I didn't want to hear any more about him, but it made me realise there was still a lot I didn't know about her. But now, as long as everyone kept shtum, and old Bill kept looking for a red Citroen and a bus conductor, it looked like they'd got away with it.

CHAPTER 19

Knocked again

The telephone ringing woke us up the next morning. It was Holmes, and could he come round. We'd had breakfast and cleared up by the time he arrived. Kathy was just about to leave, to go round the shops, when he stopped her, lifting his nose in the air and sniffing.

"You alright, Hershel," she said, "you sound like you've got a cold."

He sniffed again, louder, "Cordite."

"What's cordite?"

Looking first at me, then at her, he smiled his tight, superior smile. "Cordite, Kathy." then sniffing again, "I suspect if I were to examine the sleeve on your right arm, I might find minute traces of gunshot residue. I suspect further that you are the lady in the red car that the police are so anxious to speak to."

Kathy laughed, sniffing her sleeve, "What's cordite? I can't smell anything."

"I'm not surprised. But my sense of smell has been tested and found to be only slightly less intense than that of a golden Labrador retriever."

Kathy was looking at me, then started her fucking head nodding again, like she knew something. "You told him it was me, didn't you?"

Before I could deny it, I've now got Holmes accusing me. "So you knew it was her all the time."

It was getting awkward now, so I suggested we all sit down, have a cup of coffee, and I told Holmes the story as far as I knew it, as much as Kathy had told me.

He'd got over the disappointment of having his perfect murder ruined, and now he was full of admiration for Kathy, and I didn't like the way he kept complimenting her.

"That took a lot of guts to do that, Kathy. You're a pretty remarkable girl."

She was smiling at him, "D'you think so?"

I happen to know a bit about women, not everything, but enough to know they like flattery and attention. And knowing that Holmes was besotted with the crazy killer bitch neighbour of his, I guessed he might have a thing for homicidal women. There was one way I knew that would get rid of him politely, so I said, "We're going Christmas shopping later, d'you want to come."

The look on his face wasn't panic, more concern. He looked round at the doorway he'd just entered, making sure he had an escape route. "No, no, I won't. I'd love to, but I have some letters to write and a lot of business to catch up on. Next year perhaps."

Then he was up and out the door as quick as he could. I should have gone with him cos I didn't enjoy Christmas shopping, but I'd committed myself. I hated having to lie to Kathy, but I would have hated Christmas shopping a lot more, so instead of a whole lie, I told a half-truth.

A pal in South London owed me some money, and if I didn't get it now, there was a good chance he'd knock it all out. So what I'd do, is shoot over there, pick up the money, and be back in a couple of hours, in plenty of time for shopping. She was happy with that, so off I went.

I hadn't noticed last night, but I had a full tank of petrol, and it looked like somebody had cleaned the car, inside and out. There's no doubt about it, that Mick was a different class to all the rest of 'em.

Even Pat Boone singing 'White Christmas' couldn't depress me as I crossed over Tower Bridge and into the sunny streets of South London. The Singing Nun came on next and did her best to depress me, but I turned the tuner till I found a news station. While the nun had been piping 'Dominique,' I'd missed half the news. What I did manage to hear was that in the case of the double shooting at Romford, it appears that the two men had taken poison, and may have been already dead before they were shot. That was going to make for an interesting trial, if anyone did get nicked for it.

It was nice to be back in familiar surroundings and breathe fresh air. Turning right, off the Old Kent Road, by the Thomas a Beckett, I drove down Albany Road, past some proper trees, then cut off to Peckham and through to Lewisham.

The market stalls were busy with people stocking up with their fruit and veg, nuts, and Christmas trees. Some of the old market traders were still there, Joby Vickers, Mickey Paye, Tommy Everson, and something I'd never seen before down there, an Indian geezer, selling fabrics.

My pal was waiting for me in the snooker hall and paid me the bit of dough he owed me. Things hadn't changed in there, still the same smell of cigarette smoke and fried onions. The only difference was there were none of the old faces. I guessed they were all out trying to get hold of their Christmas money. Hoping my disappointment would show, I phoned Kathy with the sad news that things hadn't gone to plan, and I wouldn't be able to get back in time for Christmas shopping.

"That's alright," she said, "don't worry about it. I didn't want to say it,' case it upset you, but I hate going shopping with a man."

Typical woman. Make you tell a lie when you didn't need to. She could have told me that in the beginning. I took the opportunity to pop round and see my mum and my nan.; the old man was round the Palmerstone. I got the usual off of them two: 'You've lost weight, why don't you find yourself a nice girlfriend?'

'Yeah, I've already got one thanks, nice girl, ex-prostitute, just shot two geezers in Romford yesterday, and what's more, she did it for me.'

My cleaning lady had done her typical good job in the flat, so I got her to come round and gave her a shopping list of presents I wanted her to get for me. She was proper true blue, one of the old-fashioned mums, six kids, and a scallywag husband. One of them women who'd never asked for much and consequently never got much, so it made me feel

244

better to give her a few quid extra now and then. Anyway, I gave her the money to get what I wanted and a nice few quid for herself, and that was my Christmas shopping done. Well, that's what I thought at the time.

Kathy was wrapping presents when I got back, hundreds of 'em; presents for Madge in the Lion, Mr. and Mrs. Kray, the Barry brothers, half of Bethnal Green. Fortunately, there was loads of hooky, long firm stuff being sold cheap in time for Christmas. Mick had told me he could get hold of anything you want: radios, stockings, perfume, booze, cameras, blankets; anything you want.

The problem was, even this type of shopping was not my game. So the next day, while me and Holmes went to see the twins, I gave her a nice few quid and told her to get in touch with Mick and get presents for Mr. and Mrs. Kray, Madge, and anyone else she could think of, from me. Sorted.

Mick was just leaving when we got to the twins. Ron was up already and dressed like a fashion model when he opened the door to us. Holmes had produced a bag from under his coat which I hadn't noticed, showing it to Ron, "Just a little something for mum and dad."

We went through to the kitchen, where mum and dad were in their usual places, doing what they normally did; her busy at the ironing board and him in his chair, looking at the racing fixtures. Opening the bag, Holmes brought out three expensively wrapped packages and dished them out like he was one of the three wise men bearing gifts, "This is for you, Mr. Kray, and this is for you, and here's a little something for Maureen for making you look so lovely."

By the look on his face, I could tell that old Charles David thought the same as I did; 'what a smarmy bastard'. But Mrs. Kray loved it. Touching her hair and giggling, "Leave off Hershel, you shouldn't talk like that; you'll make him jealous."

That made Ron laugh, and even Mr. Kray was almost amused and laughed out of politeness, "heh heh,"

Reg was waiting for us in the front room, and we hadn't sat down before he was asking, "So, what's been happening?"

"Oh, nothing much, Reg," Holmes smiled, "Christmas shopping. Oh, and clearing up that business of the people parking opposite your house."

"You mean the Morrises, yeah, funny business that. One of them trod on a nail, and the other two poisoned themselves. Then a mystery woman shot 'em both. I dunno what to make of it."

Holmes got a bit serious now, "There was a reward mentioned if I remember. Your friends in the West End?"

Reg looked a bit uncomfortable, "Well, that's the problem. They won't pay up, they're saying Adie's death was accidental, and the other two had already committed suicide before they were shot by the woman in a red car."

Ron spoke up then," It would have been different if you or John had just gone and shot the three of 'em but the way it turned out, the word they used is 'ambiguous'. But it don't seem right, does it".

I could see Holmes was trying to control his temper. "No, it doesn't seem right, Ron. Perhaps if I paid them a visit, I might persuade them to see things differently."

The twins exchanged glances," No, you can't do that. Sorry but that's out of the question."

"Alright," said Holmes, "I can see you're in an awkward position, but if you could give them a message. If you would tell them that I said they are penny-pinching gutless scum, and if they object to being called that, come and see me. We'll be going now."

With that, he gave me a nod, and Ron showed us out. The look on Reg's face as I walked past him wasn't pleasant. Eyebrows that were usually going upward were now drawn down in a scowl. It wasn't nice to know that Holmes had not only give the twins the hump, but now their West End friends as well. And I knew they wouldn't say, 'Oh, Hershel said it, leave his mate out of it.' No, they'd want to do the pair of us, and all this cos of his silly mate Adrian.

Mick was in the Lion with a few of the regulars when we got there. Kathy had just finished her last shift before Christmas and was almost ready to leave. Taking us over to a quiet table, Mick asked, "D'you get your bit of dough alright?"

I said, "What bit of dough would that be?"

247

"For getting rid of Adie Morris,"

"No," I said, "it seems their friends in the West End wouldn't pay up."

He smiled, "Is that what they told you?"

That smile and the look on his face told us, me anyway, what we already suspected; they'd had the money and kept it.

"They've had the money, ain't they?"

Mick shook his head, "Listen; I'm not getting involved. You had the deal with them, not me."

"Fair enough," said Holmes, "but can you tell us who are their friends in the West End, and where can we find them."

"I told you, I'm not getting involved, but if I was, I'd say their friends are the CID at West End Central police station, and Big Frank and Bernie Silver.

Holmes was surprised, I could tell, and so was I. "Are you saying that the police paid to have those three killed?"

"I ain't saying anything," Mick said, "I've probably said too much already, so you work it out, and keep my name out of it,"

Kathy had finished her shift and dished out all her presents. Now she was loaded up with the stuff I'd asked Mick to get, plus presents from Madge and some of the punters; luckily, it all fitted into the boot of Homes' Jag. Back at hers, we sat down to talk, and Holmes began, "Why would the police pay to have them killed? Why not just arrest them?"

I didn't have an answer, so I called Kathy into the room. "Kath, can you think of why old bill would pay to have the Morrises done in?"

She laughed, "Well, apart from the fact they were horrible bastards, I would say to shut 'em up, keep 'em quiet."

"And why would they need to shut them up?" Holmes asked.

"Well, the Morrises have been paying top coppers in the West End for years. Paying, so their girls on the street don't get nicked. But just recently, perhaps it was a new copper on the beat, three of their girls got arrested and took to court. After that, Adie said they weren't gonna pay for a service they weren't getting, so old bill could go and fuck theirselves."

`Holmes was paying attention now, "And how do you happen to know all this?"

"I know lots of things, Hershel." she winked at him, "You'd be surprised at the things I know, but that's not all of it. There was a story going round that the Morrises were going to take over Soho. Can you imagine if they did that, all those clubs, bookshops, brothels, all paying money to them instead of the police. Then they'd have to rely on their wages and pensions. No, they couldn't nick 'em and risk it all getting in the papers, so they did what they've done before, and had 'em killed. Them coppers when they get going make the twins look like boy scouts."

249

CHAPTER 20
Christmas 1963

Homes was looking serious. "So, they've done it again, haven't they." Kathy must have known he was talking about the twins, and not wanting to hear it, she went out of the room and shut the door.

"Right,' I said, 'forget about them, forget about Old Bill, let 'em keep their poxy grand. Let's go and find the geezer who's got Lou's thirty grand and get that."

"No John," he said, with a silly little smile on his face, "I'm not going to forget them. You obviously don't know me very well if you think I'd do that."

I wanted to say, "I know you're fucking nutty, ain't that enough," but I didn't.

" Alright," he went on, "we'll see if we can get Lou's money. But as far as the twins are concerned, they still owe us a thousand pounds besides Adrian's money, and they're just compounding the interest."

I knew it wouldn't have done me any good to argue with him, so we left it at that, and he went home.

As soon as he left, I dug out Lou's address book she'd got from Maggie, and I was looking through it when Kathy came back into the room. There were a few names I knew from the old days but no TV personality that I recognised. There was nothing for it; I'd have to cut

Kathy in. So I said, very casually, "that TV geezer Kath, what was his name?"

"What one's that?" she said, smiling. She was beautiful when she smiled.

"The one who's got Lou's money, Hershel reckons we should go and get it off him."

"Oh him, he ain't got it anymore, love."

I suddenly went cold. I'd just lost fifteen grand, less a bit for Kathy. The easiest fifteen grand I was ever going to get, and now she's telling me he ain't got it anymore. My head was spinning. So who's got it? Please tell me he ain't given it to Old Bill, or worse still, the Morrises.

"Wh..wh..what do you mean he ain't got it anymore?" The shock of it had made me stutter.

"What I said, he hasn't got it anymore; someone else has." She was smiling like this was amusing to her.

"Who," I said, "who's got it?"

She put her arm round my shoulder and kissed me on the cheek.

"Well, Maggie's got half of it, and my accountant's got the other half."

For a minute, I couldn't talk. Maggie's got my fifteen grand, and her accountant's got Holmes's. What the fuck is going on!

"Your accountant, what do you need an accountant for?"

"Well, he's more of a friend really, an old client of mine, but he is an accountant. He invests my money for me."

"What money?" I said,"' You work in a fucking pub."

"Don't swear, John," she said, "I don't like it very much. I do other things, you know, not the old game. I buy and sell things, and I broker things. Mickey knows, and the twins know."

"So, how does this old client of yours invest your money?"

"Property John, bricks and mortar. It will be something for us when we're older."

When we're older. I don't remember ever telling her anything to make her think we'd be together when we're older. I told her I loved her, I know, but you tell that to all of 'em cos that's what they like to hear. You don't expect 'em to take it seriously, though.

Once she'd said that, I knew it would make the conversation about Christmas awkward, and I was right. She started it, "What are we going to do about Christmas then? Do you want to have it round here or at yours, or Madge said we could go round there if you want."

"Well," I said," I always go round my mothers' for Christmas. I thought you'd be going up north to be with your family."

"No." she whispered, smiling, and the dimples showing in her cheeks, " You're my family now, John. It's alright. We'll go round your mothers if that what you want."

That's not what I wanted at all, but there was no way out of it without upsetting her, so I said, "Yeah, that's great," and tried to look pleased.

The following day Kathy remembered she still had a few more presents to get. And I remembered I hadn't got anything for her. She was at the door when I called her back, "Listen," I said," I didn't know what to get you, so take this and get whatever you want; if that's not enough, let me know before the shops shut." And I gave her a lump of money, about four hundred pounds, which was a lot of money in those days. She looked at it and smiled, "Can I get whatever I want?'

"Yeah, course you can."

"Well, I won't need all this," and she gave me half of it back. "I'll see you later," and she was gone.

She hadn't been gone long before there was a knock at the door; my first thought was the Morrisses, then I realized, they wouldn't be knocking on any doors. It was the twins. They came in, Ron looking in the kitchen and seeing it empty, "Can we talk?"

I switched off the radio. "Yeah," I said, Kathy's out, come in here."

They sat opposite me in the front room, and Reg spoke first, "I think your mate was a bit upset about that money."

"Well, he was a bit disappointed. We put a lot of work into that."

"Yeah, we realise that," Ron said, "that's why we've pulled up two hundred pounds of our own money, so there won't be any bad feeling."

He put two brown envelopes on the coffee table.

Smiling at them, and thinking, 'You greedy pair of bastards,' I said, "No, there ain't no question of bad feeling, we know it's not your fault."

"Well that's good," they both said it at the same time as they got up. "We'll be in the Carpenters later if you fancy a drink."

As soon as they were gone, I picked up the two envelopes they left on the table, weighing them in my hands, they seemed about the same, so I put them in a drawer and switched on the radio. There wasn't even a mention of the double murder in Romford. It was old news now, the number of shoppers in Oxford Street was topical.

Holmes rang, and I told him about the twins' visit and their generous donation. We agreed to meet later at the Carpenters, and that was a mistake. We went in my car, and the nearest parking place we could find was about half a mile from the pub.

Apart from the familiar faces of the firm, it looked like the Kray Twins Fan Club had turned out. There was hundreds of 'em. As packed as it was, Holmes still had a bit of clout as the champ, and they cleared a path for us to get to the bar. After thanking the twins for the money, Holmes called one of the barmaids over and casually counted out a hundred pounds. "Give everyone a drink. If there's anything left when you shut, share it out with the others."

That was his polite way of saying 'fuck you' to the twins.

And you have to remember in those days you could get ten pints of beer for a pound. Straightaway, she rang the bell, which normally called time. "Hershel the Champ has just stuck a oner in the jar for you all to have a drink on him. So what do you say."

Well, Holmesy got cheered, good lucked, God-blessed, and slapped on the back till he couldn't stand it anymore. So we took our drinks and went and stood in a corner out of the way.

"What are you gonna do for Christmas?" I asked him.

"Nothing much; I'll be going up to Norwood for dinner, then back to mine. What about you?"

"Well," I said, "Kathy's invited herself round me mother's for dinner, so I might stay in Penge for a couple of days."

"Oh, that will be nice for her, won't it, meeting the in-laws."

I didn't answer cos I knew without looking he was trying to wind me up. It was like a madhouse in there, so we left and went round the Lion; and that was just as bad. All the Christmas drinkers were out. I know it's the season of goodwill and brotherly love, but I hate 'em. They come out at Christmas time and New Year's Eve, and they want to shake your hand, slap you on the back, kiss you, and some of the women are just as bad. It just wasn't comfortable in there, so we had one drink and left.

Kathy wasn't home when I got back to hers. But she came in soon after, loaded out with more shopping bags, West End ones, Selfridges, Burberry, Liberty. I guessed that's what she'd bought for herself with the money I gave her, but I was wrong. Now we'd agreed to have Christmas dinner round my mothers' I couldn't wait to get out of the East End.

While Kathy was clearing the fridge, taking what we wanted, and chucking the rest, I put all her bags into the boot of my car. She'd already packed a suitcase with her clothes, so in less than an hour, we were on our way.

There was a bit of traffic on the roads, last-minute shoppers hurrying to get home. Once we were over the river, twenty minutes, and I was pulling up at my flat.

There were presents on my kitchen table, the ones I'd asked my cleaning lady to get, and she'd bought wrapping paper. On the worktop, she'd put my mail and a few Christmas cards, which reminded me that I hadn't sent any. Kathy said if I told her who the presents were for, she would wrap and label them, while I went to get us a takeaway from the Chinese restaurant in the High Street.

Being back in my own flat, it seemed like I'd been gone for ages. Now I wanted to get round some of the pubs and hear the local gossip. Kathy didn't fancy it, so I left her to her parcel wrappings and went up the Robin Hood.

It was only when I got inside, I thought, "what the fuck am I doing." It wasn't any better than the East End, jam-packed with the once-a-year Christmas revelers. I managed to find Harry in the crowd, and he felt the same as I did, "Fuck this," he said, "I'm going home."

I didn't go in any other pubs that night. One look through the doors was enough. There were parties going on in some of the houses I passed, one of them was a proper old-fashioned knees up. The front door was wide open, people standing outside, and inside, someone who never learned to play the piano properly, pounding 'Roll out the Barrel' on the keys. I stood and listened for a while 'cos it was nice to hear and see people enjoying themselves. Someone at the door shouted, "Are you coming in, or are you gonna stand there all night."

I said," No but thanks anyway."

Someone else said, "Well fuck off then." And that made them all laugh. It was nice to be back.

When I got home, there was a mountain of presents piled up in the middle of my front room. There were paper decorations around the walls and hanging from the ceiling. "Do you like it?" she said.

I did like it, but suppose I didn't. With her so happy and excited, I wouldn't say no, would I? But I did like it, and I liked her for doing it. "It's lovely," I said, "and so are you. You're beautiful."

Well, you would have thought I'd given her the crown jewels. I don't think I ever saw her as happy again as she was at that moment, Christmas Eve 1963.

She woke me up on Christmas morning with breakfast in bed, Kennedy's pork sausages, bacon, eggs, mushrooms, and coffee on a tray. And she looked stunning. The bedsheets were too clean to risk eating over them, so I took the tray to the kitchen, and we had breakfast there. Once I'd had a bath, shaved, and got dressed in my Christmas finery, we got down to presents.

"I hope you like it," she said, handing me a parcel.

I ripped the paper off, and it was a presentation box of Tabac aftershave, talcum powder, and a shaving soap bowl. And I'd given her two hundred quid. "Yeah, it's lovely, just what I wanted, thanks. What did you get for yourself?"

"Oh, I got this. Do you like it?"

And she's waving her hand in front of me, and on her finger is a three stone diamond ring. The colors flashing from the stones told me it was kosher, and not one of Mick's jargoons.

"Mick got it, with the money you gave me, and it's real. D'you like it?"

"Yeah, it's lovely. Do you like it?"

Now she's got her arms round my neck, kissing me like I was irresistible. "I love it, and I love you. But, oh, I forgot, I got you something else." It was a little package, and when I opened one end, a box slid out. A cardboard box with Omega written on it. Inside that, was a red leather box with the Omega logo on it, and inside that, was an 18-carat gold Omega Seamaster De Ville watch. She was looking at me. "Do you like it? I can take it back if you want; I've got a receipt."

"Course I like it. I love it. It's the best thing anyone's ever bought me. And you're the best thing that's ever happened to me."

Perhaps because it was Christmas that I said that, or perhaps I really meant it. I probably did. Anyway, she believed it, and it made her happy. And that's what Christmas is all about, making people happy.

There was still a load of presents on the floor. "What about these," I asked her.

"They're for your family. I got a couple of bits from both of us. You don't mind, do you."

"No, of course I don't mind, but you shouldn't have bothered."

After we cleared up the breakfast things and chucked all the presents on the back seat of the car, we drove round to my old house. It was only around the corner, just off Maple Rd. I'd already told my mum that Kathy was coming, so it wouldn't be a surprise. What was a surprise was when she opened the door. "Hello John, hello love, guess who's here."

And through a gap in the door, in the front room sitting down, was the crazy killer bitch, Holmes's neighbour. I grabbed my mum by the arm, "What's she doing here?"

Pulling her arm away, she opened the door, and who do you think was sitting there drinking sherry, Holmesy. "Sherlock and his friend came to wish us Merry Christmas."

With that, he's sprung up out of the chair and shaking my hand. "Happy Christmas, John." Then he's claimed hold of Kathy and he's slobbering all over her, and his eyes darting up to the ceiling, looking for mistletoe. I'd only seen him yesterday, and he's acting like we've been apart for years.

Then, not to be outdone, the killer bitch has jumped up and was rubbing her face on mine both sides, like the French do, and making a

260

grunting noise." Mwa mwa, Happy Christmas, John. This must be Kathy; Sherlock's told me so much about you."

Then she's done the same to her. I'd only just noticed the old nan sitting in the corner, with a Sherry bottle next to her, trying not to laugh. Me and her were on the same wavelength.

"We were just about to leave," Holmes said, "we're going up to Norwood."

Then he's done a bit more kissing, my mum, me nan, slobbered on Kathy again and they were off.

Once they were gone, I had a chance to introduce Kathy to my mum and nan. Surprising to me, they got along like a house on fire, with no awkward questions and nothing to embarrass me. Not till they started opening the presents. My dad had come back down from the bedroom he'd retreated to when Holmes and his girlfriend arrived. His reason for going, he said, was cos he hadn't shaved, and he still hadn't when he came down.

He should have felt as guilty as I did cos Holmesy had bought him a solid silver cigarette box, and I'd bought him a shaving brush and a cigar. I'd bought my mum and nan the same thing, a bottle of Tweed perfume and some talcum powder. Holmes bought my mum a scarf from Burberry and slippers from Liberty for my nan. That was typical of him. He couldn't miss a chance to mug you off, even if he wasn't there to see it.

Luckily Kathy bailed me out with the presents she'd bought from both of us; a silver Dunhill lighter and a box of King Edward cigars for my dad, stockings and a bottle of Diorling perfume for my mum, and a cashmere cardigan for the old nan, plus some other stuff. Once that was all out of the way, the old man said, "D'you fancy a light ale in the Palmerston?"

And that's what we did. Kathy was happy to stay behind and help my mum in the kitchen, and my nan was happy to sit and watch the TV, drinking sherry. So everyone was happy.

We got back from the pub just as they were about to dish up the dinner, and it was lovely, the turkey was cooked just right, the stuffing, the potatoes, the gravy, everything was perfect. Afterwards, Kathy made herself more popular when her and my nan offered to wash up so my mum could sit down and put her feet up. All in all, it was a lovely Christmas day; and what made it better for me was the impression Kathy had made on my family.

Would it have been different, I wondered; if they knew she was an ex-brass from up north who'd shot a couple of people not so long ago. I think it might have been.

As lovely as the day had been, I was pleased to get away and back to my flat. My mum had packed a bag with cold turkey, ham, mince pies, and sausage rolls in case we starved to death before the shops opened the next day.

We stayed at mine till New Year's Eve, when Madge was desperate for Kathy to work that night in the Lion. I could see that Kathy was missing the East End; whether it was working in the pub, or just the East End itself, I don't know. Whatever it was, we went back to hers, stopping on the way to top up her fridge.

That night I took her down to the Lion to start her shift. A few of the regular faces were in there, but no one I particularly wanted to talk to, so I had a couple of beers and went back to hers. She phoned me from the pub at midnight to wish me a happy new year. In the background I could hear the drunken cockney voices bellowing out Auld Langs Syne as if it meant anything to 'em, and I thought how lucky I was not to be there. The following day, New Year's Day, I realised I missed South London as much as she'd missed the East End, and I went back home.

CHAPTER 21

Enugu

It was good to be back and doing the things I used to do before we got involved with the twins. Kathy came over and stayed sometimes, and I stayed at hers sometimes. But it wasn't the same as it used to be, and I don't think we were either.

My pal, the long firm man, had knocked out all his profits already through betting on horses, so I loaned him a bit of working capital to get going again. Another good thing about being back was that it gave me a chance to see more of my mum and nan, so I used to pop in for a bit of lunch now and then.

Holmes had taken his dad's wartime friend, his neighbour, the killer bitch, on a road trip round Northern France visiting some of the places where she'd been during the war. They were back now, and he was catching up on some of the things he'd neglected while we were messing about in the East End.

I'd been back for a while, and the East End was becoming a distant memory. Then, one afternoon, I was polishing my shoes in the kitchen when the phone rang. It was Kathy with a message from Ron; could me and Hershel meet him in the Carpenters the next day. Whatever the things were that Holmes had neglected and was now catching up on, they must have bored him stiff cos he was only too pleased to drop everything and see what Ron had to offer. I'd picked up Kathy on the way to the Carpenters, and when we got there, there was no sign of Ron or Holmes.

Sometimes, without knowing it, you can feel that someone is looking at you, and that's what I felt as we stood at the bar. Looking round, I saw two fellows quickly turn their heads, and I knew I was right. One of them was Arthur. He wasn't one of the firm but used to mix with them, and everyone knew him. He was very smart in the way he dressed, more so than most of them. I guessed he was about 45, short, with jet black hair smoothed down with Brylcreem and one of the neat Errol Flynn mustaches. He came over.

"I hear you wanted to see me."

Putting my drink down, I said," No, not me."

He nodded his head for me to follow him away from the bar. "About the furniture." He was tugging my sleeve, so I moved away from the bar. Then, looking over his shoulder, he said, "I hear you wanted to see me about some furniture."

"No." I said, "I don't need any furniture." And went to walk away.

"What about your girlfriend," nodding in Kathy's direction. "What about buying something nice for her."

"She's got furniture. She's got a houseful of it."

"What, flameproof?"

"Probably, it's G plan."

"G plan," he snorted. "You know that's foreign, don't you. Scandinavian. Eighteen months and that'll fall apart. What are you gonna do then? They won't give you your money back."

I knew I should have walked away, but I thought I'd play him at his own game. "No, she's had it two years, and it ain't fell apart. It's getting more solid if anything."

He changed tack then, "What about your old mum? I bet you'd like to buy something for her, wouldn't you."

"I already have. I bought her a nice Chesterfield and matching armchairs."

A pained look came on his face, "Oh my good God. Do you know what that's stuffed with?"

I shrugged, cos I didn't know. His face came nearer to mine. "Horsehair, and there's only one thing more flammable than that, and that's petrol."

He paused then, looking into my eyes to see what effect that information would have on me. Then he carried on. "She wants to get rid of that while she can. I'm telling you, John, all that antique stuff is old-fashioned now. What is in today, and what you'll see in all the top West End houses is Louie Catoors, and that's what I can get you."

"What's Louie Catoors?" I asked him.

Looking over, first one shoulder, then the other. "What's Louie Catoors? Louie Catoors is the latest thing in furniture; it's elegant, and what's more, it's flameproof. So you wouldn't have to worry about your mum sitting down for a fag and going up in a puff of smoke cos she's sitting on horsehair."

"Well, that wouldn't happen, I said, "cos she don't smoke."

"She wouldn't have to, John. I don't suppose you've ever heard of spontaneous combustion, have you."

I had to think for a bit. "Yeah, I've heard of that. But she wouldn't do that. She's not that kind of person."

I'd noticed Holmes had come into the bar and called him over. "Hershel, this is Arthur. You know you were talking about getting a new sofa."

"Was I, when was that?" Holmes looked a bit puzzled. And Arthur was on him in a flash.

"Hershel, this could be your lucky day, son."

That gave me a chance to slip back to the bar and talk to Kathy. It wasn't very long before I noticed Arthur trying to edge away from Holmes. He got closer to the door, then suddenly put his drink down on a table and was gone, leaving Holmes with his mouth open and an unfinished superlative on his lips. The reason for Arthur's speedy departure, I found out, was that he'd got his Louies mixed up. The furniture wasn't Louie Catoors, it was Louie Cans, and that's what Holmes was explaining to him when he felt the urge to leave.

About five minutes after Arthur had gone, Ron came in, looking thoughtful and smiling nice as could be and shaking us by the hand. "Hello chaps, we've missed you round here these last few weeks."

"And we've missed you, Ron," Holmes said, smiling as if he meant it.

I bought him a drink, and we took a table out of the way. Ron's first words as he sat down, "Right, Africa, Enugu, are you up for it?"

Me and Holmes looked at each other, "What's the deal?" I asked.

"Well, the deal is this. Les and Manning are out there at the moment, laying the groundwork. They'll be back soon, and me and Reg are going out there with them in a couple of weeks. And I want you two to come with us. You as my secretary." He said this to Holmes, "And you, John, as my butler."

"Your fucking what?" I nearly shouted it out, but Ron was laughing,

"No, I'm joking. What we want, is for you two to keep an eye on the others when me and Reg ain't around. What d'you say?"

"As long as you don't think I'm going to be ironing your shirts or anything."

"No, course not. You won't have to do anything, just keep an eye on the others, be like a holiday for you. We'll give you fifty quid a day each and your expenses. Have a think about it and let me know by tomorrow."

Holmes was looking at me and nodding, and I didn't need a lot of persuading.

"Yeah, we'll have that Ron, fifty a day and exes."

Ron was happy. He clapped his hands together." Right, get your passports sorted out, and be ready for the next two weeks."

It was exactly two weeks after that meeting with Ron in the Carpenters, and I was in a cab with Holmes on the way to the London Airport. And three hours after arriving, we were in the air, alongside the twins, Les Bishop, Freddie, and Bob Manning, on our way to Lagos, Nigeria. Les had said the flight would take about seven or eight hours, and he was right. Stopping once at a place called Kano, we got to Lagos at about 10 pm and had to adjust our watches to local time.

Les seemed to know the drill and got us cabs to the hotel, which he'd booked in advance. The first thing to hit you when you got off the plane was the heat. It was damp. Ten o'clock at night, and it was like you'd stepped into a sauna. It seemed to rise up out of the ground and cover you.

Once we were in the hotel and had a quick wash, it was down to the bar, where the others were already drinking; and apart from the heat, it was like being back in Bethnal Green. The next morning it was hotter still, a damp, clammy heat. Les had arranged for two VW minibuses to take us back to the airport for our flight to Enugu.

The plane for that flight was not what I was expecting. It looked like one of those old transport planes you used to see in the old war films, where they used to chuck supplies out of the side doors; perhaps that's what it was. There was a lot of smoke from the engines when they fired up, and I was gripping the seat in front of me as we bumped down the runway.

Once we were in the air, looking out of the window, all you could see was trees. Occasionally you'd see a village or a small township, and you might see a road, but that would soon vanish again into the jungle. After a couple of stops, it took us about three hours to reach Enugu, and the flight crew, who looked like Indians, made a perfect landing on the bumpy runway. When I say they looked like Indians, they were Indians and wore turbans, probably Sikhs. I wondered how they came to be in Nigeria, miles from home, flying an old airplane. But that was another one of the many mysteries in life that I never found the answer to.

Getting out of the plane with our luggage, I expected to see a VW minibus; but instead, there was a Rolls Royce, an Austin Princess, and two coppers on motorbikes. Les went and spoke to the chauffeur, and it turned out the Minister of Commerce and Industry had sent the Roller to pick up the twins, who he was anxious to meet. Les didn't look too happy when they took Holmes with them and drove off with the two motorbikes in front to clear the way. We all piled into the Princess, which took us to the hotel, while Holmes and the twins went to meet the minister.

Later, in his room, Holmes told me about the meeting. After being welcomed to the country and told what an honour it was to have them there, they'd sat round a big table in the minister's office with the minister and his mates and discussed the various licences and permits that would be needed for the work to proceed. Except the twins weren't really listening. They were more interested in knowing about the nightclubs, car dealerships, and cab firms in Enugu town. In the end, after a lot of handshaking and congratulating each other, Reg said that their chief finance officer would be in touch to sort out the details of the licences. To make their stay in Enugu more enjoyable, the minister had given them the use of his Roller and chauffeur for the remainder of their visit.

The next morning there was a briefing downstairs in the bar. While the twins were visiting the site of the new complex, Les and the other two would arrange the meetings to discuss permits and licences, and that left me and Holmes free to wander round the town, which is what we did.

I must admit, I was surprised. I'd come out here expecting to see a load of mud huts and a few government buildings made out of wood. Instead of that, there was a functioning town, like any town in England; a bit run down in places, but working. They had electricity, roads, traffic, shops, bars, nightclubs, a hotel. They had an airport.

It made me stop and think, why would they need two gangsters from the East End of London, and a couple of shady businessmen, with no knowledge of construction, to build a town for them? Holmes must have read my mind. We were in the centre of the town, and he was staring at a Coca-Cola sign over a shop. "Does anything about this seem strange to you, John?"

"Like what?"

271

"Why would these people need two East End gangsters to build a town for them, when they've done all this by themselves?"

I think we may have got the answer to that in the next few days at the meetings. The twins had insisted that me and Holmes attend these meetings, me to check the figures, and Holmes, cos he spoke the lingo, to listen out and make sure they weren't having us over. They only had to speak perfect English to do that. There were licences and permits for everything. Permits to sink a well, to store explosives, to clear the forest, heavy machinery permits. Les and the others were so eager to get things moving they went along with everything and signed cheques for over twenty grand's worth of permits and licences. What must have appealed to 'em was a clause that if diamonds were discovered on the land, half of the profits would go to the Ministry of Development.

The twins had spent the week being driven round the country, meeting local dignitaries, and being treated like visiting royalty. The permits and the thought of finding diamonds and not declaring them was worth twenty grand to them, so all in all, it was a good week's work. Because we had to do something to justify our being out there for fifty pounds a day, Holmes had prepared his usual well-written report for the twins. The meetings' dates, times, and locations; who was there and who said what to who. I'd supplied the figures, the permit's name, and what it cost. After looking it over, they seemed well satisfied, so everyone was happy. When I say everyone, I'm not sure if Les was. I don't think he liked the idea of me and Holmes being at the meetings, and he probably had his own reasons for that.

Two days before we were due to leave, Ron treated us all to a night out in one of the local nightclubs. It was nice in there, cool, after the heat of the town at night. An interesting five-piece band was playing what sounded like traditional Nigerian music, then, out of the blue, "Hello Dolly." But this was much livelier than any Hello Dolly I'd heard before, with electric guitars and a deep drumbeat. People were dancing, and there was a friendly atmosphere in there.

It wasn't hard to spot what looked like the criminal element, mainly by their dress and the amount of gold they wore. I assumed that all the single ladies were hookers, and a lot of them made it plain that that's what they were.

Holmes had got a taste for the local Star lager, and before you knew it he was up and dancing with one of the hookers. And he wasn't just dancing, but doing it like they do, shaking his arse and stamping his feet. He must have been good at it, cos soon the girls were lining up to dance with him. And he was talking to 'em in their own lingo. Then when he went to the bar, he had a flock of 'em round him trying to buy him a drink. Later on, the barman said he'd worked there for five years, and that was the first time he'd ever seen a hooker buy a drink. I guessed that must have been Holmes and Hitler's strange power in action.

Two days later, we were all packed and ready to leave. Ron had got Les to pay me and Holmes with company cheques, which he wasn't happy about, but he did it. We left Enugu at ten in the morning and got into Lagos in time to catch the flight back to London.

CHAPTER 22

The Musgrave Ritual

The Highgate thing started on a Tuesday, about a week after we got back from Enugu. I was spending more time back in the East End now. It was while we were away, I realized how much I missed Kathy, much more than I missed South London, and now I wanted to spend as much time with her as I could. We were just about to go out when the phone rang. She passed it to me, "It's Ron; he wants to talk to you."

"Hello Ron," I said, "what's happening?"

"Hello John, I really wanted to talk to Hershel. Can you get hold of him? Ask him to ring me."

And that was it. The last time I had a message like that was when that nutty Harry wanted to bash Holmes's head in. Anyway, I rang Holmes and gave him the message, and me and Kathy went for a walk in the park.

Later that evening, Holmes rang, "Are you busy?"

"What, right now?"

"No, not right now, John, tomorrow. I've spoken to Ron and been presented with a mystery which I think you might find interesting. What do you say?"

He should have known by now that I don't find mysteries interesting, not like him. But remembering the last one, Mr. Edmunds, and we'd had a little earner. I said OK, and he said he'd call round in the morning.

I was up and waiting at the door when he arrived, but he still managed to slip past me and start slobbering on Kathy's cheek. Probably something he'd been practicing in France. She was amused by it cos she knew how much it annoyed me.

Finally, I managed to drag him away and into his car, and off we went to Highgate. On the way, he told me the story that Ron had told him. A friend of theirs, Billy Pierce, lived in this big old house at Highgate. While ripping out old window shutters during some renovations, he came across an old American ten-dollar gold coin in mint condition, wrapped in paper; and on the paper was some sort of riddle.

What made this interesting was that Billy Pierce's great or great-great grandfather got done in 1856 for nicking a load of gold bars and a load of ten-dollar gold coins off of the boat train bound for France. **THE FIRST GREAT TRAIN ROBBERY**. Could that riddle be an indicator to where some treasure might be hidden?

Once we got to Highgate, Holmes soon found the house. It was one of those big old Victorian lots, hidden behind tall hedges, with bays and dormers all over it. Billy Pierce met us at the door and showed us in. You could see that most of the stuff in there was original, the ceramic floor tiles, the bannisters on the stairs, and the big old pine doors with their brass fittings.

Billy himself was about the same height as Holmes, about six foot, a bit chubby, probably early forties, with dark hair just showing a bit of gray at the sides. He seemed nice enough. Holmes introduced us, "Hello Billy, I'm Hershel, this is my good friend John. Ron said you had a little puzzle we might be able to help you with."

"That's right," he said, "come down to the kitchen, and I'll show you."

We followed him along the hall, down a couple of steps, into a massive kitchen. I guessed it was one of those houses that must have had servants years ago, cooks and maids and all that. While he made coffee, we sat at a big old pine table and looked at the coin and the cryptic note it had been wrapped in. Written in that lovely old, slanted handwriting that the Victorians were so good at, it said:

When the sun comes above the stack-----So that before the red is the black-------

And beyond the black is the green--------then below the green is the brown----

which covers the yellow.

"What do you make of it?" Bill asked as he put the coffee cups on the table.

Holmes was staring at him, sniffing, and I began to fear the worst. "Would you by chance have a billiard room in the house?" he said.

"Yeah, we have. That's where I found the note and the coin. I'll show it to you."

Holmes held up his hand like he was stopping traffic. "No rush, we'll finish our coffee. By the way, did you enjoy your kippers this morning?"

Bill looked puzzled, "What?"

"Kippers," said Holmes, "you had kippers for breakfast, didn't you?"

Bill was shaking his head. "I don't like kippers; they give me indigestion."

"Are you saying you eat the kippers, and yet you don't like them?"

"No, what I'm saying is, I don't eat kippers because I don't like them, and I don't like them because they give me indigestion."

Holmes looked at him a bit skeptical," Oh, very well, if you insist."

I could see Bill was getting annoyed," Yeah, well I do insist. D'you think I'd lie about eating a kipper. Anyway, why are you so interested in what I had for breakfast?"

"I'm not particularly interested," Holmes said, "it's just that I detected minute particles of kipper on your shirt and noticed a faint odour of kipper on your person. Oak smoked in Yarmouth if I'm not mistaken."

Billy was nodding, cos he understood now. "It's my wife. She was born and brought up in Yarmouth, and I think kippers must have been her staple diet cos she can't get enough of 'em. She has 'em sent down from there once a week. And she has an annoying habit of eating and talking at the same time and spraying food. It's not so bad when she's not eating; then it's just spit. It was her who ate the kippers."

278

"Well, not quite all of them," said Holmes, getting up from the table, "You must love her very much. Shall we go to the billiard-room?"

We followed him out into the hall and another large room with French doors that looked out onto a garden. Apart from four chairs against a wall, the room was completely bare. There was no billiard table, and the only thing that said there might have been one once was a marking board on the far wall and eight indents on the pine floorboards. I could see Holmes was disappointed. "I was hoping to see a snooker table."

"You should have come ten years ago," Bill said. "before the twins came and borrowed it."

The thought of someone borrowing a snooker table weighing about a ton seemed to amuse Holmes, and he started that chuckling and gurgling that he did when he found something funny. Eventually, he stopped and looked at the board on the wall. "Thurston. I shall assume this is the lower end of the table." Then producing a measuring tape from his pocket. "Take this, John, and hold it at the center of that far indentation."

We measured where the legs of the table had been, lengthways, sideways, and diagonally, while Bill looked on a bit puzzled. "I ain't being funny," he said," but what are you doing? I found it by the French doors."

Holmes smiled his superior fucking smile, and I knew we were in for a lecture. "Do you play snooker, Bill?" Bill shook his head, "No."

"Then you may not understand. But I'm sure the solution to this riddle lies on the green baize of a snooker table. When the sun comes above the stack. The sun, I think, represents the white ball and the stack is the fifteen reds. Only the blue and pink aren't mentioned, very interesting. I don't think there's much more we can do at this moment. I have your telephone number, and I'll be in touch in the next day or two." He turned to me, "Can you think of anything else, John?"

"Yeah," I said, "it seems to me that if this is the bottom of the table, the green, brown, and yellow would be in a line pointing directly to the centre of the French doors. Do you mind if I have a look outside?"

Bill said, "No, go ahead, the key's in the door."

While Holmes and Bill tapped and inspected the floorboards, I went into the garden. Outside there was a slab path running the perimeter of the building, then a solitary tree set in a lawn, about thirty feet from the house. Further away was a wood-framed greenhouse fronted by another slab path. I rubbed my shoes on the stone before I came back in and locked the door.

We left Bill on his doorstep, picking minute traces of kipper from his shirt, and drove down to Soho. Leaving the car in Archer Street, we walked round the corner and up into the Windmill Street snooker hall. They were used to seeing all sorts of characters in there, so no one took much notice when Holmes produced his tape and began measuring the points where the balls sat on the table.

After leaving Holmes outside the snooker hall, I didn't hear from him for a couple of days, and when I did, he didn't sound happy. "John, this thing is driving me mad. Would you like to come over and perhaps apply some of your snooker expertise to the question?"

I haven't got snooker expertise, and he could have just said come over, but that was his smarmy way of talking.

Old killer Jane was just leaving as I got to his front door. "Hello John," she said, and held out her hand. As I went to shake hands with her, she's pulled me in closer and kissed me on the cheek. Before her and Holmes started doing this, I'd only ever seen it in films, usually where there were French people involved, but they'd took to it like ducks to water. She was definitely a very striking woman, and her perfume was something special, something you wouldn't buy down Petticoat Lane.

The door was still open, so I went straight up and found Holmes sitting in his front room, surrounded by sheets of paper. He shuffled them all together and passed them to me.

"Look at those," he said, as he sat rubbing his eyes, "and tell me what you make of it."

In two seconds, I understood why he said it was driving him mad. There were triangles, pentangles, right angles, straight lines, kite shapes, every single geometric shape you could think of. Not only that, but they were drawn in colours, with measurements, some in inches and some in millimeters. There was no way I was going to let those papers drive me mad, so I put them down on the sofa next to Holmes. He was rubbing his eyes again, "Well, what do you think?"

He'd put me in an awkward position cos I didn't want to mug him off, being as he was meant to be the detective and knowing how vain he was. I wasn't as convinced as he was that it was anything to do with a snooker table. In fact, I wasn't convinced at all. That was, I thought, what Holmes would call a red herring. He'd got it wrong from the off when he assumed the sun represented the white ball and the stack was the fifteen reds. That would have been the pack. After looking at Holmes's mathematics, coloured lines, and measurements, all of which made no sense, I'd come to the conclusion that when the riddle said the sun, it meant the sun and not a snooker ball. And when it said the stack, it meant the chimney stack in the centre of the roof and nothing else. When I put this to him, he smiled and closed his eyes. I could almost see his brain ticking over, trying to justify his scribblings. Then he jumped up off of the sofa and did his usual, walking round the room and holding his head.

"You may have something there, John. It seems I've trained you well. If that is the case, then the red is obviously the red roof tiles, 'and below the red is the black,' and that would be the black guttering."

"What about the green and the brown and the yellow?" I said, "Could that be a tree? With the green leaves, 'then below the green is the brown, which covers the yellow.' That could be the brown bark of the tree, and the yellow is the gold buried underneath it."

He was smiling now in his sarcastic way. "That might be the case, John, if there was a tree next to the gutter. Did you see one?"

"Not next to the gutter," I said, "but there is a tree in the garden. I don't know what make it is, havalook."

I took a leaf from my pocket that I'd picked from the tree and handed it to Holmes. Taking it over to the window, he held it up to the light.

"Hmm, Acer Rubrum, very interesting. Better known as the red maple."

As soon as he said that, it all clicked into place. 'When the sun comes above the stack, so that before the red is the black.' The red has got to be the red maple, and the black is the shadow it casts. 'And beyond the black is the green,' the green grass over the brown dirt that covers the gold. Holmes still didn't get it.

"The red maple, ingenious. The leaves are green till the autumn when they turn brilliant red. I suppose the sun and the stack were designed to throw us off the scent."

I can't do the patronising smile that Holmes does, but I did the next best thing. I spoke to him like I was instructing a little kid. "No," I said, "when the sun comes over the stack, it throws a shadow in front of the tree. The black is the shadow, and at the end of the shadow is the green grass that covers the brown dirt that covers the yellow gold."

I knew better than to expect any appreciation from Holmes, but I certainly didn't expect his reaction. He clapped his hand to his head. "Oh my god," he said, very dramatic, "Musgrave."

I guessed this was another one of his imaginary friends, and I knew I shouldn't have said it, but I did. "Who's Musgrave?"

"The Musgrave ritual," he said," It was one of old Sherlock's favourite cases. He solved the mystery by measuring the shadow of a non-existent tree with the aid of a stick and a piece of string."

My first thought was, what a load of bull, and my second thought was, I've got old Dr. John's journals at home, I'll check it out.

We talked about the possibility of finding any gold in the garden, and we decided, if there was any, and we found it, it would be best if Billy didn't know. If he did know, then the twins would know; and if they knew, then they would want their whack off of Billy and off of us as well. That's if they didn't want it all. The object, as Holmes saw it, was for us to get money off of them, not the other way round. So the problem was how to dig up Bill's garden without him noticing us doing it. Holmes was confident he'd be able to arrange a way, so we left it at that, and I went home to Penge.

In my old bedroom at my mum's house, I dug out some of Dr. Watson's old diaries. It didn't take too long to find an entry titled The Musgrave Ritual, and this is what he wrote:

284

This evening I was coaxed into inviting Holmes to recount to me one of his so-called adventures. It was something that occurred before we met, which he called the Adventure of the Musgrave Ritual. The story that he told was bizarre enough, insomuch as it involved him measuring to within two inches of accuracy, the 96-feet shadow of a non-existent elm tree, using two parts of a fishing pole and a ball of string. However improbable such a feat might seem, it may have been possible; except that, in the case of the Musgrove Ritual, it would have meant that two trees and their shadows had not altered shape or grown an inch in two hundred years. I casually mentioned this to Holmes, and sadly was asked the question that is a favourite of scoundrels and bullies, "Are you calling me a liar?" Aware that if I pursued this, he would become petulant and take out his anger on Mrs.Hudson, I let the matter drop.

After reading Dr. John's notes, I took the time to read The Musgrave Ritual, and he was right what he said. Just a pity he never had the guts to call Holmes a liar to his face. But I suppose when you're dealing with a geezer who beats up dead people with a stick, you learn to mind what you say. Apart from all that, I realised that we might have the same problem. That maple tree could have been in the ground for a hundred years, so who knows where the shadow ended when the geezer first wrote that riddle.

I decided that while I was waiting for Holmes to get in touch, I'd find out all I could about the growth rate of red maple trees. The next morning, I was up, bathed, shaved, dressed, and breakfasted, and standing outside the gates of the park when it opened.

After scratching his head with the keys, the gatekeeper admitted he didn't know much about trees, but if I came back in half an hour, Bernard would be there, and he could tell me anything that I wanted to know about any tree that I wanted to know about.

While I was walking round the park waiting for Bernard to turn up, I looked at the shape of the trees; they were nearly all rounded at the top, and so were their shadows.

What with that, and not knowing when the maple tree was planted, I guessed it would mean digging up half of Bill's back garden. Not only digging up his garden, but putting it back together again, so he didn't know we've done it. And we don't even know for sure if there's anything buried there, just some nonsense on an old bit of paper.

Feeling a bit fed up and ready to forget about the whole thing, I was about to leave the park when I saw the geezer who opened the gates and another man who I guessed was Bernard. He called me over.

"I hear you want to know about red maple trees."

"Well yeah," I said, "a mate of mine is thinking of getting one; he wondered how fast they grow each year."

Bernard smiled, looked at his mate, then at me, confirming his audience. From the way he talked, he gave the impression that he'd waited for years to tell someone what he knew about the red maple tree. He spoke with enthusiasm that most people only have when they talk about sex or their football team, something like that. He let it all come flooding out.

"Acer rubrum, that's their real name. Your Acer rubrum will grow about a foot to two feet every year till it reaches full height, and that might be forty to seventy feet tall, depending on the soil. Tell him not to plant it too near the house because it spreads out and the roots spread out. He might want to get himself a metal detector and see if there's any pipes in the ground cos the roots can damage 'em. Those roots can lift up a path, you know."

Old Bernie was still talking, but I'd stopped listening. A metal detector. Why didn't I think of it before? Better still, why didn't Holmes think of it? He's meant to be the brainy one. It was rude of me because he had much more to say about the Acer rubrum, but I walked off and left him talking, giving his mate the benefit of his expertise.

When I phoned Holmes, he was about to leave, to visit Bill at Highgate. He was going to convince him that whatever gold there was, had been hidden in the frame of the billiard table. The one that the twins had borrowed and didn't return.

"It might take a week or two," he promised, "but if there's any gold in Bill's garden, we'll find it." Perhaps I should have mentioned the metal detector then, but I didn't. I wanted time to practice the gloating look that I'd have when I produced it.

That afternoon I was back in the East End, round Kathy's, having a cup of tea. Just being away for twenty-four hours, I'd forgotten how beautiful she was. "Why do you keep staring at me?" she asked me, smiling, cos she knew why I was staring at her. She knew years ago back in Doris's café.

Last night in the Lion, the twins had been asking if she heard from me or Hershel. I was tempted to phone 'em at home, but I thought it would be nice to tell them in person and see their reaction, and I wasn't disappointed.

Later that evening, we went out for a meal, then went down the Carpenters. It hadn't got busy yet, but there was a few of the regulars in there. Perhaps one of them phoned the twins, or it may have been coincidence, but within ten minutes of us getting there, they walked through the door. Reg went and sat a table away from the bar, and Ron called me over.

"Hello John," he said, "How d'you get on with that thing of Bill's?"

I gave my best impression of a look of disgust. "Fucking nice waste of time. It turns out there was some gold hidden in the frame of a snooker table. And he lent the table to someone years ago and never got it back."

They were looking at each other. Reg said," Did he say who he lent it to?"

288

"He might have done," I said, "but it don't matter. Whoever had it must have found the gold by now."

" That was us." Reg said, "We borrowed a table off of his old man when we had the billiard hall. But we couldn't get it in the door."

"So the gold could still be under the table," I said. "What happened to it? Do you know where it is now?"

"Fucking Tommy Abbot," Ron was scowling and kicking the table. "Gave us thirty quid for it. Said he had someone for it."

It wasn't easy, but I tried to look distraught. "And you don't know who he sold it to."

Neither of them answered, so I left them staring at the table, thinking of the fortune in gold that had been theirs and slipped through their fingers. Mick had come into the pub, and a bit later, the twins joined us at the bar. They were a bit philosophical about the gold. "Well, it wasn't ours in the first place, so we didn't lose nothing."

Then Reg said, "All I hope is that fucking Tommy Abbot never found it."

"Well, if he did," Ron said, laughing, "he certainly didn't buy any clobber with it. He wore the same suit for ten years."

That lightened the mood a bit, and even Reg permitted himself a smile. After a few more drinks, Ron was warming up. He wasn't always too pleased to have women in the company, but he said to Kathy, "I must say you look very nice tonight, Kath."

"Why, thank you, Ron," she said, "and so do you."

He said, "Yeah, but **I** always do." And burst out laughing. Reg laughed too; so more out of politeness than anything else, I laughed as well. Then Mick and Kathy joined in, and because Ron and Reg were laughing, a couple of the firm standing nearby started laughing too, without knowing what they were laughing about. That was the power of the twins in those days.

Me and Kathy left before the rest of them; but it had been a nice night. That was probably one of the best nights I ever had in company with the twins. Everyone was happy, and there was no tension, no threats, no violence: a rare night, but a nice one.

Holmes rang the following day, asking did I fancy a ride up to Great Yarmouth, a business trip. There was nothing I wanted more; cos the thought of sitting around in the flat or else in one of the pubs, waiting for her to finish work, didn't appeal to me. It never occurred to me to ask her to come cos I knew she'd be happier at work and doing her own bits and pieces.

Half an hour after he'd phoned, Holmes was outside knocking on the door. Knowing his recent habit of slobbering on Kathy's face, I didn't let him in; I said, "Be right out," and shut the door. It was always an effort for me to leave Kathy, but I did it, and I left with a kiss and a warning that I thought was exclusive to my mother.

" And don't get in any trouble."

We picked up the A12 going north, and the traffic wasn't too bad for that time in the morning. The further we went from the centre of London, the better it got. As we passed round the outskirts of Romford, I noticed Holmes was smiling to himself, and I guessed he was thinking about the Morrises and his part in their demise.

Soon we were out of the suburbs, driving through the countryside, and it was a weird feeling. It was like a freedom. A release from the grey streets of East London, where you couldn't see a hundred yards in front of you without seeing a building, a house, a block of flats, a double-decker bus. I would bet there was people in London who'd never seen a horizon, not a proper one.

Now I could see for a mile up the road in front, and in the distance, I could see a hill, maybe ten miles away. That was a horizon. And if you couldn't see a horizon, along the side of the road, there were trees; ash trees, birch trees, elm trees, oak trees, and hedges. Sometimes you'd see a kestrel hovering over the hedges, looking down, looking for a meal.

We didn't really talk much on the way up there. All Holmes would tell me was that he had to see a couple of people; he obviously didn't want me to know too much, and I didn't really want to, so that was ok. I guessed I was just there for the company.

When people say you can have too much of a good thing, I think that's what happened to me. After an hour or more of looking at the road and the trees and horizons, I was getting a bit bored with it all and was glad when we got to Lowestoft.

I like to see the different sorts of buildings in these coastal places. They seem to have something in common wherever you go, something you don't see in London. After Lowestoft, it was back to road, trees, and horizons; and if you came to a rise in the road, you could see for miles. One thing we both noticed, was the number of dead animals and birds we passed. Holmes took the time to identify them for my benefit. "That's a partridge, that one's a pheasant, that's not a rabbit, it's a hare."

More than once, I saw a solitary wing lifting from the road, flapping as if it was waving to the passing traffic; and each time, Holmes said it was a blackbird. That was the worst part of the journey for me, seeing all that dead stuff. That's what the motor car's brought to the countryside.

Before I knew it, we were passing houses again, then more and more till Holmes took a right turn and over a bridge, and we were in Great Yarmouth. After driving about for a while to get his bearings, Holmes pulled up outside the Holkham Hotel pub. It was pretty busy inside, mostly holidaymakers, but I managed to find a table while Holmes went to the bar.

He must have known the guvnor cos they were shaking hands and chatting like dear old pals. Then I saw Holmes take an envelope from his coat and pass it to the geezer, who, without looking at it, put it in his pocket. With two beers in his hands, Holmes came over to the table, eyeing everything up the way he always did.

"What's all that about," I asked him.

Leaning forward, and staring at me with his creepy eyes, I felt his hand on mine. "John, I'm going to ask you to indulge me. Just for a week or so."

I pulled my hand away. "Just what do you mean by indulge you. I don't even know what that means. But it sounds a bit pervy to me."

He was genuinely amused by that and sat there chuckling for a while. "What I want, John, is for you not to ask me any questions, and within a week, I'll be able to tell you everything. That is indulging me."

I was happy with that, so after finishing our drinks, he went off to see a couple of people, and I had a walk along the front to find some fish and chips.

It was nice to stroll along the front again, and it hadn't changed much since I was last here. Maybe there were a few more hot dog places and a few more amusement arcades. And the music blaring from the open doors was Millie now, singing, 'My Boy Lollipop'. Last time it had been Acker Bilk and 'A Stranger on The Shore'. But it didn't matter to me what the music was on a seafront or a fairground; if it was loud enough, it always sounded good.

We'd arranged to meet back in the Holkham, and I was already in there when he came back. It had been interesting, listening to all the different accents in the bar and trying to put a name to 'em. The

Scousers and Brummies and Geordies were all pretty easy, and the locals; but there were accents from up north that you couldn't identify, only that they were northern. By the time he came back, Holmes had finished all his business and was ready to leave.

We took a different route out of Yarmouth to the one we came in on. Then, a near enough straight road took us to and around Norwich and onto the A11. There was more to see on this road. Still plenty of trees and horizons, but we passed some interesting places. Places like the Snetterton racetrack, and the Elveden war memorial, stuck right in the middle of the countryside and nearly as tall as Nelson's column. I only knew this cos Holmes told me.

Then we passed near Mildenhall airbase, and further on, straight through the High Street at Newmarket, where Dennis, the geezer I got my racing tips from lives. All the time Holmes was telling me things about the places we passed, how they got their names, what happened there in 1645. The name of this place means Alef's farm in the mud, in Anglo Saxon. I ain't sure if he wasn't making it up, but it didn't matter, and it made the ride interesting.

We stopped twice on the way back, once at the Red Lodge transport café for a cup of tea and again at Woodford, where Holmes wanted to look at the statue of Churchill. When I say 'look at', he was gazing at it the way a normal person might look at a statue of Sophia Loren or Ava Gardner, and it made me feel a bit uncomfortable. After he'd finished staring at Winston Churchill, we drove back into London.

Within half an hour of him dropping me off at Kathy's, I'd had a ham sandwich and was soaking in a hot bath. It was the sound of Kathy coming through her front door that woke me up and made me realize I'd fallen asleep, and now the water was cold. Once I was dried off and dressed, I went into the front room to find her in a funny mood. Holmes would probably describe it in one word, but I would say, as happy as a dog with two tails.   "What are you so happy about?" I asked.

"I'm happy 'cause I've got you," she said laughing, "and I've just made four hundred pounds this afternoon".

"Oh." Straight away, I asked myself the question that anyone else would ask. How does a very attractive ex-prostitute make four hundred pounds in an afternoon when the average weekly wage is about twenty-five pounds?

Perhaps she guessed what I was thinking, 'cos she said, "Don't look like that. I sold a parcel of cigarettes, actually it was a vanload".

I stopped her there. "How did you get hold of a vanload of cigarettes?"

"I didn't," she said," I never even touched it, never even saw it. The people who chored it found their buyer had been nicked the same day, and they were stuck with 'em. Anyway, someone in the Lion put 'em onto me, and I put 'em onto someone I know, who bought 'em, and I wound up getting five hundred pounds for my whack. By the time I gave the twins their share and a drink for someone in the Lion, I finished up with a nice four hundred."

That was nice that the twins got their share. That's what it was like in those days; anyone who had an earner had to pay the twins for the privilege of living in the East End. Knowing she felt indebted to 'em, I didn't bother to say anything. She was still in a happy mood.

"And I'll tell you what I am going to do with you," she said, "I'm going to take you up the West End and buy you a nice new suit, and shoes to go with it. Would you like that?"

For a brief moment, I knew what it felt like to be a pimp. No one had offered to buy me a suit since my dad did when I'd just left school. There was no way, though, that I was going to spoil the mood she was in, so I said, "Yeah, I'd like that, 'course I would."

We went up the West End a couple of days later, and I got measured for a new suit. Naturally, I went to Sam Arkus in Berwick Street, and it was good to see Soho again. We walked around the streets with our different memories. 'The Little Hut' tea stall in Greek St., where I used to get a mug of tea when I was a teenager and watch the men playing dice. Where I watched three of the street girls run off laughing, after they'd picked the pocket of one of the men they'd been dancing with in the street.

Some people recognised and remembered Kathy, some of the market traders, and shop keepers; and they all seemed pleased to see her again. Soho hadn't changed too much; that is till we got down to Gerrard Street. The clip joints were gone. Where there used to be clubs there was now Chinese shops and cafes; they weren't even big enough to be called restaurants. It was like a part of the culture of Soho had been taken over and replaced. What made it worse, was when we walked round the corner into Lisle Street, Doris's café was closed, and it didn't look like it was ever going to open again.

I looked at Kathy, and she smiled, "Oh well." I could see it had affected her, perhaps more than me. This was like losing something you knew you could never get back.

It was two weeks later, on the day I was going to collect my suit, that Holmes rang to ask if I was ready to go to work. I didn't need asking twice, so, after picking up my suit from the shop, I got a cab round to Balfour Mews. Jane wasn't there when I arrived, but her perfume was still in the air. I'd never smelt anything as nice as that and made up my mind to get some for Kathy. After letting me in, we went upstairs, and Holmes told me his plan and the preparations he'd made for it.

He'd arranged for the Pierces to have a week's holiday in Great Yarmouth, beginning tomorrow. That had been the reason for our visit. While we were there, he'd sorted out their hotel accommodation, and he'd also got hold of some notepaper from the Great Yarmouth Chamber of Commerce. On that paper, he'd written and informed the

Pierces that for their dedicated support of the Yarmouth kipper industry, they'd been entered in a draw, and won first prize; a week's holiday for two at the Holkham Hotel, with kippers for breakfast every morning. They'd confirmed, by telephone, their grateful acceptance, to the guvnor of the Holkham, who'd confirmed it to Holmes.

So tomorrow while they're on their way to Norfolk, we'll be digging up their back garden. In case of nosy neighbours or passersby, Holmes had decided we'd be rigged out to look like water-board workers. He suggested that I go to Millets and buy myself a donkey jacket, denim jeans, a pair of boots fit for digging, and a shovel. "And what are you going to be wearing?" I asked him.

"Don't worry," he said, "I'll do my share of the digging."

He was well aware that he wasn't answering my question; I knew that he would turn up dressed as the boss, and I was going to be the humble labourer.

I'd been thinking about possible outcomes, and I said to him, "Ain't you worried, after going up to Yarmouth, and laying out a nice bit of money, that there might not be any gold there at all?"

It must have occurred to him, but he wasn't bothered by it. "No," he said, "not at all. It will be worth it to me, John, just to follow in the footsteps of old Sherlock and the Musgrave ritual."

"We could have a bit of a problem there," I said, "cos like old Sherlock and the Musgrave Ritual, we don't know for sure when that tree was planted and just how long the original shadow was."

It was obvious from the different expressions that were crossing his face that this was something he hadn't thought about. And while he did think about it, for one instant, I saw the look on his face of someone who wanted to shoot the messenger. That look reminded me that I needed to get down to Millets before they closed, and before he offered me something to drink.

After getting a cab back to the East End, I picked up my car and drove down to the Mile End Road, where I found a section that was like the Saville Row for building workers. There was a Millets, and next to it, an army surplus shop, where I'd taken Ron once when he needed to buy a machete. Further down was one of the old-fashioned hardware shops, and if you couldn't find a pick-axe handle or machete in the surplus shop, you might find one there. I soon had everything I needed, and it gave me plenty of time to drive over to Penge and pick up the metal detector. That had come courtesy of the gas board at Sydenham; a pal of mine's cousin worked there, and for twenty pounds, he wasn't too fussed about whether he got it back or not.

The next morning, I got dolled up in my jeans and donkey jacket, and if there was a fashion magazine for labourers, I could have been on the cover. There was not a smarter labourer than me in the country right then, or a more uncomfortable one either. It may have been because it was new, but the shirt I'd bought was scratching me like sandpaper.

Luckily it was only for one day. Kathy wasn't impressed by my new look.

Looking at me a bit suspicious, she asked, "Why are you dressed like that, and why have you got a shovel?"

I didn't want to lie to her, but there's no way I was going to tell her the truth, so I just looked as serious as I could and said, "Why do you think, Kath?"

"Oh fuck." she said, holding her head with both hands," You're gonna bury someone."

She knew the rules in the East End; you didn't grass, and you didn't ask questions. That was as good as Old Bill saying, "You do not have to say anything if you do not wish to do so." Still looking serious, I said, "Kath, you know I can't say anything, don't you."

She kissed me on the cheek and whispered,   "Yeah, of course I do. Just be careful."

That was enough for me, and I was out the door and gone before she could say anything else.

Round at Holmes's, he made me take my boots off before I could go upstairs. Didn't matter they were brand new; just because they were labourer's boots. Funny geezer. Since the last time I saw him, he'd been mooching about in the Highgate area, checking the times and height of the sun. What that meant was that we had a couple of hours to kill, time enough for him to cook us an excellent breakfast. And time enough for him to tell me again where it all came from, except this time, there was ham from Bavaria; no one else I knew did that. When it was time to go, he left me upstairs while he fetched a little grey A35 van round the front. I put the shovel and the metal detector in the back, and off we went. We were halfway to Highgate when Holmes asked me, "What was that other thing you put in the back, John?"

"That was a cat," I said," a cable avoidance tool."

"And why would we need that?"

"I'm hoping, that if it can detect metal cables, it will detect metal coins or metal bars. I'm hoping it might save a lot of digging."

He didn't say anything, but I knew he wished he'd thought of it, and that's why he didn't say anything. Somewhere along the Holloway Road, he took a left and pulled up in a quiet road. Reaching behind his seat, he produced another navy raincoat and a peaked cap with a water-board badge stuck on the front, then from a pocket of the raincoat, he took a false mustache and pressed it on his upper lip. I had to look out of the window to stop myself from laughing.

The tall hedges at the front of Bill's house allowed us to park the van out of sight from the road, which was handy. At the side of the house was a bolted gate which led into the garden, and while I held his coat, Holmes clambered over and unlocked it in record time. After taking the C. A. T. and spade from the van, I went into the garden to find Holmes halfway down the lawn, holding a stick at arm's length and gazing up at the sun. Then he stood at the end of the tree's shadow and started pacing forward to its trunk.

I'd already estimated that the tree would have been about eight to ten feet high when it was planted, and the shadow would be fifteen feet long or thereabouts. So while he was fucking about, I lined up the sun, the chimney stack, and the tree, paced out about four yards and switched on the CAT. Swinging it in an arc, I zigzagged slowly forward, and in about two minutes, I got a reaction.

Holmes must have picked it up with his bat-like sensitive hearing cos he put down his stick and came over. After locating the spot with the strongest signal, I carefully cut out a square of turf. To avoid us both being disappointed, I said, "It might only be a pipe." And I started digging.

Holmes had spread his raincoat by the side of the hole, and a pile of earth soon grew on it. It was less than eighteen inches deep when I hit something solid.

Holmes's bat ears heard that alright, and he flung himself on the ground, scraping the loose dirt away with his fingers. Pretty soon, we had the shape of a box, and I had to persuade him to let me dig some more with the spade. Finally, with enough space round it, we managed to lift it out.

Once we'd got it onto the path and cleaned off some of the dirt, I could see that it was made of copper and fastened with an old brass padlock. Some house bricks that were laid up near the greenhouse went into the hole to take up the space that the box had left. After I'd filled it in and tapped down the turf, you might never have known it had been disturbed at all.

When the box was in the van, and we were ready to leave, Holmes went back to lock the gate from the inside and came over the top of it like an agile chimp, still wearing his water-board cap.

Driving back to Holmes's I got this feeling that I've had lots of times before. When you've got a safe to open, and you don't know for sure what's in it; it's a buzz. I don't think Holmes ever felt anything like that. The buzz for him was probably just finding that box, don't matter if there's five grand in it or if it's empty. He calls it the thrill of the chase. But at the same time, I don't think he'd give up his share if it ain't empty.

We got the box into Holmes's kitchen, and he fetched a hammer and chisel to knock the padlock off. After giving it a few knocks to loosen the lid, it came open, and we could see it wasn't entirely copper; it was a wooden box lined with copper.

But it was what was inside that took my breath away, gold bars and plugs of gold ten-dollar pieces, wrapped in a sort of waxed paper. I'd seen piles of money before, but this was more exciting. It was like the treasure you'd dreamed of finding when you was a kid; after watching films like Sinbad the Sailor or Treasure Island, and it was ours, we'd dug it up.

If Holmes was as excited as I was, he didn't show it, although he did allow himself a little smile as he weighed one of the bars in his hands.

From one of his cupboards, he produced a set of scales, the old type with the weights, and we set about weighing it up. It totaled thirty-two pounds and a couple of ounces.

Assuming it was all pure, and the gold price, as Homes said, was forty-five pounds, it came to just over twenty-three thousand pounds.

We discussed what we were going to do with it; the options being splitting it down the middle, selling it together, and splitting the money, or Holmes would buy my share for ten grand. And that's what we agreed on. I felt a bit guilty about Billy Pierce not getting any, till Holmes suggested we cut him in for a third share of it.

I thought then, the twins would probably take it off of him, and that would hurt him more than not having it at all. So it was best he didn't know anything about it. Holmes did say he'd find a way to give Bill a few quid in a way that wouldn't make the twins suspicious.

There was one more thing. I asked Holmes if we couldn't call it quits now with the twins, count this as the money that they owed us and what they owed Adrian, but he wouldn't have any of it. "No way, John," he said, "No, if this was their money, I'd say yes, but it wasn't. No, one way or the other, they're going to pay us with their own money."

After I left Holmes, my first thought was to get out of the clothes I was wearing. Kathy wasn't in when I got back to hers, so I had a quick bath and got changed into my proper clothes.

The donkey jacket and stuff, I put into a couple of carrier bags and drove down to Fieldgate Street. There was a dosshouse there with railings outside, so I pulled up and stuck the bags on the railings.

The thought of some poor homeless geezer finding them clothes made me feel good about myself. It compensated in a way for Billy not getting his share of the loot. Plus, him and his old woman had already had a holiday for nothing.

As I was about to pull away, I looked back and the clothes were gone, and there was no-one in sight. The thought that went through my mind, as I drove back to Kathy's; was whoever took them clothes, was he going to wear 'em or sell 'em. Then deep down I knew it was none of my business what he did with 'em; they were gone, and I had better things to occupy my mind.

CHAPTER 23

Jane

That thing at Highgate was the last bit of excitement, if you could call it that, for a long time. When someone noticed that Bill Pierce and his wife were not answering any calls, and someone else noticed that I'd been seen putting a shovel in my car, a rumour went round that me and Hershel had done 'em in and buried 'em.

So they must have been pretty disappointed when Bill turned up a few days later in the Carpenters, sun-burned, and handing out kippers wrapped in newspaper to whoever wanted them.

For the next few weeks, I didn't do anything much. A couple of times, me and Kathy went away for the weekend, down to Brighton and Bournemouth; but I could tell she would rather be in the East End. If we went in a pub she would be watching the bar staff all the time, wanting to be one of 'em.

We spent some time together at mine, had a couple of meals round at my mum's. It was strange, she didn't miss Yorkshire or the West End, but she missed East London. Somehow, she'd become a cockney.

Holmes, I found out, was as bored as I was. He'd had a couple of cases to look at, but they really didn't interest him. I think he really missed the bizarre life that went on around Bethnal Green. Sometimes he'd ring me, and we'd go out for a drive somewhere, or walk round one of the parks.

I got to know his neighbour, Jane, a bit better, who he was giving one, and thought no-one knew about it; a bit like old Sherlock and Mrs. Hudson. Once you got to know her, she was quite a nice person, and she actually was a killer. One day when we were all out together, I got her to tell me about it. It turned out she'd been brought up in France as a kid and grew up speaking fluent French and English.

When the war came along, she enlisted and got recruited into the special operations mob. The result of that was, after training, she got parachuted back into France to work with the resistance. And that's where she did her killing.

The first one was a German soldier, then a Frenchman, who they thought was a spy. Then the mayor of a town who was an out-and-out Nazi. The way she told me this, I guessed it wasn't the first time she'd told that story, and she was obviously proud of what she'd done.

At the end of the war, she got a medal off of General De Galle himself and some more off of our government. So she was, in fact, a war hero. It did cross my mind to tell her I'd killed four people, and my girlfriend had shot two as well, but she'd just think I was trying to top her up, and I didn't want to do that.

While we were out at Henley one day, I asked her, and she told me that the perfume she wore was Joy, by Jean Patou.

It seemed strange to me then, but in all the time I spent with them, I never saw either of 'em get the hump or sulk about anything. Never once heard one of 'em swear. They were very relaxed with each other, always smiling and happy. And if you looked at them, you could imagine them doing one of those exotic dances together, like a tango or something.

I couldn't forget the words of my old nan, though. "Wait till she's 80 and he's in his 60s, see how they get on then,"; but she could put a damper on anything when she was in the mood.

Since we'd got involved with the twins, I'd got a different impression of Holmes. Previous to that, I'd always thought of him as being a bit mimsy, as well as a bit slippery. But since I saw the way he handled the three geezers in the Borough market, plus Benny, although I could have done him, and then the way he knocked that Harry round the ring, I knew I'd been mistaken.

On top of that, I'd come to believe he really did have the strange power over women and dogs that he said he shared with Adolf Hitler. I'd only seen it work on women, cos Gaynor was definitely besotted with him, and I guessed Jane was too, then there was the brasses in Enugu, and Ella Mae in St Louis, who called him her 'dynamic cracker.'

Regarding dogs, the only evidence I'd seen was the poor thing outside the twins' house. But if he said it, I was prepared to believe him.

The thing that actually made me respect him was when I heard, sometime later, that Billy Pierce had won ten thousand pounds on some lottery or raffle or something.

At the time, I thought that Holmes had actually given him his share of the gold money; but when I thought more about it, those coins were over 100 years old in mint condition. We'd only priced them at their bullion value, but they could be worth a fortune individually to a collector. So I had to respect him twice as much, once for giving Billy ten grand that he didn't have to, and once for making me satisfied with ten grand when I could have had more.

As the summer went on, I started to get bored. For the first time in a long while, I didn't have an income. Although I had plenty of money, more than I needed, I had no income. It was Holmes's obsession with getting his money off of the twins, and his keep your enemies closer philosophy, that had kept us both trapped in the East End.

Ever since leaving the R.A.F., I'd always been active. Whether it was ducking and diving or betting on horses and greyhounds, I'd always done something. Now I was getting lazy and I needed some action. Then one afternoon, like an angel answering a prayer, Ron rang me at Kathy's.

"We're going to Africa next week. Are you ready?"

"I am," I said, "but I don't know about Hershel."

The line went quiet, and I could hear him talking to someone else, then, "Get hold of him and ring us. Let us know what he wants to do."

Holmes may have been waiting for that call cos he said, "Tell them I'm ready right now."

I phoned Ron right back, and we agreed to meet the next day in the Lion.

As we talked, I could see that the twins were getting excited about this visit. Now at last, it seemed that they might be getting some return for their investment. It seems they have a large number of contractors lined up, and each of them was going to put up five thousand pounds as some sort of contingency payment to allow them to work on the Enugu project. That was going to amount to a lot of money.

Brother Charlie was coming this time, as well as the others. By the time we'd finished talking, there was nothing said which couldn't have been said on the phone; and the end result was we had to be at the London Airport by 8 am on Tuesday.

During the next few days, I did a bit of shopping in the West End. My first stop was Harrods, where I bought three bottles of Joy perfume: one for Kathy, one for my mum, and one for Jane. Then some shirts and stuff, suitable for the oppressive heat of Enugu.

There is nothing so nice as spending money that you haven't worked for. Whether you've won it or stolen it, it don't matter. It's a wonderful feeling. And it's a feeling that most straight people never get to know. The downside is that it's something you have to control, or you could go into a spending frenzy, and I've seen that happen. You could find yourself buying things you don't need, like a piano that you're never going to learn to play or a coffee percolator when you've already got a perfectly good one. That's why you have to control yourself.

Holmes had invited me and Kathy for a meal with him and Jane in the Dorchester, which was nice. Personally, I would just as soon go to the local Chinese restaurant, but she wanted to go, so we went.

By the time she'd put on her makeup, and diamond earrings, and got dressed, she looked like she belonged in there. And I'm pretty sure the doorman nodded to her as we went in, as if he recognised her.

Another thing that surprised me was she knew all the right knives and forks and spoons to use, while I had to watch them cos I didn't have a clue.

Jane looked stunning too, she'd had her hair cut, not short, but shorter than before. For jewelry, she had matching diamond and emerald earrings and necklace, which brought out the colour of her eyes.

I was probably biased, but I looked round and thought to myself, 'me and Holmes have got the two best looking tarts in the gaff.'

It may have been the Joy perfume that united them, or an instinctive bond that homicidal women have; whatever it was, her and Jane got on like a house on fire. The meal was nice, all five courses of it, and after that, I got a bit flavoured on Champagne, so much so that I snatched the bill off of Holmes and insisted on paying it. That could have been a spending frenzy starting to kick in.

CHAPTER 24

Kray twins to the rescue

The next morning, I was up early. My case was already packed, and I was ready to go. Kathy had got up before me and made my breakfast, and she looked just as beautiful as she had the night before. Bang on 7.15, Holmes was at the door with a cab, and by 8 o'clock we were saying hello to the others in the airport.

Besides the twins and Charlie, there was Les and Freddie, Manning, and a Canadian fellow named Richard. Charlie being there made the trip enjoyable. Apart from the physical similarities in their features, it was hard to believe that him and the twins were brothers. Whereas Charlie with outgoing and friendly, compared to him, the other two were morose. The twins were always polite enough; they'd apologise if they happened to push you out of the way. But Charlie wouldn't push you out of the way in the first place. That was the difference, he was considerate, and they weren't.

It was gone 10 o'clock before we could get on the plane and another half hour before it took off. Once we were up, looking out of the window, it was surprising how much green there was in this country of ours. I soon got bored with that, though, and went to sleep.

The rest of the journey was the same as before; we stayed overnight at Lagos and got the old plane to Enugu in the morning. When we got to Enugu airport, we were met by the same transport as before, except for the motorcycle escort. Charlie and the twins hopped in the Roller, the rest of us in the Princess, and we all went back to the hotel.

That night there was a meeting in the bar to decide the plan of action. It was agreed that the next day we'd just settle in and get down to business the day after. While we had our own rooms on the first floor, Ron and Reg had separate bungalows in the hotel grounds. I suppose that was a status thing. I don't know about the others, but I slept well that first night. And in the morning after breakfast, me and Holmes took a cab into the town.

It was nice walking about down there. The people we met seemed pleasant, smiling, saying hello. One fellow was surprised when he greeted us in his own lingo, and Holmes retaliated with a burst of it. That must have meant something, cos the man was nodding his head and shaking Holmes's hand like he was an old friend. Just after that, on the same road, Holmes got talking to someone else, who directed us to a car hire firm.

It didn't take long to get signed up, and we were soon on the road in a Peugeot 404. After driving about for a while on the outskirts of the town, we went back into the centre and parked up by a bar with tables outside.

Although it was still hot, the heat wasn't so much of a problem for me now. I'd bought some cheesecloth shirts in Charing Cross Road. They were cheap and colourful, but they did the job.

For over an hour, me and Holmes sat there drinking beer and relaxing, watching the daily life of Enugu go by. When I say the everyday life of Enugu, that came in all shapes and sizes and different shades of brown. There was one geezer went by dressed like a lawyer out of Lincolns Inn, with a three-piece pinstriped suit and a Homburg hat on his head. Other times you would see men in their traditional clobber, which was like a sack dress with tight trousers underneath, and all in bright colours.

Then there was a very pretty girl, about 18, in a tee-shirt and blue jeans walked by with what looked like a big pile of laundry balanced on her head.

You can only sit out in the heat drinking beer for so long before you realise it's not much fun. When that happened, we paid the bill and drove back to the hotel.

The twins weren't there when we got back; they'd been out in the Roller sightseeing. Charlie, Les, and Richard, the Canadian fellow, were in the bar playing poker and invited us to join them. I'd never played poker much and certainly never won any money playing it, and I didn't this time either. Within a couple of hours, Holmes had cleaned us all out.

Now there are some people who can't believe they can lose at poker unless someone is cheating; I think that was the case here. No-one actually said it, but there were snide remarks, "I've never seen luck like that before." ...." Do you realise you've won five hands on the spin."

Like you should feel guilty for winning.

Ron came in as the game was finishing. They'd sent the Roller home, and Reg was having a shower in his bungalow. We sat round a table while Ron told us about his day, "Whatever you do," he said, "don't get yourself nicked out here."

He went on to tell us about his visit to the local prison. Somehow, he'd persuaded someone that he was interested in sociology; and that someone had arranged for him to visit the local nick.

What he described made Wandsworth seem like the queen's garden party. And Wormwood Scrubbs, which is known as a filthy prison, seem like the chef's kitchen at the Savoy. The smell in there was so bad, he said, that it clung to you, and he'd had to chuck his clothes when he got back and get one of the staff to burn 'em.

Reg had come in the bar as he was telling us this; he didn't go to the prison but went into town and had a look around. He must have been near to where we were cos he saw the same geezer in the homburg hat.

As we were talking about our day, Ron kept interrupting with more gruesome reminders of the prison, the fellow who'd been cut and had two fingers hanging off, the dead body in the yard with flies buzzing over it, waiting to be taken away. In the end, I was glad to get back to my room; and I think Holmes was too. We left them talking in the bar and arranged to meet in the morning.

We all met up at breakfast the next morning and got our orders for the day. Charlie, Les, me, and Holmes were going to get the contractors list off of one of the ministers. Freddie, Manning, and Richard were to visit the site where the new town would be developed. The twins had other business to attend to.

For some reason, Les Bishop didn't seem to be too fond of me and Holmes. Nothing was ever said, but you just got the feeling. He chose not to come in the car with us to the meeting, but got a cab with Charlie, and we followed.

The meeting was held in the offices of a government building in the town. We sat on one side of a long polished table, and the Minister of Development and two of his henchmen, all in their traditional robes, sat on the other side. Les did the introductions on our side, and the Minister did the same for their side.

I could see Holmes staring at them, one by one, and I knew he was bursting to tell 'em what they had for breakfast or what road they walked down that morning. The Minister noticed it too, "Do you find our clothes interesting, Mr. Coombes?"

All eyes were on Holmes. He sat up straight in his chair and gave a slight bow of his head, and then he started talking to them in what I assumed was their own lingo. Well, he didn't just say a few words but gave a proper little speech, stopping to hold his head now and again, posing, like he always did.

When he'd finished, he sat back in his chair with a self-satisfied smile on his face and waited for a reaction. And that's what he got, when the three of em with big grins on their faces started clapping. The Minister was saying, "i mere nke ọma", and repeating it.

After that, the meeting went well, with smiles all round, and the Minister gave a large manilla envelope containing the contractors list to Holmes. "The other list is not yet completed," one of the aides said, "If you come back tomorrow at the same time, it will be ready for you."

We hadn't got out of the building before Les snatched the envelope from Holmes. "I don't know why he gave this to you," he said," when you're not even part of the company."

Holmes didn't say anything at first, then he winked at me and said, "onye nzuzu." I had no idea at all what that meant, but I nodded as if I understood, and Les didn't like it one bit. He stuffed the envelope in his briefcase and stormed out of the building.

Later that night me, and Holmes went back to the New Era Club, where he'd made such an impression on our last visit. It looked like the same punters in there as before and the same band. Our table was on the edge of the dance-floor, where we could see the bar and the main door, who came in and who left, pretty much everything.

I spotted some of the resident lowlifes at the bar and some of the working girls. We were on our second beer when one of the girls slid off her stool at the bar, came to our table, and asked if I wanted to dance. I said, "No, but he does."

Holmes was already pushing his chair back to get up. They were the only two on the dance-floor, dancing pretty normally to a slow tune and looking like they were stuck together with adhesive. When the music changed to one of those lively African numbers, they must have been right in tune, the pair of 'em, cos they separated, shaking their arses, then came together again, both lifting their legs at the same time and stamping down in time to the drum. The band got louder and faster, and more people joined them on the floor; pretty soon, it was like party time in Enugu.

The whole place was buzzing. And it was nice, just sitting there, thousands of miles from the East End, watching people dancing and enjoying themselves, and listening to that music.

After a while, Holmes and his dancing partner came back to sit at the table. I'd expected him to get rid of her after the dancing, but he didn't. Instead, he'd brought her back, probably for his "research." After buying her a drink, he quizzed her about her background and a load of other stuff that was really none of his business. She didn't mind talking, though.

Her name was Precious, and she came from out in the country, where her family were farmers. Now she worked in the offices of a transport company in Enugu. Well, that's what she said. But she didn't explain why she hung about with the hookers at the bar, dressed like one, walked like one, and acted like one.

Holmes must have twigged this, but if he did, he didn't let on, and she stayed with us drinking and chatting, enjoying the music. Once or twice she asked what the time was, then, later on, she grabbed my wrist to get a better look at my watch, like she was Cinderella and had to be home by midnight.

Another thing I noticed, was when she went to the ladies, which she did more than once, a couple of the girls at the bar would slide off of their stools and join her. I watched the local gangsters at the end of the bar, and what looked like the guvnor of 'em. He was a big lump, with slanted eyes and plenty of those tribal markings on his face.

As I turned away from watching them, Precious was whispering in Holmes's ear, making him smile. "John," he said, "quoting Captain Oates, I'm just going outside and may be gone for some time. Precious has something she wants me to see."

I'd never heard it put like that before, but I said, "OK, just remember what the MO told you."

As soon as they left, I watched the geezer with the stripes on his face nod to a couple of his mates, who finished their drinks, and they all trooped out. I've got to be honest; I didn't rush to go out after them. I didn't even want to go out there at all. Holmes had chose to take some random tart out of a club in a foreign country, into a dark night. And now I had to put myself at risk to bail him out.

Looking round, I couldn't see anything that would help me, apart from a Star lager bottle on the table, so I picked that up and made for the door.

Outside it was the reverse of what I knew back home, when you leave the warmth of a club and go out into the cold night air. Here, you leave the cool fan-driven air of the club and step out into the clinging damp heat of the Nigerian night.

Apart from the thumping music from inside, the town was quiet, an occasional car or bicycle would pass by, but there was no sign of Holmes or the other little mob. I walked round into the car park, looking for our car, when suddenly out of the darkness there was five of them in front of me.

" Hello," It was the fellow with the scars. "Are you going home already?"

"No," I said, "I'm looking for someone."

"Yes, so are we," he said.

What a spiteful looking bastard. Apart from his slanty eyes and scars all over his face he had a horrible smile, like he wanted to bite you. A couple of the others had moved round behind me, and I knew then this wasn't going to end well.

"I wonder if you would tell me the time by your watch," he said.

Without looking down, I said, "It's just turned half past ten," and went to walk past.

He stood in front of me, and the others came in close. "You're a very rude fellow," he said, "now give me the watch."

I got that horrible tingly feeling, then suddenly cold all over. "Holmes," I shouted as I tried to push past. And the next thing I was on the ground with three of 'em on top of me, and someone clawing at my wrist.

The screech of car tyres skidding to a stop about a yard from my head made them jump up out of the way; but they didn't run off or anything. I got to my feet and was pleased to see the twins climbing out of the Rolls Royce. Ron was brushing the dirt off of me, and Reg said, "What's going on?"

"Geezer's trying to nick my watch," I said,

I think, seeing there was only three of us and five of them must have given them a bit of confidence, cos they started crowding round us. Then one of them produced a long horrible looking knife, and without saying anything, pointed it at me, nodding his head.

Ron held his hands up in a surrender position, "Hold on, we don't want any trouble. What do you think Reg?"

Reg said, "I think we should give them what they want." Then he turned to the big geezer, cos he could tell he was the guvnor. "Alright my friend, we don't want any trouble, we're going to let you have it."

He turned to me and winked, "Give me the watch, John."

Taking off the watch I handed it to him and pretended not to notice him slide it into his pocket as he held out his hand to the big fellow. "Here you are."

If that man had come from the East End, he wouldn't have been fooled so easy. And if he hadn't been grinning, he wouldn't have been spitting blood and teeth as Reg's fist exploded on his chin. He staggered back and walked into a left hook from Ron which crumpled him to the ground. Before he'd hit the ground, Reg was head butting another one, kneeing him up the bollocks at the same time. Ron had hold of the geezer's arm who was holding the knife, punching him repeatedly in the temple, till the knife dropped to the floor. and he followed it. While Reg and Ron were kicking the three on the ground, another one was trying to explain to me that all this was nothing to do with him, till I hit him across the nose with the beer bottle. With his hands clasped to his face and blood oozing between his fingers he tripped over one of his mates and ended up with Ron kicking and stamping on him.

The last one, looking like he'd suddenly remembered he'd left the fridge door open or something, turned round and ran. He hadn't gone about five yards before his feet seemed to rise up off the ground as if he was levitating, then with a dull thud, he came down flat on his back. He'd run straight into Holmes, who was now dragging him back.

There was now five of them on the ground. None of 'em were unconscious, but it might have been better for them if they were. Every time one of 'em tried to get up Ron and Reg would kick 'em or punch 'em back down. Somehow Ron had got hold of the knife off of the ground, and while Reg was stuffing all the money he had into the chauffeur's hands and telling him to drive off and say nothing, Ron was slicing up their victims.

It's hard to keep quiet while someone is hacking at your face with a knife, so naturally there was a lot of screaming and yelling going on. In Bethnal Green that would have been enough to keep people indoors, but here they came one by one out of the club; just in time to see our car drive out the other exit.

Ron did more laughing on the way back to the hotel, than I'd seen since that first day we met in the Old Horns. He was really happy. "Did you hear what that geezer was saying, Ha ha ha. I've got hold of his arm and I'm punching his head like a melon, and he's saying, 'I kill you. I kill you'." We all laughed at that and it took away some of the tension. Then we all told our stories of how it had come about.

I'd seen the little firm creep out after Holmes, so I'd followed them. When I was in the carpark they appeared out of nowhere and tried to mug me for my watch. That's when Ron and Reg turned up like the cavalry, just in time.

Reg told his bit. They'd been out for a meal and decided to look in at the club. They pulled into the car park just as the three geezers jumped on my back

323

Holmes then told us he'd left the club with Precious to get a bit of fresh air. That's what he called it. She tried to pick his pocket, so he dumped her in a puddle by the roadside and was on his way back to the club when he saw the commotion. And the poor fellow running away, ran straight into him, and a right uppercut.

Ron hadn't quite finished, "I think I might have done a terrible thing tonight," he said, 'Them scars they have mean they belong to a certain tribe. Well I striped em up so bad they won't be able to tell what fuckin tribe they belong to." That made him laugh some more, and we all joined in, even if it wasn't that funny.

What else wasn't funny was the thought of spending time in the local prison with the flies and the maggots and the dead man lying in the yard.

Back at the hotel, we parked up and went to Reg's bungalow at the rear of the main building. There was plenty of blood on the pair of 'em; more on Ron, who looked like he'd just come out of a slaughterhouse. They didn't seem embarrassed at all when they stripped off all their clothes, right down to their socks, while me and Holmes sat watching, and trying not to appear interested. I guessed it wasn't the first time they'd had to do it, after one of their little blood fests.

Their clothes and shoes were all bundled into a sheet, and given to me to give to Charlie get rid of. "I think it will be best if we go back to London for a while," Reg said. "We'll get the first flight out in the morning. While we're gone, I want you to keep your eye on Les and

Manning. Keep a note of who they meet and where they go and ask Charlie to come and see us."

There were 40-gallon oil drums at the back of the kitchens that were used for burning waste, so I chucked the sheet and its contents into one of them and waited till it caught light. Inside the hotel, the others were all in the bar, so while Holmes went upstairs, I took Charlie aside and gave him the twins' message.

In Holmes's room, he sat on the bed and I sat in a chair, and we looked at each other. I said, "We'd better sort out a story."

He nodded, "Right, we left the club and in the car park there was a group of people fighting. Not wanting to be involved, we got in our car and drove off. We didn't know anyone there and we wouldn't recognise anyone, and that's all we know."

I left him then and went to my room to wipe the blood from my shoes and wash my shirt. After a shower, I went to bed, and lay there wide-awake thinking about the night's events. It's hard to sleep when you're expecting the police to come into your room at any time and cart you away to the fly and maggot infested prison; eventually though I must have dozed off.

It was nearly nine o'clock when I woke up, looking round slowly to reassure myself I was still in my room and not a prison cell. I got dressed quickly, knocked on Holmes's door, and we went down for breakfast. The others had just finished as we arrived. Charlie told us that the twins had had to go back to London. They'd took the morning flight to Lagos. We tried to look surprised,

"Oh why's that Charlie?"

He shrugged and smiled, "Business, that's all I know."

There was a meeting in the bar after breakfast, and they'd already started when we got there. Les was talking, addressing Freddie, he said, "If you and the others go and check the factory sites, Charlie and me will go and pick up the other list of contractors."

"And where's that Les?" Holmes asked.

Les didn't even look at him, shuffling some papers on the top of the bar, he said, "It's where we went yesterday, but you won't be going."

Suddenly you could feel a bit of tension in the room. "Les," Holmes said it quietly, but loud enough for us all to hear, "Reg said that John and I should attend all the meetings."

Putting the papers down, Les stared at Holmes, a bit contemptuous, "Did he. Well Reg isn't here, is he. And when he's not, I'm in charge. And I'm saying we don't need you there, so you're not going. Got it."

The animosity coming from Les was guaranteed to get your attention. Holmes was smiling, "So what is the purpose of our being here. Are you saying you're going to pay us to do nothing?"

Les gave a short laugh, "No, I'm not paying you at all."

That's when I piped up. "Hold up. Ron said we'd get fifty quid day all the time we were out here."

"Well, you'd better take it up with Ron. I didn't employ you, and neither did the company."

And that's how it was left. Charlie shrugged his sympathy, and the others just looked embarrassed.

CHAPTER 25

Et debitum solvit

We sat in Holmes's room. "Right." he said, "The die is cast."

I'd heard that saying before, probably off of him, and never knew what it meant. "What are you talking about?"

"Les has thrown down the gauntlet, and I'm picking it up. Actually, I'm picking it up for both of us."

"Holmesy," I said, "he ain't thrown anything down. He just said we can't go with 'em. So what's happening, in plain English."

He sat on his bed, closed his eyes, and sat in a sort of a trance for a while. Then with his eyes open, his face lit up in a big smile. "I'm going to clear the twins' debt for them, John. I'm going to take five thousand pounds out of their company. I think that's fair, don't you."

I sat down in a chair then cos I had to think. I know they knocked us for some money over the Morrises. But Holmes would have done them in for nothing anyway; he'd have done it on principle. Then they'd took a bit of money over that thing with Adrian, and they never stopped Teddy Kray from sending the photos. But that didn't add up to five grand.

And what was worse from my point of view, I was feeling a bit indebted to the twins for what they'd done last night. They'd got out of their car and fronted five dangerous geezers to help me out. Not everyone would have done that. And for all I know, they might have saved my life. They'd risked, not only their own lives, but being nicked and flung in a stinking prison in a foreign country. And now Holmes was asking me if it was fair to nick five grand off of 'em.

"No," I said, "I don't think they owe us that much."

"Well that's what I'm taking," he said. "You don't have to have any if you don't want to."

For a little while I thought about refusing the money. Then I thought; if I didn't take it the twins would never know. I'd be like the anonymous donor, and what's the point of that? "Alright," I said," I'm in."

"I thought you would be." The sarcastic bastard said, with a smile.

We watched from his window as the cabs came to take Les and Charlie to their meeting, and the others to the factory sites. As soon as they were out of sight, Holmes said, "Right, let's go to work."

Les Bishop's room was directly opposite, and while I waited in the corridor, Holmes unlocked the door, and slipped inside. In less than five minutes he came out, smiling, and locking the door after him.

Back in his room, I didn't even have to ask him the question. He held up the key. "This key, John, it fits all the rooms, yours, mine, everyone's. I made it after our last visit."

He showed me then, the copy he'd made of the list of contractors. Their names addresses and contact numbers. And every one of them was going to put up five thousand pounds in cash. Not only that, but he'd taken a company cheque out of the book. It made me stop and think, there were two lists of names, and each one of 'em was gonna part with five grand. That's a lot of money, perhaps it might be better to stick it out; but Holmes wasn't thinking like that.

"If only John," he said, "if only you were more than semi-literate you could write a book about the wonderful things I do. You could be my Boswell."

Him talking like that made me uncomfortable, so I made an excuse and went downstairs to the bar. When he'd finished complimenting himself and whatever else he was doing in his room, he came down and told me his plan to get the money.

First, we drove out to the west of the town and cruised around, till he stopped outside a bar, The Imperial Bar and Restaurant. After satisfying himself about the location, we drove to the other side of town and did the same thing; cruising the streets till he pulled up outside a hotel, the New Excelsior. It was impossible to know what went on in his nutty mind, but just looking at the front of that hotel made him start giggling to himself. He stopped for a moment.

"Sorry about that." Then started again as he drove away. It took us about ten minutes to get back to the centre of town, and we stopped outside the Texas Bar and Grill. While the hotel's food was OK, I fancied a change and Holmes did too. We ordered steak and chips, along with a local rice and tomatoes dish, and it was excellent.

Leaving the car, we walked down the road to the main Post Office. There were telephones in there, and I watched as Holmes dialled the number of our hotel. When he spoke, I looked round quick, thinking one of the locals had got in the phone booth; but it was him. In a perfect Nigerian accent, he asked for and got Mr. Leslie Bishop on the phone.

"Hello Mr. Bishop, how are you sir? I have to be very discreet Mr.Bishop; I work for the Ministry of Develoment...... The problem is sir, I have a close relative who is on your contractors list, but near the bottom you see. He would be very happy sir to pay a substantial fee, if his name could be pushed up. Pushed nearer the top."

I couldn't hear the conversation at the other end, but Holmes carried on, "I think that's very reasonable Mr. Bishop, If we can meet tomorrow 12 midday at the Imperial Bar and Restaurant on Garden Road. I will bring the money, sir, and I think it best if you come alone. I think one of your people is a bit of a nosy parker sir......yes, that's the one. Thank you Mr.Bishop, I'll see you tomorrow."

Putting the phone down, he winked at me and smiled, "Was that good?".

I agreed with him as he dialled the next number, The New Excelsior hotel. He spoke into the phone, but it was Les Bishop's voice I heard. "Hello, my name's Bishop, and I'd like to book a room for tomorrow please. ... that's fine, I'll be arriving in the morning, thank you."

He then produced his copy of the contractors list, and in Les Bishop's voice, phone two of them and invited them to meet tomorrow, at the New Excelsior, to sign up and pay their deposits. "Why two?" I asked him, "I thought we were only taking five grand."

"Insurance John, just in case one of them doesn't turn up.'

It took us another half hour to find a shop that sold the type of safari jackets that Les wore; and when he tried one on, brushed his hair different, and puffed his chest out, I was looking at Les Bishop, or at least what would have passed for him.

That night we packed our cases and got ready for leaving in the morning. Holmes thought it would be best if we avoided the others; let them think we were sulking. While we were cleaning up Holmes's room, making sure there was no evidence left, there was a knock on the door. It was Charlie.

"Hello chaps, you alright. We haven't seen you all day."

Holmes said, "Yes, we're fine Charlie. We've been in town having a last look around. We're leaving in the morning."

Charlie looked round the room, at the packed cases. "Well, I'm sorry about that," he said," There's nothing I can do. I'm not even on the payroll. I'm just an observer like you."

"I hope you have better luck observing than we did Charlie." Holmes said.

Charlie laughed, and we shook hands with him. "See you back in London."

And he left. I liked Charlie, and I would have to say, after Mickey, he was the best of all the East Enders that I'd met. I was glad it wouldn't be his money we were going to steal.

In the morning, we were up and out of the hotel early, probably before the others were awake. There were street vendors in the town, selling hot food off of carts at the side of the road. With the car windows down, the smells were appetising, but not appetising enough to make us stop and eat at any of them.

We finally pulled up at a café that looked pretty busy, and had breakfast there. The breakfast, that Holmes recommended, was some sort of spiced mashed up beans with an omelette and bread. And not only was that good, but the coffee was excellent too. It was nice just to sit there, looking round at what was rush hour in Enugu. Except nobody rushed.

The fastest person I saw walking in Enugu was the fellow dressed like the Lincolns Inn lawyer. And running, was the mugger in the car park, but he only managed a five-yard sprint. I hadn't thought about it before, but now when I did, I could see that nobody hurried. They just went at their own leisurely pace and seemed to get where they were going in the end.

After leaving the café, it took us about five minutes to get to the railway station. There was plenty of parking there, and we found a spot out of the way. From the back of the car, Holmes took his Safari jacket out of his suitcase and laid it on the seat. He also took out a book, which he gave to me. "Something to read while I'm gone. I'll meet you back here at two o'clock."

Then with his jacket folded over his arm, and his suitcase in his hand, he strolled over to the cabstand.

I learned that day it's not easy to kill four hours in a foreign country, when you don't know your way about. And the book Holmes gave me didn't help, THE HISTORY OF THE PELOPONNESIAN WAR. He probably meant it as a joke, but I made a promise to myself, once I put it down, never to pick it up again. I left it on a table at one of the roadside bars.

Holmes was waiting for me when I pulled up back at the railway station.

"How'd you get on?" I asked him.

He didn't have to answer cos I could see by the smile on his face, he'd been successful. Rubbing his hands together, he winked at me. "et debitum solvit."

Because I was hot and sweaty and a bit tense with the waiting, I said a bit rudely, "And what the fuck is that supposed to mean?"

"It's Latin, John, it means 'take me to the airport, my good man'."

Three hours later, we were bumping down the runway in the old propeller driven plane on our way to Lagos. And three hours after that we were in the Federal Palace Hotel, eating lobster and drinking Champagne.

In the time I'd been waiting for Holmes, nearly four hours, I'd sorted out any guilt feelings I might have had about taking this money off of the twins. I thought about how they'd reneged on the deal over Adrian, not that I cared much about him, but it was the principle. Then there was the time they tried to get us mugged in the Borough Market. Then there was the way they nicked most of the money we should have got for topping the Morrises, And there was the time I got hijacked into driving Reg to shoot that geezer. Thinking about it, and considering our pain and suffering, I came to the conclusion that twenty-five hundred pounds was not too much for what I'd put up with.

Imagine how happy I was, when it wasn't twenty-five hundred pounds, it was five grand each; cos Holmes had signed up the two contractors. Then my natural greed justified taking five grand off of 'em. The rest of it was like a fine for all the bad things they'd done.

The first flight we could get back to London was 11 am the next morning, and it got us into London Airport at just after six at night. Kathy wasn't home when I rang, and she wasn't at the Lion. I didn't fancy going round to hers with this money on me, so I said cheerio to Holmes at the airport, and got a cab home.

Holmes rang me the next morning. He'd spoken to the twins and arranged to meet them lunchtime at the Regency. That gave me time to go down to the shop at the top of the high street, and stock up my fridge. I had it in my mind that I'd be spending a bit more time in Penge, than before. Kathy didn't answer her phone when I rang, and she wasn't in the Lion or the Carpenters.

Holmes was sitting outside the Regency, in his Jag, when I pulled up, and we went in together. Reg called us into the office, and there were chairs enough for us all to sit down.

"So what happened?" he said, his eyebrows going up, "How come you're back already?"

I left it to Holmes to tell them the story of how Les blocked us from going to the meetings, and as there was no point in us staying, we came home. Ron's eyebrows were closing down to the top of his nose.

"I fucking knew it," he was growling, "I knew we couldn't trust him. Wait till he comes home, he's going to top of the list."

His death list was legendary in the pubs round the East End, It was like a Who's Who. Most of the people on it were other gangsters, but there were policemen, newspaper reporters, club owners, the odd shopkeeper and publican. And now Les had gone to the top of the list. It wasn't the best time to do it, but Holmes brought up the fact that we hadn't been paid. Reg was frowning, like he couldn't believe it.

"What, didn't Les pay you?"

"No, he said you hired us, so it's down to you."

"That fucking bastard." Ron was kicking his chair round the room.

Reg said, "No I'm sorry, but you were there on company business. As soon as he gets back, I'll get him to write you both a cheque."

So they'd nicked another few quid off of us; but I didn't begrudge it, and neither did Holmes.

When I finally got to see Kathy, it wasn't the reunion I'd been expecting. After leaving the twins I went straight round to hers. She hadn't been up long and was still in her dressing-gown, and she didn't look great. Her eyes were red like she'd been crying.

"What are the suitcases in the hall?" I asked her. "You going away?"

"No John, you are." She was crying softly, wiping her eyes on her sleeve. "I've packed all your things. Everything of yours."

I was in shock. "What's all this about?

She'd gone into the front room and sat down. "You didn't phone me once John. Not once."

"Fucking hell Kath," I said, "We were working."

She was nodding her head again. "So was Charlie, John. He rang Dolly every night."

I thought, 'thanks Charlie,' but I said to her, "So what. That don't mean I don't love you just as much, does it?"

"Don't it, John? You don't love me the way that I love you, I don't think you can. You don't love me enough to stay in the East End, do you?"

I sat next to her, not saying anything, thinking of what I could say to talk her round. But she was right; I didn't love her enough to stay in the East End. And I knew she wouldn't be happy away from there.

It was childish and I shouldn't have done it, but I took off the watch she'd bought for me, dropped it on the sofa next to her, and said,

"well fuck you, and fuck the East End too."

With the suitcases in the car and driving down toward Tower Bridge, I was already regretting what I'd done. She didn't deserve that, When I thought about it, all she'd ever done up to now was to love me unconditionally. And I knew that if I'd asked her, she would have come and lived in South London, and tried to be happy, even if she wasn't. It just seemed a bad way to end a relationship that had been so good.

As soon as I got home, I rang to apologise, but she didn't pick up the phone. Later I tried ringing her at the Lion and the Carpenters, and it was three days before she'd speak to me.

When I finally did get to apologise for the way I'd spoke to her I think she was pleased.

"Thank you, John," she said, "I'm glad you said that. You know that I'll always love you, don't you?"

"I'll always love you too, Kath, and I'll always be grateful for what we had."

"Goodbye then, John." And she put the phone down.

We heard later through Mick, that another of the Enugu contractors had signed up with Les and paid his five grand. Charlie had wired the money straight home, and for a short time, the twins were spending like drunken sailors. The money was all gone, when a little while later, Charlie phoned to say that Les and the others had been nicked and flung into the filthy Enugu prison.

It turned out that the contractor they'd signed up wasn't happy and wanted his money back; the money that the twins had been spending. Because his brother–in–law was the chief of police, it meant that Les and the others would stay in jail till he did get his money back.

Now the twins were calling in debts everywhere, and some people who had no idea that they owed the twins any money, suddenly found that now they did. They even went so far as to ask Charlie's wife, who they hated, to contribute to the fund, and got a knockback. Probably because they owed us money, me and Holmes never got asked to put in, we were exempt.

It was hard to believe that they'd have trouble raising five thousand pounds between the two of them, but that was the case. In the end, they got the money together, wired it out to Charlie, and Les and the others got released.

From the stories they told, Ron wasn't exaggerating when he said how filthy the prison was. Instead of the Rolls Royce escort, they'd got on arrival, they got one supplied by the local constabulary when they left for Enugu airport. And that was more or less the end of the Enugu project. I guess me and Holmes and some of the ministers were the only ones who showed a profit from it.

I think I must have been holding Kathy back, cos after we split up, she really cracked on. With her accountant and with the backing of the twins, she bought out Mr.Edmonds, and took control of the Great Metropolitan Loans Company.

Stories came back that she was financing a lot of the big robberies that were going on, as well as long firm operators on both sides of the river. Then there was property; her and her accountant were buying and selling property all over London.

Me and Holmes mostly stayed away from the East End, but I'd kept in touch with Mick, and we'd all meet up occasionally. Through him, we met some other East End gangsters, and I have to say they were a different class to the firm. They were independent men; they went out and got their own money. There's no way they would be cowed and bossed about, like the others were. They were nice people.

The few times I saw Kathy we talked like old friends; as if we'd only ever been friends, and nothing more. And I never saw that magical smile again, the one I first saw years ago in Soho. It was sad to think that even if you both wanted to, you could never get back what you'd had; it was gone forever. I knew though, that there would never be anyone else in my life like her.

As for the twins, we kept them at a distance as much as we could. They must have realised by now, that we knew they'd robbed us. Not once, but every time they could. What they didn't know, and that's what made it more satisfying, is that me and Holmes had robbed them for a lot more.

I did worry that, knowing Holmes and how vain he was he might want to let them know. And he came near to it in the Lion one night. He was whistling to himself, and Ron asked him, "What's that tune?"

Holmes said, " It's a Beatles song Ron." Then he started singing; not in his own voice, but like a Scoucer, like George Harrison:

"Listen, do you want to know a secret?

Do you promise not to tell? Whoa oh oh

I've known a secret for a week or two

Nobody knows, just we two oo."

And he's winking at me.

 Reg said, "what, do you like the Beatles then?"

"No Reg, I hate 'em," said Holmes. "But I like that song."

Printed in Great Britain
by Amazon

83853965R00205